I0672412

Murder in Custer State Park

Playhouse Mystery Series

Adele Gibbes

~ Firehole River Press ~

This is a work of fiction. Names, characters, places and incidents are products of the author's imagination or are used as fictitiously and not to be construed as real. Any resemblance to actual events, locales, organizations, or persons, living or dead is entirely coincidental.

Firehole River Press
Bozeman Montana
For bulk sales and book club offers contact:
fireholepress@gmail.com

Copyright 2013 by Firehole River Press
978-0615935560
http://www.playhousemysteries.blogspot.com

Dedicated to my wonderful mother, as well as the wildlife, scenery and amazing staff at Custer State Park. I'd also like to acknowledge the talented staff of the real-life Black Hills Playhouse. I'm still rapt in the spell of the Black Hills. Thanks to my readers for taking a journey into Murder in Custer State Park.

Acknowledgements

The journey to Murder Custer State Park began in August of 2009. Fresh out of college, I set out across the U.S. to explore our National and State Parks. My mom and I fell in love with the charm and majestic beauty of Custer State Park in the stunning Black Hills. We camped for three weeks at Center Lake, less than a mile from The Black Hills Playhouse.

Through long days spent hiking and picnicking in Custer, an idea was born. Inspired by the tradition of The Black Hills Playhouse as well as my own history working as a costumer, I sought to create an atmosphere of mystery to reflect the splendor of South Dakota.

I'd like to thank all the park staff who provided me with amble information in researching this book; the Custer City Chamber of Commerce and area businesses; National Park Service and Travel South Dakota.

Most importantly I thank YOU, the reader for taking a chance on the Playhouse Mystery Series. Each book in the series follows Merritt Andrews through her adventures in the drama and murderous world of costume design and the theatre.

For plot purposes I took creative license with a few minor details. The Custer Playhouse is a fictional reimagining of the real-life Black Hills Playhouse. The Black Hills Playhouse is one of the oldest and most preeminent stock theatre companies in country.

You'll find travel links and some fun facts about Custer State Park at the back of the book.

A portion of proceeds from the sale of this book will be donated to The Black Hills Playhouse and Custer State Park.

Map of Custer State Park

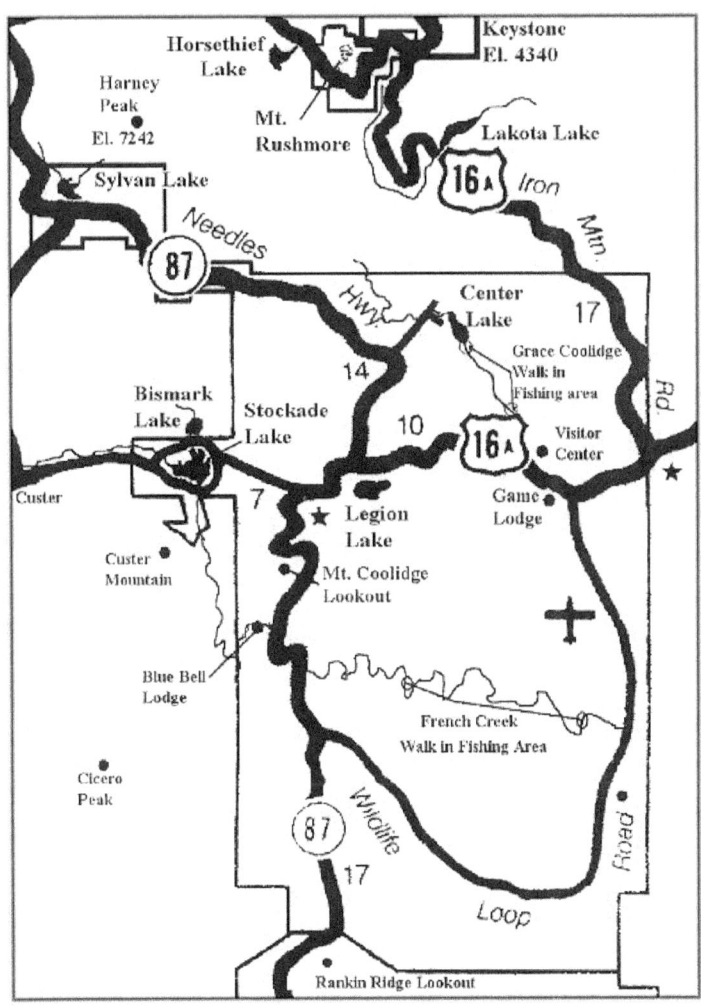

Adele Gibbes

Chapter 1

"Welcome to Custer State Park," an affable park ranger in his mid-forties named Todd Miller, greeted Merritt Andrews as she pulled into the western entrance of South Dakota's premier park.

Merritt is a twenty-three year old standing just over 5'8 with thick shoulder-length auburn hair and green eyes. She recently graduated from the University of North Carolina at Chapel Hill with a B.A. in Theatre, with an emphasis in costume design. For her first post-grad job, Merritt's college advisor arranged for her to spend a summer working in the Black Hills of south western South Dakota as assistant costumer for the historic Custer Playhouse.

"My name is Merritt Andrews and I'm working for the Custer Playhouse this summer. Mr. Gordon told me to check in at this entrance, upon my arrival into the park."

"I'll need your license and car registration so that I can issue you an employee park pass for the season," the ranger requested.

As the costumer handed over the necessary documentation, the ranger noticed the license plate on her Honda Civic.

"Wow, North Carolina. You have traveled a long way. Is this your first time in Custer State Park?"

"It is and I couldn't be more delighted," the costumer enthused. "The scenery here is magnificent. Not to mention the fact that the Custer Playhouse is one the best summer stock theatres in the United States."

"The playhouse has been a Black Hills institution for over sixty years, entertaining thousands of park visitors each year with top notch performances. It'd be a shame, if the old theatre is forced to shut down," Miller sighed.

"Is the playhouse's future in doubt?"

"It's a sore subject around here, and one I'm sure you'll hear plenty about," Miller abruptly shifted the subject. "Nevertheless I'm sure that your troupe will have an excellent run this year."

"I'll do my best to ensure that there aren't wardrobe malfunctions," Merritt jested.

"You'll do fine," Miller replied as he returned her license and registration information. "I'm going to put a Custer State Park resident sticker on the right side of your rear window. This will allow you unlimited access into the park throughout your stay at Custer State Park."

"Can I trouble you for a park map and directions to the playhouse?" The costumer requested.

"Here is a copy of our park tourist guide, the *Tatanka.* Everything you need to know about Custer State Park is in that guide: detailed maps, trail information, scenic drives, recreation opportunities and restaurants."

"Tatanka," Merritt stated, as she surveyed the fifty-page park guide. "That's an interesting word. What does it mean?"

"It's the Lakota word for 'Bison,' something you'll see a lot of around here," Todd chuckled. "Custer State Park is home to a herd of over 1400 bison, or 'buffalo.' As tame as the beasts may seem, they are wild and dangerous. Do yourself a favor and steer clear of them when possible; otherwise they'll gore you to bits."

"I'll heed the warning," Merritt replied sincerely. The only time she'd ever seen a Bison was at the North Carolina Zoo. She anticipated seeing an emblem of the American west in its native habitat during her park stay.

"Smart girl," Ranger Miller replied before giving Merritt a detailed set of directions.

"Thank you for your help Ranger Miller."

"I look forward to opening weekend at the playhouse."

As Merritt drove into the park, she admired the striking scenery. For a mid-May day the weather was a perfect sixty degrees with a bright blue cloudless sky. The granite spires of the Black Hills coupled with large forests of ponderosa pine and sweeping valley floors offered some of the most picturesque views that she'd ever seen.

With over 71,000 acres, Custer is the largest state park in South Dakota and second largest in the United States. Named after General Armstrong Custer, who explored the area in 1874, the park was founded in the early 1900s as a wildlife preserve and state forest. By 1919, Custer Forest became Custer State Park, and has since become a headquarters for conservation, recreation and family fun. The park boasts a diverse array of wildlife, scenic drives, hikes, and not to mention an abundance of streams and lakes prime for fishing, swimming and boating.

Custer's geography is a place of stunning extremes. In the northwestern corner of the park you'll find Harney Peak, the tallest mountain east of the American Rockies and west of the European Alps. Contrast that to the park's southern corridor where you'll be met with a landscape of sweeping grassland prairie and big skies.

Within the park's boundaries, South Dakota operates nine campgrounds along with four unique resort lodges: the stately Game Lodge, the rustic Blue Bell, the sweeping Sylvan Lake Lodge and family friendly Legion Lake Lodge.

The Custer Playhouse is located on Center Lake Road, off Highway 87 on the Needles Scenic Highway.

The Playhouse grounds encompass seven acres and include a number of wooden structures including a large indoor playhouse, staff dorms, a dining area, rehearsal hall, prop and costume area, paint and set design studio, along with several additional miscellaneous buildings to aide in summer stock production.

As Merritt pulled into the gravel driveway she was flagged down by a theatre representative

"I'm Merritt Andrews and I'm working as a costumer for the playhouse this summer. Is this where I check in for duty?"

"You've come to the right place," a brunette in her mid-twenties smiled. "I'm Claudia Cosgrove and this is my third season working as a stagehand. You won't find a more dedicated and group of theatre people this side of the Mississippi. "

"It's a pleasure to meet you," Merritt shook Claudia's right hand through the car window.

"The pleasure is all mine," Claudia smiled, directly her to a temporary parking spot in a nearby gravel lot. "Check in and registration is in the theatre lobby."

"I'm Merritt Andrews, reporting for duty," the costumer approached the orientation desk.

"Miss. Andrews, I heard rave reviews about your talent as a costume designer from your advisor at UNC-CH, Doug Bennett. It's an honor to meet you." A dark-haired forty-five year old gentleman, donning horn-rimmed glasses greeted the recruit. "I'm Gully Gordon producer and stage manager for the Custer Playhouse."

"I'm Beth Seeley, the head of the ticket office and the business manager." An attractive middle-aged woman with blonde hair and blue eyes introduced herself.

"And I'm Kat Warner, the script supervisor for our summer production *Dakota*." Kat stands just over 5'6 and is in her mid-thirties. She dresses casually and wears her thick brown hair in a shoulder length shag cut.

"Kat is Custer's resident playwright," Gully cut in. "Miss Warner is the genius behind this season's playhouse production, *Dakota*."

"Don't give me all the credit," Kat contested. "Custer's music director, Artie Shaw composed the original music and lyrics for *Dakota*."

"It sounds like a fascinating play," Merritt put forth. "I look forward to reading the script."

"You'll love it! The story showcases South Dakota's rich history by bringing to life such historical figures as General Armstrong Custer, Crazy Horse, Wild Bill Hickok, along with Custer State Park founder Peter Norbeck," Beth informed. "The buzz surrounding *Dakota* has bolstered our pre-season ticket sales."

The group continued to chat for several minutes, as completed her registration. She was asked to sign several documents, including a theatre contract, which outlined her job description, pay and benefits.

"Congratulations you're officially a member of the Custer Playhouse crew!" Gully smiled as he filed Merritt's paperwork away. He then handed her a large canvas bag, which was filled with an orientation packet, Custer Playhouse tee shirt and water bottle. "For your dorm assignment, you'll be staying in the Alpine Cabin. It's one of our recently remodeled Civilian Conservation Corps units. The cabin has a sink, but the showers and bathrooms are located roughly seventy-five yards away in the bathhouse."

"You'll be rooming with my daughter Emma, who works as my assistant in the box office." Beth noted. "She has been working at the playhouse since she was fourteen. I'm sure that you'll hit it off."

"I can't wait to meet her," Merritt replied graciously before asking for directions to the staff dorms.

"To reach the dorm complex, you'll need to take a right out of the theatre parking lot onto Center Lake Road. Drive roughly 200 yards before turning into a gravel driveway, at the end of which, you'll find the dorms. The Alpine cabin is the second to last structure on your left," Kat explained.

"We're having a cook out on the quad behind the playhouse at seven-thirty where you can meet up with other cast and crew members. Immediately following the cook out the entire Custer crew is expected for our orientation meeting in the main theatre," Gully informed.

"See you there."

En route to her car, Merritt ran into Claudia.

"All checked in?" Claudia asked in an upbeat tone.

"I'm all set. I'm going to start moving into my dorm."

"To which dorm were you assigned?"

"Alpine."

"Cool. I'm in Ponderosa, which is right next door. If you need anything let me know."

"Likewise neighbor," Merritt smiled as she got into her Civic and started the ignition.

The playhouse dorm complex is situated on a clearing behind a thick patch of lodge pole pines adjacent to the main theatre complex. Fifteen cabins are scattered across the property, along with a medium sized mess hall, and bathhouse.

The Custer Playhouse cabins were built in the 1930s by the Civilian Conservation Corps, a public works organization, which was started under the New Deal proposed by Franklin D. Roosevelt. The organization was designed to provide relief to unemployed youth who had a hard time finding work during the Great Depression by providing workers with an education, and salary. During its tenure, the CCC was charged with a number of conservation projects across the United States.

Without the Civilian Conservation Corps, Custer State Park would not be the park it is today. From mid-1933 to November of 1941, four CCC camps worked to plant trees, build miles of roads, campgrounds, dams, bridges and buildings within the park. Several of the larger projects included the creation of Stockade and Center lakes. The Custer Playhouse is located within walking distance of Center Lake. The CCC workers used the company cabins while they built the dam and popular recreation lake.

The playhouse cabins are named after flora found within Custer or park notables such as founder Senator Norbeck or famous park-visitor Calvin Coolidge. Each cabin comes with a gravel parking space and a picnic table out front.

"I must be the first to arrive," Merritt thought to herself as she entered the space. The cabin décor has a rustic ambiance with modern charm. It is equipped with four beds, four sets of drawers, an overhead light, a ceiling fan and a mini fridge.

Merritt set her suitcase on the bed closest to the sink and right next to one of the dressers. She then proceeded to unload her car, which was filled to the brim. Having never been to South Dakota, Merritt figured it was better to bring too much stuff rather than too little. She'd hauled three suitcases filled with clothes, her portable sewing machine, a box of costume sewing patterns, alarm clock, her laptop, stereo, favorite albums, and a handful of camping gear across the country.

After spending two hours unloading her car and organizing her things in the dorm, Merritt phoned her parents to let them know she'd arrived in Custer safely.

Merritt, an only child, is very close to her parents, who live in North Carolina's capitol city of Raleigh. Her mom, Lynn, teaches high school English and her dad, Michael, is a pediatrician. Both were excited to hear details about their daughter's new job.

Following the phone call, the costumer explored the playhouse campus including crew facilities and nearby Center Lake.

The bathhouse is one of the newer structures on site, dating to the 1980s with the interior remodeled in 2000. It is divided into two sections, on the right you'll find the girls locker room with restrooms and showers, and the boy's locker room on the left.

The mess hall is comprised of a decent sized, though older kitchen, although with a buffet and eight large cafeteria tables. Merritt had to admit the whole set-up couldn't help but remind her of summer camp, of which she has fond memories.

From the dorms you access Center Lake via a quarter-mile forest trailhead. It is one of four recreational lakes located within Custer State Park and is popular area for swimming, picnicking and camping.

"What an ideal spot to relax," Merritt sat down a picnic table overlooking the lake. She pulled the *Tatanka* out of her Vera Bradley backpack, and spent the next half-hour reviewing the park guide, reading up on Custer's history and information on park attractions. The playhouse promises crewmembers one day off a week to allow for exploration of the surrounding area. Merritt kept his in mind she read through the variety of activities Custer has to offer.

"I should head back to the dorm and get ready for the cookout," Merritt glanced at her watch. "Perhaps my roommates have arrived?"

It was a twenty-minute walk back to Alpine from Center Lake. As Merritt re-entered her new summer home, she was met with two friendly faces.

"You must be our newest roommate," An attractive, tall and slender girl, with wavy brown shoulder length hair greeted Merritt. "I'm Rebecca Lane, also known as 'Laura Ingalls Wilder' and 'Grace Coolidge.'"

"And I'm Virginia 'Ginny' Terry, known to theater goers as the notorious Calamity Jane." Ginny has a pretty face and tall and athletic structure. She has short curly brown hair and brown eyes.

"It's nice to meet you both," Merritt shook their hands. "I'm Merritt Andrews, one of the summer costumers."

"Ginny and I were part of last summer's theatre company," Rebecca explained. "We attend the University of South Dakota as theatre arts majors. Gully is the Dean of the department in Vermillion, and Artie and Kat teach music and theatrical writing at USD."

"The University of South Dakota's Theatre Department has a wonderful reputation," Merritt noted.

"USD has sponsored the Custer Playhouse since 1946," Ginny noted. "It's a graduation requirement for theatre majors to spend at least one summer working as a stock actor or stagehand here in the glorious Black Hills."

"Does most of the Custer crew hail from USD?" Merritt inquired.

"Only forty-percent of the cast and crew are USD students or staff. Many of the actors come from larger markets such as Chicago or Denver. Some of the actors like Chet, Peter, and Marty are mainstays, having performed here year in and out for over twenty years. The Seeley's, live in the town of Custer where they teach English and history at the high school. Mr. and Mrs. Seeley are both on the board of the South Dakota Arts Council and big supporters of the Custer Playhouse, or CP as we call it," Ginny explained.

"I met Beth when I checked in," Merritt mentioned. "She seemed really nice."

"Her daughter, Emma is our other roommate. She should be here by the start of the cookout."

"Emma's great. She's a recent USD graduate herself and has worked for the playhouse since high school," Rebecca stated before changing the subject. "So tell us about yourself Merritt. What led you to become a card carrying member of the CP staff?"

"I graduated from the University of North Carolina at Chapel Hill a few weeks ago. For my first summer out of college, my advisor suggested I apply for a summer gig working at the Custer Playhouse to get my feet wet and to experience a different part of the country. He faxed Mr. Gordon my portfolio and I got the job."

"What an adventure," Ginny exclaimed. "North Carolina is a long way from South Dakota! How long did it take you to drive here?"

"The drive took six days. I did a lot of sightseeing along the way," Merritt admitted. "I spent two nights in Nashville with a friend from high school who goes to Vanderbilt. I then went to the zoo in Omaha, and I did some hiking in the Badlands National Park."

The Badlands National Park is located approximately seventy miles northeast of Custer State Park, off of Interstate Ninety. Although originally considered a harsh land by early settlers, the park is internationally renowned for its striking beauty. The topography ranges from impressive colorful spires, sharp ridges, canyons, gullies and sandstone buttes shaped by years of erosion to miles of mixed prairie and endless blue sky.

"The Badlands is a must see tour stop. The colors of the sandstone canyons are sublime," Rebecca enthused.

"The last time Becky and I visited the area, we spent half of the day enamored by the prairie dogs. They are adorable!"

"I could take my eyes off of them," Merritt agreed.

"Custer State Park also has a large prairie dog population. We'll have to hike the Prairie Trail one day to scope them out," Rebecca suggested.

"Did you go to Wall Drug to get your free glass of water?" Ginny asked, interested in Merritt's recent cross-country trip.

"How could I miss Wall Drug? It's an icon," Merritt smiled.

Wall is a small gateway town, servicing tourists to the Badlands National Park. It is best known for the famed roadside attraction Wall Drug.

In 1931, Dorothy and Ted Hustead, a pharmacist, bought Wall's drug store. The town of Wall was small and located in what seemed the middle of nowhere. With the Great Depression in full swing, the young couple struggled to make ends meet until Dorothy developed a brilliant marketing strategy to put Wall Drug on the map.

One sweltering summer day, Dorothy watched as countless cars driving by on nearby Interstate Ninety passed their drugstore by as they headed to Mount Rushmore, sixty miles west of Wall. Realizing that many of the travelers must be parched, Dorothy suggested they begin advertising free water on a highway billboard. The idea was that travelers would come for the water, but would end up purchasing other items such as ice cream, sodas, post-cards or even medication. The idea worked. Business began to boom and hasn't let up. Nearly seventy years later, Wall Drug is bigger than ever, averaging thousands of guests every summer.

"It's a bit campy, but I stop there every road trip to Custer," Ginny admitted. "I fill up on my free-water and opt in to buy of their delectable hot fudge sundaes."

The trio continued to chat for another hour until it was time to head over to the cookout. Merritt was relieved that she got along so well with both Ginny and Rebecca. The roommates have a lot in common, from tastes in music to recreational activities such as hiking, sightseeing and shopping.

"There you are!" Ginny shouted after noticing a 5'5 blonde haired girl walking across the playhouse quad. "Merritt, meet the final member of our cabin quartet, Miss Emma Seeley."

"Ginny and Rebecca told me all about you." Merritt stated as she shook Emma's hand.

"All lies I'm sure," Emma joked. "What's your role with the playhouse this year?"

"Costume associate."

"You'll be working with Dot and Bob. They are wonderful people," Emma held. "I'm working in the ticket office this summer."

"That's what your mom said. I met her when I first checked in."

"She'll chat your ear off, but I love her," Emma smiled. "We have a tough task ahead of us this summer. If we don't reach our summer sales quota it'll be RIP to the Custer Playhouse."

"A park ranger mentioned the playhouse's future is in limbo?" Merritt questioned.

"It's a complicated issue. I'm sure Alistair and Gully will go into detail about the whole saga at tonight's meeting," Emma sighed. "In short if we don't make a profit this summer, the Governor's office will shut down the playhouse and revoke our lease."

"That's terrible!"

"The Custer Playhouse has been a Black Hills tradition for over sixty years. It has launched countless careers and bolstered park tourism. I just pray that *Dakota* becomes a smash show so our curtain stays up and the lights don't go down." As Emma finished her sentence four handsome males in their mid-twenties approached the group.

"Howdy gals? Ready for some grub?" A tall dark-haired boy in jeans and a tee shirt greeted the girls.

"First we need to introduce you to our newest CP addition and costumer extraordinaire," Ginny replied. "Merritt meet Luke and Tom Barber."

"Pleased to meet you," Luke smiled a Merritt. "Resident electrician and the cuter of the Barber siblings."

"Don't listen to him," his brother cut in. "I'm Tom, the CP lighting director, obviously much better looking than my younger brother."

"This is my boyfriend Jim Carter," Rebecca introduced Merritt to a 6'2, brown hair and blue eyed twenty-two year old. "Jim is going to play Cool Cal Coolidge, my on-stage husband as well as explorer Meriwether Lewis."

"I'm Ethan Daniels, the property 'props' master. Props and costumes go hand and hand. I'm sure that we'll be working together often."

"Ethan is a newbie too; although he grew up with us in Rapid City," Luke and Tom noted.

"I ended up going to the University of Washington for film school. I graduated about a year ago."

"What brought you to Custer?" Merritt asked.

"Frankly Seattle's too rainy and L.A. is too sprawling. I figured a summer gig with the famed Custer Playhouse would be the perfect opportunity to save up enough money to move to New York."

"Ah yes, the Big Apple. A great town for theatre and film, but expensive," Merritt agreed.

"We should probably get over to the buffet before the food runs out," Luke suggested.

"I am famished," Ginny followed as the group headed to the buffet. Food services had grilled up plenty of burgers, hotdogs and a variety of other food options to make sure that no palette was left empty.

Merritt grabbed a plate and filled up on a mixture of food including a cheeseburger with no bun, salad, and baked lays.

"What no bun?" Ginny questioned.

"I'm gluten intolerant, which means that I can't eat the protein gluten, found in wheat, barley, and several other grains. Unfortunately no wheat equals no bread, cookies, pizza, etc..."

"What a bummer."

"Pizza is the only thing I really miss. Other than that it's not too bad. They have a lot of tasty gluten free products now," Merritt replied before as the group sat down at a large picnic table.

"Why *is* he here?" Emma groaned halfway through dinner as she noticed a man in a black suit and briefcase crossing the lawn.

"Who is that?" Merritt questioned, sensing the irritation in Emma's voice.

"Mike Trump. He's an envoy from the Governor's office. He petitioned to have this season cancelled back in January. He claimed that our buildings were not up to code and therefore a safety hazard. Luckily the Arts Council and volunteers from across the state were able to fix all the violations in time for us to open. The Governor's office was none too pleased very angry when we met their challenge."

"Why is the governor so opposed to the playhouse?"

"Money. His office thinks the park would earn more revenue if they demolished the theatre and used the land to build a convention center and lease the property to a concessionaire," Emma explained. "The South Dakota state legislature supported our theatrical presence in the park by vetoing the Governor's proposal. The governor has attempted to undermine the legislature by working with the Attorney General's office to figure out a backdoor approach to accomplish their mission. Their first tactic was to peg the playhouse buildings as structurally unsafe. We rose above that challenge, so Trump has concocted a new way to evict us."

"Which is?"

"If we fail to yield a profit this season the state won't renew our lease, which is up in September of this year," Emma fumed. "They claim lack of money card to scare taxpayers, but in reality the playhouse pays for 98% of its own budget. The State gives us less than $3,000 per year."

"Surely the Park Superintendent is against the playhouse shutting down?" Merritt asked. "It promotes tourism to Custer."

"The last superintendent, Bobby Cooper was terrific, but Wade Harden is a jerk who is the pocket of one of the lobbyists vying to gain a potential concessionaire contract! Harden has publicly stated that he supports the termination of our lease."

"I'm confident that if we put our best efforts into making *Dakota* a first rate production that the playhouse will generate enough revenue from ticket sales to stay open!" Merritt assumed.

"The playhouse is promoting the production as much as we can," Emma stated. "We're running ads in regional newspapers and television and radio stations. Alistair and Gully are also organizing few campground shows with a few cast members enticing park visitors to buy tickets."

"I'll be happy to help with marketing efforts in my free time," Merritt offered.

"I'll hold you to it," Emma replied with a smile. "We'll need all hands on deck, if we're going to outsmart Trump and company."

Chapter 2

The cookout lasted for approximately forty-five minutes before CP members migrated into the theatre for the orientation meeting. The Alpine group sat down on the third row back from the stage. A series of director's chairs with microphones were set up on stage, along with a projector screen.

"Welcome to the summer season of the Custer Playhouse. I'm Gully Gordon, the co-producer and stage manager for *Dakota*. Also on stage we have our talented director Alistair Fitzgerald, assistant director Blair Westcott, resident playwright and script supervisor, Kat Warner, music director Artie Scott, ticket sales and marketing gurus Beth and Bill Seeley and Custer Playhouse President Mr. Jeffrey Beaumont. Over the course of the meeting each of us will be detailing this year's production, schedule and theatre goals. Later on each of you will have a chance to introduce yourselves and your integral roles in pulling off a top rate production," Gully explained. "I'll turn over the floor to Miss. Kat Warner and Mr. Artie Scott."

Kat approached the podium with a tall, lanky gray haired male in khakis, loafers and a loose fitting pastel Oxford shirt.

"Hello. I'm Artie and this is the lovely Miss Warner. Collectively we are the creative minds behind this year's production *Dakota*. Under usual circumstances the playhouse puts on three to five productions during our summer season, however, considering this year's budget, our board decided it was best to concentrate our energies on one stellar show. And I can assure you that Kat and I have written a dandy. *Dakota* is a mix of drama, music and history guaranteed to captivate even the pickiest of audience."

"When Artie and I set out to write an original production for the Custer Playhouse's 64th year in Black Hills, we wanted to create something that was unique to this region and expressed the spirit of South Dakota. *Dakota* is a historical play divided into two parts. The first half focuses on South Dakota's prehistory through the mid-1800s. The first scene focuses on the story of the Lakota people's settling of the land, accompanied by Artie's Lakota ballad *Song of the Plains*.

The second scene is focused on Lewis and Clark's time in South Dakota as they lead the Corps of Discovery up the mighty Missouri River, which flows through the eastern and central sections of our state. In scene three we fast-forward to General Armstrong Custer's exploration of the Black Hills and the discovery of the gold at French Creek in Custer State Park.

A song entitled *The Way West* demonstrates the battle for land as settlers populate the area, at the expense of the native Lakota, who are determined to protect their sacred home. This culminates in the narratives of U.S. General Armstrong Custer and Lakota leader Crazy Horse and their differing point of views. Artie consulted with Lakota tribe leaders and our own Marty Tate and Peter Wiseman to write a heartfelt ballad entitled *My Lands are where my Dead Lie Buried*, which is taken from Crazy Horse's famed quote explaining to the white settlers where his people's land is located. The song is sung half in English and half in the traditional Lakota language and uses tribal instruments.

In the final scene before intermission, we turn our focus on Deadwood and the infamous shooting of Wild Bill Hickok by that scoundrel Jack McCall. The first half will end with the play's title song *Dakota.*

After a thirty-minute intermission, the audience will return to a scene depicting Laura Ingalls Wilder. An adult Laura reminisces about her childhood on the South Dakota prairie and sings a ballad entitled *My Prairie Home.* Laura will act as a story-telling bridge between the old-west and moving into the twentieth century and beyond.

The next set of scenes is set around the founding of Custer State Park, Mount Rushmore and the Crazy Horse Monument. The final scene will feature famed Custer State Park resident and playwright Badger Clark reciting his well-known Cowboy Prayer poem. The curtains will briefly close. The audience applause sounds, the curtains reopen with an encore of the song *Dakota,* before the cast take their final bows."

"It sounds like a wonderful historical play," Ethan whispered to Merritt as Kat finished her summary.

"I can't wait to read the script," Merritt whispered back before turning her attention back to the stage, as Director Fitzgerald took the microphone.

Alistair Fitzgerald is short, but what he lacks in height he makes up in poise and his vocal projection. He seems to have a knack for fashion, wearing a pair of well-pressed linen slacks, an Oxford shirt, and Ascot and alligator loafers. Mr. Fitzgerald wears a thick-rimmed pair of designer glasses and keeps his thick gray hair well-coiffed.

"Good evening," Alistair's dynamic voice projected throughout the theatre. "I'm Director Fitzgerald and this is my tenth summer working as the stage director for the Custer Playhouse. I have two degrees in fine arts from NYU and UCLA. Throughout my career I have acted and directed television, Broadway productions and a number of repertory and stock theatre productions. At the advice of my beautiful wife Celeste, who serves as the CP Call Girl, I settled down in South Dakota and have been teaching theatre and film courses at USD in Vermillion on the other end of the state since 2000.

Kat and Artie have supplied us with a fabulous play. It's my goal as the director to make the history of South Dakota come to life in an engaging stage production. In order to do so I'll need your help. Every member of this cast and crew will play an integral role in ensuring that *Dakota* is a success," Fitzgerald stated before asking his assistant director to address the crowd.

"I'm Blair Westcott," Blair is tall and wears her thick blonde hair pulled back in a ponytail. "As for my background. I just earned my Masters of Fine Arts Degree from USD back in December. This is my fourth summer with the Custer Playhouse. In 2007, I worked as an actress, playing Dorothy in *The Wizard of Oz*. As much as I enjoyed my time in the spotlight, working behind the scenes is more up my alley. In 2008 and 2009 I worked as a script supervisor and stagehand. This year I'll be acting as Mr. Fitzgerald's assistant director.

At check-in you received an orientation packet. This packet includes a copy of the script, a personalized schedule, performance dates and other pertinent information regarding the production and general park safety information.

Please review the information and let me know if there are any problems with scheduling. This goes for both cast and crewmembers.

Opening night is Thursday June the 17th. This means we have less than four weeks to rehearse, finish our sets, design the costumes and assemble props. That's a tall order and I expect everyone to meet the challenge.

We'll discuss the production timeline during tomorrow's meeting, which will be held right here in the main theatre at ten a.m."

After finishing up her statements, Blair sat back down, and Mr. and Mrs. Seeley took the stage.

"I'm Bill Seeley and this is my wife Beth. We both are residents of the town of Custer City. We have been working with the Custer Playhouse for the better part of twenty years. Both Beth and I are on the boards for the South Dakota Arts Council and Custer Playhouse. Beth manages the ticket office with our daughter Emma. I work as a publicist and marketer for the playhouse. I also sell concessions during performances."

"As many of you are aware, the Custer Playhouse is facing financial hardships. With the down economy, people don't have the extra money to contribute to the playhouse fund like they used to. That's why ticket sales are more important than ever this season. Unless the playhouse makes a profit this year we will lose our lease when it expires in the fall.

In order to bolster ticket sales, we are working very hard to promote this year's production. The week before opening night Bill and I have arranged to set up booths at various park locations such as Sylvan Lake, Game Lodge, Legion Lake, and Blue Bell and in Custer City to sell tickets and inform the public about our work to save the Custer Playhouse.

The playhouse will also sponsor several theatre nights where actors will perform select scenes from *Dakota* at park campgrounds. In order to pull this off, I'll need volunteers. In the coming weeks I'll be posting sign-up sheets in the mess hall," Beth stated before motioning for Jeffrey Beaumont.

"I'm Jeff Beaumont, Director of the South Dakota Arts Council in Rapid City and President of the Custer Playhouse board. I speak on behalf of the entire board when I say how happy I am for you to be part of our season. Since its inception sixty-four years ago, the Custer Playhouse has provided visitors to the Black Hills region with quality family entertainment. This year will be no different. *Dakota* is landmark play, which shows the Custer Playhouse at its best. I have no doubt that with our hard work and dedication will rise to meet the challenge facing the future of the playhouse. For those of you unfamiliar with the details, our governor has voiced his displeasure with the Custer Playhouse's presence within CSP from a financial standpoint. The Governor feels that the playhouse is not as relevant in a society fueled by on-demand technology, televisions and IMAX theatres. He questions the artistic merit of our organization and the true benefit of having a stock theatre in a state park. I think it's safe to say that the playhouse is a vital part of the dichotomy, which is Custer State Park. We allow visitors a chance to see affordable first-rate theatre year in and year out. We are just as much a part of this park as the Bison herd or Harney Peak. I know that theatre has never been a goldmine in dollars and cents, but our company is worth its weight in cultural gold. Whether or not we earn enough money to convince the governor's office to renew our lease or not, we will have accomplished something pure and good: bringing quality entertainment to visitors. If we are forced out, it will be with a storied legacy; a legacy that no convention center or concession stand will ever live up to. Thank you for being part of the team and break a leg this season."

The playhouse roared with applause as Beaumont finished his remarks.

It was obvious to Merritt how special the Custer Playhouse was to longstanding members of the cast and crew. She genuinely hoped that *Dakota* would be a big enough hit to convince the governor's office to renew the playhouse's park lease in September.

"Thank you Jeff for that excellent speech," Gully stated as he returned to the microphone. "Now before we call it a night I'm going to give every cast a crew member a chance to introduce themselves. When I call your name, please stand up and tell us a little about yourself."

During the course of the next half-hour members of the cast and crew spent several minutes on introducing themselves.

"I want to thank you all for coming to tonight's meeting," Gully stated after the introductions concluded. "I know you'll all enjoy living and performing in what I consider to be the prettiest state park in America. We'll have a continental breakfast tomorrow morning from eight to nine-thirty. As Blair stated earlier there is a mandatory meeting here in the theatre tomorrow at ten a.m. Have a good night and..." Before Gully could dismiss the cast and crew for the night, Mike Trump rudely interrupted him.

"Ahem," Trump shouted as he rushed to the stage. "I have something to say before you conclude this little meeting!"

"For goodness sakes, shut your pipe Trump," Wild Bill actor Chet Rawlins shouted.

"You best mind your manners Mr. Rawlins," Trump retorted. "I have *the* power to close you down."

"We're sick of your empty threats and pre-fabricated baloney," Rawlins shot back.

"I suggest that you stop being antagonistic and start listening to my so-called baloney?" Trump rejoined harshly. "Now Mr. Gordon, I'd appreciate it if you'd allow me one minute to address the cast and crew before they are dismissed for the evening."

"Be my guest Mike," Gully groaned, handing Mr. Trump the microphone.

"My name is Mike Trump. I'm an envoy from the governor and attorney general's offices in Pierre. I have been charged with overseeing the summer stage run of the Custer Playhouse. As much as I admire the long tradition of your stock troupe, the state cannot afford to invest taxpayers' hard earned money into a fledging arts project, nor can we lease valuable park real estate to an organization that deters potential from Custer's lucrative park tourism industry.

That being said, it is my hope that this season will yield a profit, so that my office can extend the Playhouse's lease for years to come. To ensure that the playhouse has a successful run, I have been asked to oversee production spending so that you do not go over budget. I have prepared an information leaflet regarding the governor's stance on this issue and fiscal goals that outlines facts versus skewed sentimental misinformation."

"Put a sock in it Trump," a voice from the crowd reproached. "You want the playhouse to fail so you can get rich from some outsourced concessionaire."

Ignoring the derogatory remarks from the crowd, Trump rolled his eyes and boldly exited the playhouse.

"Talk about off stage drama," Merritt sighed.

"I told you that Trump is a jerk," Emma sneered.

"He is here to sabotage the production," Rebecca feared.

"We'll outsmart that two bit jerk," Ginny vowed.

Following the meeting, Merritt tracked down her fellow costumers Bob Mero and Dot Darlington. Both are theatre pros with design experience in New York and Chicago. Bob is sixty-five with thick white hair and blue eyes. Dot is short and stout. She looks remarkably young for fifty. Like Merritt, Dot, along with her twin sister Dolly, is originally from North Carolina and speaks with a soft southern drawl.

The costumers spent several minutes getting acquainted, before Merritt headed back to her cabin. The time was only ten-thirty, but she had to admit she was very sleepy. After washing up and reading through the orientation packet, Merritt hit the sack. She needed to be well rested for her first full day on the job.

Chapter 3:

"Good morning sleepy head," Ginny greeted Merritt as she slowly arose from her bed.

"What time is it?" Merritt panicked, as she searched for her portable alarm clock.

"Early enough," Rebecca replied with a yawn as she washed her face at the nearby sink.

"It's just after eight," Ginny stated in a perky tone.

"You had me scared," Merritt replied. "I thought I'd overslept."

"Don't worry Ginny's our built in alarm clock," Rebecca joked. "She's one of those obnoxious morning roosters who wakes up overly peppy and doesn't require caffeine."

"I'm glad someone in this cabin is an early riser," Merritt stated, through a series of yawns. "I'm a notorious night owl."

"Me too," Rebecca followed. "If I didn't have Ginny as a roommate at USD, I'd have missed most of my morning classes."

"Good morning," Emma greeted her fellow roommates as she re-entered the cabin after her morning shower.

"Morning Emma."

"I was thinking we could head on over to the mess hall in a few minutes to grab some grub?" Ginny suggested.

"If they have coffee I'm there," Merritt pulled on a pair of jeans and polo shirt.

By the time they reached the mess hall, there was a large line at the buffet. The playhouse provides company members with two meals a day, breakfast and a late lunch. Today's breakfast options consisted of waffles, eggs and bacon, cereal and muffins.

"I'll forgo the line and stick with milk and cereal," Rebecca stated after surveying the menu.

"Cereal and juice sounds good to me," Merritt agreed.

"Waffles are my weakness. Fattening or not, I can't resist them," Ginny admitted.

"I'm definitely going for the waffles," Emma concurred.

"We'll meet you at the table," Rebecca replied before she and Merritt headed to the cereal bar.

After grabbing a bowl of Rice Chex with skim milk, a banana, a glass of orange juice and hot cup of coffee, Merritt and Rebecca sat down at a table with Jim and his roommate Justin Martin, the playhouse sound engineer.

Jim greeted Rebecca with a kiss on the cheek.

"Hey you," Rebecca beamed.

"How are you this morning?" Jim inquired before take a bite of waffle.

"Good now that I have coffee."

"I know the feeling," Jim smiled.

"Is everyone pumped about our first full day of pre-production on *Dakota*?"

"Definitely," the group agreed.

"*Dakota* is going to be one of the best productions the Custer Playhouse has ever put on. The script is fantastic and the music Tony worthy," Jim stated. "The cast isn't too shabby either."

"Hey don't forget the crew," Justin joked.

"Of course I respect you Martin," Jim rejoined. "I don't have a choice. You control the microphone."

For the next half hour, the group talked about the playhouse and their summer activity plans within the park.

"We definitely have to hike Harney Peak," Rebecca noted. "The views from the summit are spectacular."

"The Harney Peak ascent is a must-do while in Custer," Ginny agreed. "The hike is hell on the knees, but you can't find a better hike than Little Devil's Tower, Sunday Gulch or the Cathedral Spires, which are the three of the trailheads leading to the peak."

"I'm game," Merritt thought the adventure sounded fun.

"It's settled then. Before this summer's out we'll organize a hiking party to ascend the mightiest cliff in Custer."

After finishing breakfast, Merritt and her roommates headed back to Alpine to freshen up before the ten o'clock meeting. At nine fifty the girls grabbed their theatre notebooks and headed over to the playhouse, which is roughly a five-minute walk from the cabins.

"Good morning! I hope everyone had a restful night's sleep," Gully's friendly voice sounded from the stage. "Before we break into our production oriented groups, Ranger Suzy Sinclair is here to discuss park safety. I want to remind all of you that first and foremost, Custer is a state park dedicated to conserving the natural beauty and unique wildlife of this area. It's our responsibility as park residents to be respectful of the land and its wildlife. I ask that you all heed Ranger Sinclair's instructions."

"Thank you Gully. I'm grateful for the opportunity to address your fine cast of thespians and crafty playhouse crewmembers," Ranger Sinclair smiled as she approached the microphone. She is a forty-seven veteran park ranger who stands just over 5'4 with short blonde hair and green eyes. "I'm Suzy Sinclair, a senior park biologist and curator at the Peter Norbeck Visitor Center, which is located directly across the street from the historic Game Lodge. Custer State Park is an amazing place, and I'm sure you will all enjoy your summer in the park. However given the park's unique environment it's important that you understand park rules and park safety. These regulations are not just arbitrary rules, meant to aggravate you; they are in place to protect you and the park's natural resources. Failure to abide by these rules will result in fines, and possibly eviction from park property. The Custer Playhouse has a reputation of quality theatre; and if one of you decides to go rogue and not obey park regulations, you'll let the entire company down. Better to keep the drama on stage rather than off. Understood?"

"Understood," the crowd of theatre workers replied.

"Common sense rule number one: Do not feed or approach wildlife. The park's biggest attraction is also its most dangerous. Custer State Park is home to a herd of as many as 1,500 bison, more commonly known as buffalo. Bison are the largest terrestrial mammal in North America, and although these magnificent creatures look docile and safe to approach; they are quick, agile and dangerous. Bison can grow to six feet tall and weigh more than two tons. They can run at speeds of over thirty-five miles per hour. More visitors are injured or killed from bison attacks than anything else, so at all costs DO NOT approach the bison. The bison often hang out near park resorts and campgrounds, particularly the Game Lodge. You might even wake up one morning to see a bison sleeping on your doorstep. This is not just cause to let your guard down. Remember that we are on their turf. It's our duty to respect their space. When on foot stay at least twenty-five yards away from bison. When driving in the park, especially on the Wildlife Loop, remember that bison have the rule of the road. If they are blocking traffic, wait patiently for them to cross. Honking at bison won't make them move any faster, and if anything will cause the bison to get aggressive. They can do a load of damage to your car so unless you're in the mood to chat with your insurance adjustor, just be cautious and use common sense when driving around bison."

"Bison are no joke," Emma whispered to Merritt. "I've seen several nonsensical visitors meet the wrath of an angry bison in an effort to nail the perfect photo-op. Next thing you know the bison gores them with its sharp tusks, throwing the person 100 feet. They wind up with a mangled face and expensive hospital bill or worse."

"I don't blame the bison," Ginny added in. "How would you feel if some stranger started encroaching on your space? They are wild animals. They are using their natural instincts to protect themselves. Nine times out of ten it's the human, not the bison's fault when an attack occurs."

"Speaking of driving... you speed demons need to slow down. The maximum speed limit allowed in Custer State Park is thirty-five miles per hour," Ranger Sinclair stated firmly. "This speed limit is in place for a reason. The father of Custer State Park, Peter Norbeck went to painstaking lengths to map out the park roads. The roads are designed to highlight the park's scenery; not to serve as a speedway. The roads around the park curve like a snake in motion, sharp turns and unpredictable bends. Driving over thirty-five miles per hour will put you as well as other drivers and wildlife at risk. Please obey the speed laws; it'll give you more control over your vehicle, thus preventing a tragic accident from occurring."

"I just hope Chet Rawlins *pays her mind.* He almost ran me down with his car yesterday." Merritt overheard Ethan whisper to Tom Barber, sitting in the row behind her.

"Everybody knows Chet's a speed demon. He drives like a lunatic, especially when he has been drinking," Tom replied. "I'm surprised he still has his license."

"Now that we've covered bison and cars," Suzy continued. "I'll briefly apprise you of a few additional park rules and safety measures. Because of the threat of forest fires, open fires are only prohibited in approved fire grates located on campgrounds and picnic areas. Anyone under twenty-one found to be in possession of alcohol is subject to fines and prosecution. For those of you above the legal drinking age, open containers of alcohol in a motor vehicle are prohibited. It's also important to note that loaded firearms are not allowed in the park.

If you go out hiking, be sure to stay on the trails and do not hike alone. When in the park's backcountry bring plenty of drinking water. Always wear insect repellent containing DEET when outside. Mosquitoes carrying the West Nile virus and ticks carrying Lyme disease are found throughout the park. Poison ivy is abundant within the park. So if you see any plants with three leaves, stay clear. Otherwise you'll be itching like crazy without much relief.

The expression *'if you don't like the weather wait five minutes'* perfectly describes the forecast in Custer State Park. The weather in the Black Hills is constantly changing with rain, extreme hail, lightning and strong winds typical. Just because it's sunny when you start out your day, be prepared for an ever-changing climate. Keep rain gear handy at all times and stay inside during storms. If you follow these simple common sense rules you'll have a fantastic and safe summer in CSP."

Ranger Sinclair spent the next ten minutes briefly highlighting park activities such as Ranger talks, guided nature walks, nighttime programs and other CSP sponsored events that playhouse workers might enjoy on days off from the theatre.

"I'm leaving my business card, along with several flyers detailing park regulations and information in the theatre lobby. If you have any questions or concerns please don't hesitate to contact me via cell-phone or stop by the Peter Norbeck Center," Suzy stated as she wrapped up her speech. "Good luck with *Dakota*. I'm sure it will be a big hit with tourists and locals alike!"

Gully and Alistair briefly addressed the entire theatre company before breaking everyone up into small production oriented groups.

The primary cast and stock actors remained in the theatre annex with Blair and Alistair to discuss rehearsals and complete a preliminary read-through of the script. Set Designer John Hood led a select group of stagehands; along with property master Ethan Daniels to the Scene Shop, a set and paint workshop located behind the playhouse to discuss set construction. Gully rallied the remaining stagehands, along lighting and sound engineers to the Playhouse Control Booth to discuss the electrical and acoustical aspects of pre-production.

In the theatre lobby, Merritt met up with her fellow costumers Dot and Bob. Dot's sister, Make-up and Wig Artist, Dolly Darlington was also on hand for the mid-morning meeting. Dolly is slightly taller than her sister Dot and wears her thick curly hair in a short bob.

"Merritt, this is my sister Dolly," Dot introduced the pair. "Dolly spends most of the year doing television make-up in L.A. She's worked on several popular shows including *Operation Forensics*."

"I love that show," Merritt replied with a smile.

"It's a lot of fun. One minute I'm making up actors to look like corpses and the next I'm glamming up O.F. stars Tyler Jackson and Kara Michaels," Dolly enthused. "Still, no gig in Hollywood beats a summer in the Black Hills. I always make time for my stage home at the Custer Playhouse."

"Merritt is from North Carolina too," Dot told her sister.

"What a small world. Dot and I haven't lived in the Tar Heel state in ages, but we visit as often as we can. If for no other reason than to eat barbeque at Wilber's and go to the beach."

"You can't beat pulled pork and hushpuppies at Wilber's in Goldsboro, that's for sure," Merritt agreed.

The group chatted in a few more minutes before heading down to the Costume and Make-Up shops, located in the theatre's basement.

"Here we are," Bob stated as he unlocked the door and turned on the overhead lights to the Costume Shop annex.

The Custer Playhouse Costume Shop is situated in a 2000 square foot enclosed space adjacent to the Make-Up and Wig shop, and across the hall from the green room and staircase to the theatre wings.

"Let me give you the grand tour," Bob replied enthusiastically as he showed Merritt the run of things. "In the wardrobe closet we store costumes from past productions. Over the next few days we can sift through our costume stock and pull anything we can re-use or repurpose in *Dakota*. Anything we don't have on site we'll make from scratch or roundup from other theatre companies or costume shops in the area."

They continued onto the sewing room.

"This is the room where we'll spend most of our time. Each of us has our own costume design table, which is complete with Bernina sewing machine, fabric cutter, and a hoard of sewing supplies including: zippers, buttons, Velcro, hook and eyes, safety pins, measuring tape, pencils, hot glue gun and sticks, seam rippers, needles and threads, etc."

"Talk about a sewer's dream space," Merritt enthused. "Everything is so organized!"

"We've got to keep it that way. Otherwise things will get very hectic with misplaced buttons and spindles!"

Merritt recalled her first dabble in costuming during a high school production of Hamlet. All the fabric got mixed up and the costumes looked more like rag doll than disturbed royal.

"Luckily, over the years Dot and I have established a decent organization system designed to streamline efficiency and costume production," Bob smiled.

In addition to the sewing tables, the room also includes fabric storage, ironing boards, hat and dress mannequins, and a large shelf of costume books and costume patterns organized by historical era or genre.

"Here you'll find our Check and Dressing Rooms. Every night before a performance, our actors check out their costume and are fitted here. After the show the actors return their costumes here so we can wash and dry-clean and press the clothing prior to the next show. We have washers and dryers and a modified dry cleaning system down the hall, allowing for a majority of the costume cleaning to be done on site. We stagger check in times for individual actors based on how long it takes them to get fitted, their make-up requirements, call-times, etc...It's our job to keep the actors on track, and to have any costume changes set out for the actors so the show moves along as planned. As long as we stay focused and the actors follow cues this usually isn't too stressful."

"That's if we make sure that Peter and Chet stay clear of each other," Dot warned in a blunt tone. "Otherwise we'll end up with World War III."

"Dot's referring to Crazy Horse actor Peter Wiseman and Wild Bill portrayer Chet Rawlins," Dolly explained. "The two actors are Custer Playhouse staples, having performed here since the 1980s. Unfortunately they loathe one another."

"Why?" Merritt asked, curious about the origin of the actors' feud.

"They used to be good friends, until a blow-out fight in 1986. I think the argument had something about alcohol and a car wreck, but I'm not exactly sure. They despise one another."

"It boils down to the fact that Chet Rawlins is an arrogant jerk and Peter is a gentleman," Bob stated with conviction.

"That's a bit harsh," Dot gave her two cents. "Chet is the epitome of professionalism on stage."

"On stage sure, he's a top talent, but offstage? Chet is a total tyrant. He's cocky and at times impossible to work with. He nearly broke poor Celeste's heart..."

"Director Fitzgerald's wife?" Merritt pressed.

"It's a long story," Bob hesitated with a sigh, "Before Celeste and Alistair married, she was engaged to Chet. That idiot Chet cheated on Celeste, sending her into a tailspin."

"Given the history I'm surprised Director Fitzgerald would want to keep Mr. Rawlins on as an actor," Merritt replied.

"Like I said, Chet's a damn good thespian and popular with playhouse patrons. Alistair is too much of a professional to let offstage drama upset the overall production," Bob explained. "Enough with idle gossip, we've got a wardrobe to plan."

"Indeed we do," Dot, replied as the group returned to the *design studio* where to plot their creative itinerary. "Today is May the 23rd, meaning we have less than three weeks until dress rehearsals begin and only four weeks until opening night on June the 17th. Gully requests that our preliminary costume design sketches, to be turned in this Friday for approval. That doesn't give us much time to research the history behind each character's style of dress, and design an appropriate costume. Therefore I suggest that we streamline our efforts. We divide the cast list, each of us focusing on a specific set characters and actors. I'll handle the Deadwood cast of characters," Dot volunteered, "As a few years back I worked on a Rapid City production of *The Trial of Jack McCall,* and I learned a lot about Deadwood's history. It shouldn't take me too long to sketch out a few ideas, and possibly even pull the male costumes from our wardrobe closet."

"Dot's in charge of costumes for Wild Bill, Calamity Jane, Seth Bullock, Jack McCall and the Deadwood stock actors," Bob noted in his organizational notebook.

"I'll do Lewis and Clark as well," Dot added in. "I'm a Corps of Discovery buff."

"What about you Merritt? Any preferences on which characters you'd be interested in focusing on?"

"I'm flexible, but it would be fun to research costume ideas for Custer State Park notables Peter Norbeck and Badger Clark. I'm up for designing the costumes for Laura Ingalls Wilder and the President and Mrs. Coolidge as well."

"I'll put you down for those characters then," Bob annotated on the cast list. "Do you also mind working on the costumes for General Armstrong Custer as well?"

"Not at all," Merritt nodded.

"So that leaves me to focus on Crazy Horse, Sitting Bull, and sculptors Korczak and Borglum, and several stock actors" Bob stated.

"That works," Merritt and Dot agreed.

"Why don't we each spend the next three days researching and sketching out design ideas? On Wednesday we'll meet up to discuss our research and share ideas. Once we know the direction we plan to take with each character's on stage appearance we'll figure out which costumes we can pull from the wardrobe closet, and which we need to make from scratch or borrow from area sources," Bob suggested.

"I'll research hairstyles and work up some make-up ideas that we can forward to Gully as well," Dolly added in.

In theatre it's essential for make-up and hair to coordinate with the costume department to ensure an authentic and appropriate look for each character. The costume department also occasionally works with the property master to ensure that the correct on stage accessories are acquired.

"As for researching costumes per the character's historical period we have a number of resources available on site," Dot noted. "The bookshelf in the sewing room corner is full of books related to historical dress. And of course the Internet is a valuable tool as well."

"Do you know where the best place to gain Internet access is in the park?" Merritt inquired. "I couldn't grab hold of a signal from my cabin."

"Unfortunately due to the budget cuts this year, there isn't any Internet service on the playhouse grounds unless you purchase your own server. Legion Lake, and the Game Lodge offer free wireless Internet, or you can drive into Custer City and use the computers in the library."

"Legion is close by. I'll go up there tonight and start my preliminary research. Tomorrow I'll stop by Badger Clark's house and the Peter Norbeck Visitor Center to ascertain biographical information and photographs."

"I suggest that you schedule a visit to the 1881 Courthouse in Custer City, which is the home of Custer County's historical archives. The staff is knowledgeable of the area's history, particularly General Custer," Dot suggested to Merritt.

"Dot's right. The 1881 Courthouse is a treasure trove of information," Bob agreed. "My friend Cindy Darling works on site as a curator. She'll be more than happy to assist you with your research."

The group then spent several more minutes discussing their pre-production itinerary. The goal was to spend the first week on research, taking the actors measurements, and surveying what they could pull from wardrobe stock and what needed to be made from scratch or acquired from outside sources. Weeks two and three would be dedicated to sewing, and fitting actors, along with prepping for dress rehearsals.

"We'll meet back here on Wednesday afternoon to discuss our research and costume ideas. It would also help if everyone could read through *Dakota* at least once by Wednesday. Take note of any specific wardrobe notations or props that we need to incorporate into our final costume designs."

With that the group parted ways, and Merritt headed back to Alpine. She pulled out her laptop and typed out production notes, including the list of actors/characters she was charged with dressing. Merritt then printed two copies of list from the compact printer she'd hauled across country; placing one list on the wall by her bed and the second list in her production notebook.

| Dot: | Bob: | Merritt: |

Wild Bill = Chet Rawlins	Crazy Horse = Peter Wiseman	Peter Norbeck/General Armstrong Custer = Jack Webster
Calamity Jane = Virginia Terry	Sitting Bull= Marty Tate	
Jack McCall/ Capt. William Clark= Rick Summers	Korczak = Cliff Arnett	Laura Ingalls Wilder/Grace Coolidge = Rebecca Lane
	Borglum: Hank Rogers	President Calvin Coolidge = Jim Carter
Capt. Meriwether Lewis = Jim Carter	Stock Actors = Lakota and U.S. Calvary, Mt. Rushmore and Crazy Horse Monuments	Badger Clark = Leroy Stewart
Stock Actors = Deadwood and Corps of Discovery		Stock Actors: Prairie, Cowboy Prayer, Calvary, Miscellaneous

Merritt glanced at her watch; the time was just after three. Ginny, Rebecca and Emma were still busy with production meetings.

"I think I'll walk down to Center Lake and read the script for *Dakota*," Merritt thought to herself as she grabbed her Vera backpack, bottled water and the script. "Later on I'll see if my roommates want to go up to Legion Lodge with me."

The weather was perfect balmy seventy-two with clear blue skies. The air smelled of fresh pines and the sound of birds chirping filled the air. Merritt has always loved being outside. When she was a kid, her family went camping in the North Carolina Mountains every summer and fall break. Outside of the theatre, there's nothing Merritt enjoys more than a nice long hike in the woods or lakeside picnic. Custer State Park offers plenty of both.

On the way to Center Lake, Merritt ran into Ethan.

"Just the girl that I was looking for," Ethan smiled as he approached her. "I finished up talking props with John Hood and thought I'd check in with the costume department. I figure it would help if we could work together to ensure all of our *Dakota* characters have the right props and accessories on stage. I went down to the Costume Shop to track you down, but it was locked."

"Sorry that I missed you," Merritt lamented. "I agree that we need to collaborate as far as costumes and props are concerned. I know that we'll need assistance in acquiring the appropriate weaponry for the likes of Custer, Crazy Horse, and the Deadwood crew."

"Why don't we meet up later this week, once the costume department has a better handle on potential accessory and prop requirements?" Ethan suggested.

"I look forward to it," Merritt smiled.

"I'll catch you later Miss. Andrews," Ethan replied in a friendly manner before the two parted ways.

Merritt spent the next two hours at Center Lake enjoying the sunshine and reading through the *Dakota* script. She was thoroughly impressed with the story, and how well Kat and Artie had managed to interweave so many historical plots together in a seamless fashion. She anticipated the drama that would unfold on stage with the costumed actors and completed sets.

At five-thirty, Merritt headed back to Alpine, where she met up with Ginny and Rebecca. Emma was still working in the ticket office with her mom.

"How was your first rehearsal?" Merritt asked as she stepped in the door.

"We went over the rehearsal and production schedule and then did a read through of the script," Rebecca followed.

"I don't know how I'm going to deal with Chet Rawlins," Ginny let out an irritated sigh.

"Yes the notorious Mr. Rawlins," Merritt joked. "Bob Mero says he can be a handful."

"That's an understatement," Ginny replied harshly. "Once Chet gets into character he's a terrific actor. I could have sworn Wild Bill had come back to life during today's read through. His real life persona is less endearing. Chet is disrespectful and abrupt with his co-players. He defines egotistical insolence."

"If you're going to be playing opposite him in the Deadwood sequence you've got to learn not to take what he says so seriously," Rebecca advised.

"I think Rick Summers, AKA Jack McCall has the best part in the entire play. He gets to shoot Chet dead in every show," Ginny aired her frustrations.

"He's shooting Wild Bill dead, Ginny. In reality Chet is getting hit with blank bullets, surviving even the most convincing of death scenes," Rebecca replied with the roll of her eyes. "I suggest you start acting more like Calamity Jane, and shape up when it comes to Wild Bill, otherwise this is going to be a long summer."

"Don't worry. I can handle Chet," Ginny sighed. "Just as long as I don't have to fetch him his tea and wait on him hand and foot."

"Chet is addicted to this special herbal tea blend imported from England. He drinks it before and after every performance. He claims that it keeps his vocal chords fresh," Rebecca explained.

"Tea does work wonders for the voice," Merritt followed.

"The stuff he drinks tastes horrible. No one on the set will touch the concoction except Chet," Rebecca replied. "Given the strength and tone of his voice during every performance, I don't doubt the tea is some sort of magical, bad-tasting elixir."

"So how was costume meeting?" Ginny changed the subject.

"It went great! The next few days I'm going to spend researching the historical dress featured in the play," Merritt explained. "In fact I was thinking about heading over to Legion to use their wireless Internet for my costume research."

"I wouldn't mind a break at Legion," Ginny suggested. "They have a lakeside deck with tables perfect for relaxing. You can work on the computer while Becky and I run through lines."

"I'm game, especially if we can splurge and grab a bite to eat in the Lodge dining room?" Rebecca suggested.

Fifteen minutes later, the girls piled into Merritt's car and drove four miles southwest to the Legion Lodge. The area's namesake is derived from a local American Legion post that used to lease the land when Custer State Park was a game preserve.

The Lodge was built in 1913, and has a stone and wooden architecture style designed to mimic the landscape. The Lodge is sits on the banks of Legion Lake amidst a thick ponderosa pine forest and sheer granite rock walls. It is home to a family dining room specializing in deli sandwiches and burgers. A small store is connected to the dining room, vending Custer State Park souvenirs and supplies. A campground and a variety of comfortable, family-sized cabins surround the main lodge. Legion has tons of onsite recreation activities, including a beach for swimming, paddleboats and kayaks, and several nearby hiking trails including the Legion Lake Loop.

"Welcome to Legion Lake," a friendly waitress named Roberta Matthews greeted the girls as they walked through the door. She grabbed a stack of menus and led the girls to a corner table towards the back of the restaurant.

The Legion Lake Dining Room seats just over 100 guests and has a family friendly décor of wooden tables and chairs, with checkered table cloths, a sandwich bar with comfortable stools, and ceiling fans. The menu features a variety of down-home cuisine such as burgers, steaks, salads, pizzas and colorful desserts.

Merritt decided to try the Legendary Legion Burger with no bun. Ginny opted for the Lodge Club sandwich with fries. And Rebecca ordered the Cobb Salad.

"Are you enjoying your trip here at CSP?" Roberta inquired after serving their entrees.

"Actually we're working at the Custer Playhouse this summer. Ginny and I are actors and Merritt works as a playhouse costume designer," Rebecca explained.

"I simply adore the playhouse!" the waitress enthused. "What shows are you performing this season?"

"Due to budget cuts we're only producing one play this season, called *Dakota*. The gripping drama details major events in South Dakota's colorful history."

"I look forward to seeing it," the waitress promised.

After dinner, they briefly perused the gift shop and small Legion grocery store before moving out to the lakeside deck. They hung out lakeside until nine-thirty, when the sun finally was eclipsed by nightfall.

"We should head back to the cabin," Ginny suggested. "We all have busy days tomorrow and I don't know about you two, but I'd like to take a shower before all the hot water runs out."

"Agreed," Merritt and Becky replied. They then packed up their stuff and headed back to the playhouse.

The road from Legion to Center Lake Road is a treacherous stretch, curvy and hard to maneuver at night. Merritt was careful to maintain the speed limit and keep an eye out for any wildlife.

"Yikes," She slammed the brakes as they approached the final bend in the road before reaching the Center Lake Road turnoff, due to a red sports car speeding past them in a non-pass zone, barely missing the Civic.

"I can't believe how fast that car was going!"

"They driving eighty miles per hour around one of the sharpest curves on Highway 87. Not to mention the fact they flew past us in a no-pass zone. Does the driver have a death wish?"

"Their reckless driving nearly killed us," Merritt sighed before collecting her nerves and resuming the drive back to the cabin.

"You've got to be kidding me," Ginny spat out as they drove past the playhouse parking lot.

"Chet Rawlins was the idiot driving that car?" Rebecca stated in disgust. "I guess somebody didn't heed Ranger Sinclair this morning."

"It looks like Peter Wiseman is already telling him off," Ginny observed.

Anxious to get back to the cabin, the girls quickly brushed the incident aside

Chapter 4:

Merritt set her alarm for eight-thirty on Monday morning. After applying sunscreen lotion and bug spray, she pulled on a pair of Columbia shorts and her new company tee shirt, before heading over to the Mess Hall with Emma for a quick bite to eat before starting what would be a full day of costume research.

"Good morning," Ethan and the Barber boys greeted the girls as they sat down at the table.

"Morning boys," the girls assented.

"So what's on tap today?" Luke asked before taking a sip of his orange juice.

"My mom and I have a meeting with the Rapid City Chamber of Commerce after lunch," Emma replied. "They are going to sell *Dakota* tickets on our behalf. They Chamber is also interested in sponsoring a Rapid City theatre night in their downtown City of Presidents. Like the Campground nights at CSP, a few of our actors would perform select scenes from *Dakota* for the public. In turn my mom and I will be on hand to sell tickets to those interested in coming to the show at the playhouse."

"I'm sure a lot of tourists to the Black Hills stop in Rapid City for tourist info. The City of Presidents will serve as a neat backdrop for an outdoor snippet of the play," Ethan added in.

"We are also organizing a Custer Playhouse night at Mount Rushmore, the week before Independence Day," Emma noted.

"Luke and I thought it would be a good idea to record the *Dakota* soundtrack, which we can sell to the public to help earn money for the playhouse. We can pull the audio from rehearsals and then mix the soundtrack on our laptops with Pro Tools."

"Innovation in action," Emma enthused. "The music for *Dakota* is really well-written and I'm sure theatre goers would love an opportunity to take the music home as a souvenir."

After breakfast, Merritt hopped into her car and drove three miles southwest on Highway 87 to the historical home of famed South Dakota cowboy poet Charles Badger Clark. The cabin, affectionately known as the "Badger Hole," is nestled in a thick wood of Ponderosa pine, in proximity to Legion Lake.

The Badger Hole is a four-room cabin with a front porch stretching the entire width of the building. Its homey interior includes a living room with a stone fireplace, a kitchen with a wooden cook stove and several bedrooms and a wall brimming with books. The typewriter where Clark penned many of his famous literary works, under the glow of kerosene light, is on display.

Sam, a forty-five year old park ranger and curator greeted Merritt as she entered the rustic stone and wooden cabin. "Welcome to the home of South Dakota's first poet laureate and Custer State Park resident, Charles Badger Clark!"

"I'm working as a costumer for the Custer Playhouse this summer. In this year's production we feature several scenes with Badger Clark, including a musical number inspired by his poem *The Cowboy Prayer*. I am hoping to acquire biographical information and review photographs of Clark to ensure accuracy in his costume design," Merritt requested.

"I'd be happy to assist you with your research," Sam offered. "Charles Badger Clark is one of the most colorful characters in park's history and a preeminent master of Cowboy Poetry. He was born the youngest son of a popular Methodist minister in Iowa in 1883. Shortly after his birth, the Clark family moved west to what was then, the Dakota Territory where his father preached in the towns of Huron, Mitchell, Deadwood and Hot Springs. As a youth, Badger was restless and did not want to be pinned down with a set career. His penchant for smoking embarrassed the founders of Dakota Wesleyan University, where his father was an elder.

After finishing school, Clark spent six adventurous years in Cuba and Arizona. During this time he fell deeply in love with ranching, cow punching and what he referred to as '*the last of the old, open range.*' To describe his passion for the life of ranching, he sent a letter in verse to his stepmother, who in turn submitted it to a magazine, thus starting Clark's career as a professional author. His literary works focus on the spirit of the American West; it's raw, rugged and beautiful scenery, and living a life of independence.

As self-confessed individualist, Badger Clark abhorred the idea of committed himself to a set career guided by a punch clock and whistle blowers. He opted rather to pursue his own interests on his own time under the freedom of Dakota's open skies. He built this cabin in 1927 and lived here until his death in 1957 at the age of seventy-four. Within the Badger's Hole, Clark would entertain guests, read from his extensive library, write poetry, and reply to fan mail in between long hikes in the surrounding woods."

"He sounds like a fascinating figure," Merritt's interest piqued.

"That he was," Sam replied. "He was known for being a people person, with sharp wit and rich speaking voice. And although never one for a set career, Clark eventually accepted speaking engagements to make enough to support his modest lifestyle, and as a way to interact with people from across the nation."

"I regret that I haven't heard more of Clark prior to coming to the Black Hills," Merritt lamented.

"Although he achieved a degree of recognition as a South Dakota poet laureate, Clark was reluctant to court fame, which left him largely unknown outside of his home state. Add in the fact that his best-known poem, "A Cowboy's Prayer" was widely reprinted under the sobriquet 'Author Unknown,' further contributed to his anonymity," Sam explained. "I sure it doesn't bother Clark though. He lived a wonderful life here in Custer and his literary works, though not extensive fully capture the spirit of this land."

"Do you sell an anthology of his works?" Merritt's interest piqued.

"We have a great selection of works by Clark, along with several biographies and other miscellaneous Badger Clark themed items in our gift shop," Sam replied. "I suggest you purchase a copy of Clark's pamphlet "Custer State Park History." It only costs a few dollars, and I think it will assist you with your research. Another must read is Clark's poetry book *Boots and Bylines*."

After purchasing a few items from the Badger Hole gift shop, Sam gave Merritt a packet detailing Badger Clark's life along with several photo-print outs detailing his style of dress.

"As you can see in this photograph, Badger Clark had a distinctive fashion sense. He wore riding breeches and boots, a military blouse, flowing tie, officer-type jacket and broad-brimmed hat."

"These photographs will be most helpful as I create a costume that will bring his larger-than life persona alive on stage. Thanks so much for all your help!"

"It was my pleasure! I can't wait to see the finished product on stage," Sam replied.

"I think you'll really enjoy the play. Leroy Stewart plays Badger Clark."

"I know Leroy. He's a retired park biologist who always had a knack for entertaining park visitors. He'll portray Badger Clark perfectly."

"I had better head on over to the Peter Norbeck Visitor Center. I still need to research Peter Norbeck and the Coolidge's today," Merritt noted.

"Ah yes, Peter Norbeck, a governor, senator and the father of Custer State Park. He was a great man," Sam noted. "As for the Coolidge's, I'd suggest that you stop by the front desk at the Game Lodge to gain information on the President's stay in Custer in 1927."

"I'll heed your advice," Merritt smiled. "Thanks again for your help."

"Oh and Merritt, feel free to bring by a stack of flyers for the play. Given the fact Badger Clark will be featured in the cast, I'm sure many cabin visitors would be interested in seeing the show."

"I'll bring the flyers by as soon as they're printed up," Merritt promised before exiting the cabin and driving six mile southeast to the State Game Lodge and Peter Norbeck Visitor Center.

As she neared the Visitor Center, Merritt was forced to hit the brakes as twenty bison and calves crossed the road.

Bison are a symbol of the American west, known for their hump shoulders, dense shaggy brown and black hair covering their heads and necks, appearing somewhat like a beard. A set of brown eyes is situated on their face, directly below a pair of sharp curved horns, which sticks out from each side of the bison's head.

In awe of the magnificent creatures, Merritt patiently kept her foot on the brakes as the bison meandered across the highway. Once the road was clear, Merritt continued on towards the Peter Norbeck Visitor Center.

The Peter Norbeck Visitor Center is one of two primary information centers located within Custer State Park. The other Visitor Center is a smaller facility located off the Wildlife Loop Road in the southwest corner of the park. The Peter Norbeck Visitor Center sits atop a large grassy hill, just across the road from the Coolidge General Store and the historic State Game Lodge and nearby Chapel.

The Civilian Conservation Corps built the Peter Norbeck Visitor Center as the park museum during the winter months of 1934 to 1935. The young men worked to design a structure that would fit the surroundings of Custer State Park. They used native materials of logs and rocks, with an interior outfitted to educate the public on the park's natural and cultural history.

The Peter Norbeck Visitor Center contains a wealth of park information, including exhibits on wildlife, Custer's history, and tourist opportunities within the area. Throughout the summer the Peter Norbeck Visitor Center is a hub for Custer's educational programming efforts, included guided nature walks, junior naturalist programs and discussions on park wildlife and history.

As Merritt entered the facility via a set of large wooden double doors, a tall and attractive park ranger with short dark hair and blue eyes, who looked to be around her age, greeted her.

"Welcome to the Peter Norbeck Visitor Center," a handsome ranger greeted her. "Is there anything particular that I can help you with today; Information on Park History, details on area hikes, the scoop on area wildlife?"

"My name is Merritt Andrews and I'm spending my first summer out of college working as a costume designer for the Custer Playhouse. This year's production, *Dakota*, tells the story of South Dakota's state history and also the history of Custer State Park. As I'm charged with designing costumes for the historical characters featured in the play, I was hoping you could help me gather some biographical information and possibly show me some photos of Peter Norbeck and the Coolidge's during their stay in the park."

"It sounds like an interesting play. I'd love to help!" the Ranger replied enthusiastically.

"This is my first summer in CSP so I'm little green in regards to the Park's history."

"Where are you from originally?" the ranger asked with interest.

"North Carolina. I just graduated from UNC a few weeks ago with degrees in Business and Theatre-Costume Design."

"You've got to be kidding? I'm originally from Winston-Salem. I graduated from N.C. State's forestry school back in 2008."

"What a small world!" Merritt exclaimed. "I grew up in Raleigh, just down the street from State, near Cameron Village."

"I used to do all my grocery shopping in the Village at Harris Teeter."

"Me too," Merritt responded, still surprised by the coincidence.

"I'm Josh by the way, Josh Ford," he smiled, shaking Merritt's hand.

"It's a pleasure to meet you Josh, or should I call you Ranger Ford," Merritt hoped to see more of the ranger over the summer.

"Josh is fine," he laughed. "You'll love it here," Josh promised. "Custer State Park is one of the best parks in America. The wildlife and ecological diversity is outstanding. There are tons of recreational activities to partake in from hiking, to scenic drives, to swimming and fishing. Not to mention the area attractions in the Black Hills region such as Mount Rushmore, Crazy Horse, Jewel Cave National Monument and Wind Cave National Park."

"You don't have to sell me," Merritt stated. "I've been here just over forty-eight hours and I'm already enamored with region."

"It's always nice to have a fellow North Carolinian on site, *even if they did go to Carolina*," Josh joked. N.C. State's biggest rival is Carolina. When it comes to sports, State fans abide by the mantra 'ABC' or anybody but Carolina.

"I guess I can stomach a Wolf Packer. Now if you went to Duke...well we wouldn't be speaking right now," Merritt teased.

"Since we can tolerate each other, in spite of our college affiliations, we should hang out this summer," Josh suggested. "I'd love to give you a guided tour of Custer State Park."

"That would be great!" Merritt replied enthusiastically. "My work schedule is a bit erratic, but I usually have Monday's off."

"Why don't we meet up on Memorial Day?" Josh suggested. "We could enjoy breakfast and then drive Custer's famed Wildlife Loop?"

"How could I refuse a personal Wildlife Loop tour with Ranger Josh Ford?" Merritt smiled, admittedly smitten.

The pair exchanged cell-phone numbers so they could firm up their plans later in the week.

"Now that you've swept me off my feet, do you mind helping me with my costume research?" Merritt requested in tongue in cheek tone.

"Peter Norbeck affectionately known as the *Father of Custer State Park* was born on August the 27th 1870. He was the oldest of six children born to Scandinavian immigrants eight miles of what is now Vermillion South Dakota. During his tenure he served as a South Dakota State Senator from Spink County, as Lieutenant Governor of South Dakota, the ninth Governor of South Dakota and s a United States Senator. Interestingly enough, Norbeck was the first South Dakota governor to have been born within the borders of the state.

Norbeck had a love of the land in his home state, particularly this corner of the Black Hills. As a progressive conservationist he saw a need to preserve the land for future generations. Throughout his career, Norbeck vigorously fought for the establishment of state and national parks, forests and wildlife preserves, believing that the natural areas contained local heritage and could be used as tourist attractions to generate revenue, particularly in his home state of South Dakota. He was a pacesetter in issues of conservation, park and forest management and sustainability of natural resources.

Norbeck was partially responsible for reintroducing bison, bighorn sheep, elk, and pronghorn into the park, and working to preserve their populations from going extinct. If it weren't for Norbeck, Custer State Park wouldn't exist, and neither would other popular area attractions, including Mount Rushmore and the development of Jewel Cave National Monument and Wind Cave National Park.

In 1912, serving as Governor at the time, Norbeck crafted a deal, which would allow school holding lands to be consolidated into a nearly 48,000 acre tract, which would be named Custer State forest. On July 1, 1919, the state legislature voted to change Custer's status as a state forest to Custer State Park, thus becoming South Dakota's first State Park.

As he explored the park on foot and on horseback, the desire grew within him that others experience the beauties of Custer as he did. Knowing that he would have a hard time convincing tourists to navigate the steep ridges and varied landscape of the on foot, Norbeck began to dream of roads. He didn't want commercial roads within the park, but rather roads that showcased the scenery. Norbeck first worked to develop the Needle's Highway, which straddles the famed Black Hills granite spires known as 'the needles.' In 1927, Norbeck, who by that time was a Senator, worked closely with Mount Rushmore sculptor Gutzon Borglum to lay out the Iron Mountain Road, a winding parkway running between Mount Rushmore and Custer State Park known for its pigtail bridges, tunnels and scenic views of Mount Rushmore and the Black Hills."

"The park roads perfectly frame the grandeur of the scenery. It's worth driving under thirty if it means experiencing the landscape to its fullest," Merritt replied.

"I'm glad you understand the concept of the park's roadways. Frankly if it were up to Mr. Norbeck, visitors would park their cars and walk. He loved the land and wouldn't do anything to taint its natural beauty."

"Do you have any photographs of Senator Norbeck to assist me in designing his costume?" Merritt requested.

"Of course," Josh replied as he pulled out copies of photographs from a park information binder. "Being a statesman, Senator Norbeck is often seen where a polished suit and a straw skimmer hat. We also have a picture here of Norbeck sporting more rugged gear on the trails in the park. I also have a few photographs I'll print out for you of President and First Lady Coolidge," Josh offered. "Senator Norbeck pushed for his good friend President Coolidge to spend his annual three week summer vacation in the Black Hills of South Dakota in Custer's State Game Lodge. Norbeck's goal in luring Coolidge to the Black Hills was an effort to convince his friend to federally back the Mount Rushmore project and promote tourism to Black Hills. The plan worked. The Coolidge's enjoyed the area so much they extended their three-week week vacation to a three-month summer stay. The State Game Lodge was transformed into the "Summer White House." Reporters flocked to the region to cover the President's stay in Custer. The resulting windfall of publicity is credited for launching the area's modern tourism industry."

"So Silent Cal decided to back the Mount Rushmore project after becoming so enchanted by the Black Hills?"

"Both Norbeck and Mount Rushmore sculptor Gutzon Borglum worked overtime to convince Cool Cal that the federal dollars to back a massive stone carving would be a sound investment. They organized an elaborate dedication ceremony with the President on hand and Borglum asked for Coolidge's assistance in composing a suitable inscription for the carving. The strategy worked and when Coolidge returned to Washington at summer's end, he endorsed legislation to provide funding for Mount Rushmore. And, for the record, investing South Dakota's natural resource and tourism was a sound investment. Over 2.7 million visitors from around the world visit Custer State Park, Mt. Rushmore and the Black Hills every year."

"Who knows if we'd have those four famed faces in stone if Norbeck hadn't convinced Coolidge to spend his summer right here in Custer State Park?"

"Thankfully we don't have wonder 'what if.' Norbeck's push to preserve the Black Hills paid off. Mount Rushmore is a legacy in stone that will stand forever as a patriotic symbol of our nation. Now it's our duty to continue their vision and act as good stewards, managing the land and resources to preserve this area for future generations."

"I whole-heartedly agree," Merritt replied with a smile.

"Listen, I hate to cut our meeting short, but I'm due to conduct a Junior Naturalist Program in about five minutes," Josh lamented. "I'll call you later this week to firm up our details for Memorial Day."

"I look forward to it," Merritt smiled.

"Oh and Merritt, you might want to walk over to the State Game Lodge. They have an exhibit on the Coolidge's stay there. You'll also enjoy the building's architectural integrity."

Listed on the National Register of Historic Places, the graciously appointed Saint Game Lodge was built in 1922 in a small valley, adjacent to a dense forest and mountain cliffs. Grace Coolidge Creek winds along the Game Lodge corridor, babbling through a riparian ecosystem of moss and ferns. The creek is hot spot for trout fishing.

In addition to serving as the "Summer White House" for President Calvin Coolidge in 1927, President Dwight D. Eisenhower also stayed at the Game Lodge for several days in 1953.

The Game Lodge offers a wide variety of accommodations, from historic and elegant suites to newly renovated economy rooms and pine-shaded cabins. The Creekside Lodge, built in 2008, sits on the lot to the right of the Game Lodge and offers thirty additional rooms.

The lodge interior is a comfortable blend of rustic and upscale with hardwood floors, molding, high ceilings, stone fireplaces and original Tiffany lamps.

The dining room is located past the lodge's gift shop and art gallery, where each summer artisans display handmade arts and crafts. Casual excellence perfectly describes the atmosphere of the Game Lodge Dining Room, which serves hearty breakfasts, family lunches and the best of culinary cuisine at dinner.

Fortunately the lunch crowd had died down by the time Merritt arrived, and she was seated a table right away. Per the suggestion of the server, she opted for the lunch buffet, which features an array of fresh home style Dakota favorites, such as the Buffalo Stew and hand carved roast beef.

Merritt started off with a salad of fresh mixed greens, dried cranberries, fruits and vegetables before a main course of Buffalo stew and a baked potato. For dessert Merritt indulged in hot apple pie with a scoop of vanilla ice cream.

Thoroughly stuffed after lunch, Merritt decided to go on a short walk before spending the rest of the afternoon camped out in the Creekside Lodge lobby working on costumes designs and research.

There are a number of scenic trails in the Game Lodge area. Since Merritt was short on time she opted to walk the Creekside Trail. The trail starts off by the Coolidge General Store, which was built in 1927 to house reporters and White House staff during the president's stay in Custer. Today it is a grocery and souvenir shop.

Once on the trailhead, the path runs two miles alongside the Grace Coolidge Creek. The hike highlights the riparian ecosystem of the creek and is a perfect spot to see whitetail or mule deer.

After her walk, Merritt hung out in the lobby of the Creekside Lodge for about three hours before heading back to the playhouse cabins. Ginny and Becky returned from rehearsal approximately half an hour after Merritt arrived at Alpine.

"Look who is home," Merritt greeted her roommates as they walked in the door. "How was rehearsal?"

"It was good. Chet was cordial and Becky and I aced our lines," Ginny shrugged. ""How was did your costume research progress?"

"I've just about pinned down the costumes designs for Badger Clark, Senator Norbeck and President and First Lady Coolidge."

"What design angle do you have in mind for my character, Grace Coolidge?" Rebecca inquired.

"I'm aiming for a 1920s drop waist summer dress, with stockings and T bar shoes and a cloche hat," Merritt explained.

"Sounds cute," Rebecca smiled. "What will my on stage husband President Coolidge be wearing?"

"Probably a three-piece suit and skimmer hat, but I also have a photograph of Coolidge wearing cowboy chaps and western attire during his visit. I'll inquire to see which looks, Alistair and Gully prefer."

"Game Lodge is a great area. Did you see any bison?"

"From a distance," Merritt bit her lip. "While I was doing costume research at the Peter Norbeck Visitor Center I met a Ranger named Josh. He's also originally from North Carolina, and offered to show me around the Wildlife Loop on Memorial Day."

"Look at you Miss Andrews. Two days in the park and you already have a date."

"It's not a date per se," Merritt objected.

"*Right*," Ginny and Becky rolled their eyes. "What do you say we head over to the Mess Hall and grab some grub, and you can give us all the details on dreamy Josh?"

"Fair enough," Merritt laughed.

Chapter 5:

Tuesday morning, after a Mess Hall breakfast of milk and cereal, Merritt drove eight miles southwest to the town of Custer City, also known by locals simply as "Custer."

Situated on the western edge of Custer State Park, the gateway town lies in an open valley surrounded by dense forests juxtaposed by mountains of thick raw granite and needle-like spires. Its proximity to area attractions such as Jewel Cave National Monument, Crazy Horse and Mount Rushmore, and CSP serves as a beacon of tourism.

Steeped in history, Custer is the oldest established town in the Black Hills. The town derives its namesake from General George Armstrong Custer, who set up an encampment on the present-day site of Custer City in the summer of 1874, during his sixty-day exploration of the Black Hills. While encamped in the Custer City area, gold was discovered in nearby French Creek, which led to the Black Hills gold rush.

By 1875, gold diggers had settled in the area only to find out that French Creek didn't yield much profit from gold. The gold discovery near Custer was quickly eclipsed by the gold strikes of Deadwood Gulch, seventy miles to the north. Despite the declining population as gold seekers moved to more lucrative mines, Custer hung on to become a stable city, not founded on the promise of gold as much as the hope of creating a lasting community in the beautiful Black Hills.

Custer's main street is lined with historic buildings, charming shops and a multitude of restaurants. Throughout the summer, the town is home to several festivals including "Gold Discovery Days", which celebrates Custer's golden history.

Located in the heart of downtown Custer the historic Courthouse Museum structure dates to 1881, nine years before South Dakota became a state.

For ninety-two years, the 1881 Courthouse was the hub of Custer County, serving as a center for government, social gatherings, and occasional church services. In 1974, a new courthouse was built in town, leaving the historic courthouse vacant. In 1976 the Custer County Historical Society moved into building and turned it into a museum, dedicated to preserving the history of the area.

"Welcome to the 1881 Courthouse," an outgoing curator in her late fifties greeted Merritt as she entered the museum.

"I have an appointment to see Cindy Darling about doing some costume research on behalf of the Custer Playhouse."

"You've come to the right place. I'm Cindy, the head of archives and history here at the 1881 Courthouse Museum." Cindy replied as the pair shook hands.

"It's a pleasure to meet you Ms. Darling."

"Please call me Cindy. So when spoke on the phone you said you wanted to learn about General George Armstrong Custer..."

"I'm charged with creating his wardrobe. Most of his scenes take place during the 1874 Black Hills Expedition, but there is a scene encompassing the Battle of Little Big Horn in Montana. I was hoping that you could give me some biographical information on General Custer and possibly view any photographic archives you might have from his time in the Black Hills?"

"Follow me to the Custer Expedition Room, which houses exhibits and archival information about General Custer."

Merritt followed Cindy to a large exhibit room, filled with a wealth of information on the life and times of Genera George A. Custer.

"Before we plunge into the Black Hills Expedition of 1874, I think it wise to give you a biographical background on General Custer. George Armstrong Custer was born on December 5th 1839 in New Rumley Ohio to father Emanuel Henry Custer, a farmer and a blacksmith and mother Marie Ward Kirkpatrick. According to family letters, he was named after George Armstrong, a minister, with the hopes he would join the clergy.

As boy Custer spent most time living with his half-sister and brother-in-law in Monroe Michigan. He moved to Hopedale Ohio to attend school, and graduated in 1856. After working as a teacher in Cadiz, Ohio, Custer enrolled in the United States Military Academy at West Point. While at West Point, Custer was no model student. Each of his four years he nearly got expelled for excessive demerits, particularly for pulling pranks on fellow cadets.

He graduated with a low ranking in 1861, just as the Civil War broke out. Under usual circumstances, a cadet with a ranking as low as Custer's would fare poorly, earning an obscure posting or mundane job with the army at best. However with the Civil War kicking off, the Union Army needed officers and quickly. G.A. Custer was commissioned as a second lieutenant in the 2nd U.S. Cavalry, immediately joining his regiment at the First Battle of Bull Run, where he was charged with delivering messages from Army commander Winfield Scott to Major General Irvin McDowell."

"I didn't realize that Custer was an officer in the Civil War," Merritt commented.

"If it hadn't been for his infamous last stand at Little Bighorn, Custer would have probably been best remembered for his time served in the Civil War. His performance as an aggressive commander impressed high-ranking officers, thus allowing him to work his way up the ranks from low-ranking West Point cadet to a temporary ranking of Brevet General during the war. After the war, during his stay with the Regular Army, Custer was awarded the rank of Lt. Colonel."

"What battles was General Custer involved in?" Merritt inquired.

"After the First Battle of Bull Run, Custer was reassigned to the 5th U.S. Calvary where he fought under Union General McClellan, in the early days of the Peninsula Campaign, which took place in south-eastern Virginia from March to July of 1862. After fighting in the Battle of Antietam in Maryland on September 17th of 1862, Custer began serving under Major General Pleasanton, who became his mentor. On June 28th 1863, three days prior to the Battle of Gettysburg, Pleasanton promoted Custer from captain to the Brigadier General of volunteers. This put him as one of the Union's youngest generals at age twenty-three

Despite having no command experience, newly ranked General Custer, wasted no time in implementing his attack plan. He implanted his aggressive character on his brigade, a style that critics claimed to be reckless or foolhardy. He was not afraid to take personal risks on the battlefield, which could either land his men into serious trouble, or serve as a brilliant winning strategy. On July 3rd, after nearly falling prey to the Confederate army, Custer rebounded, leading in charges and hand-to-hand combat on Gettysburg's East Cavalry Field. Although Custer lost more men than any other Union Cavalry brigade, with casualties of 257, Custer's men broke the back of the Confederate assault and played a key role in the battle."

"He certainly served in several famous battles," Merritt replied with interest.

"During the war, Custer met, courted and married Elizabeth Clift Bacon," Cindy explained as she pointed to a black and white photograph of the couple. "Although at times the pair had a tumultuous relationship, they were very much in love. Mrs. Custer refused to wait at home while her husband was on the battlefield or away on military assignments. She often followed him on his tours of duty. After his death at Little Bighorn in 1876, Elizabeth Custer was a fierce advocate of her husband, refusing to allow him to be a scapegoat for the disastrous battle. She was General Custer's staunchest supporter and ally after his death, writing many novels about his life and final battle."

"She sounds like an interesting woman," Merritt stated before they moved to a nearby group of displays, detailing Custer's time in the Black Hills. "Now that you have a basic background of Custer's early years and Civil War tenure we can turn our focus to his time in the Black Hills. After the Civil War, Custer continued on with the army and in 1866 was assigned to the newly formed Seventh Cavalry Regiment with the official title of Lt. Colonel, as his title of Brigadier General was only a temporary rank for the war. Custer was still awaiting elevation to a full colonelcy when he fell on the Little Bighorn in 1876," Cindy explained. "Until Custer's expedition, the Black Hills had remained mostly closed off to the non-native American populations, and landscape a mystery. On July 2, 1874, Lt. Colonel Custer set out for the first U.S. expedition to the Black Hills of South Dakota from modern day Bismarck, North Dakota, then known as Fort Abraham Lincoln of the Dakota Territory. The official aims were to look for suitable locations to build a military fort, and to find a route to the southwest. Custer also wanted to search for gold and other minerals, which could yield a mining profit.

It's important to note that in 1868 the U.S. signed the Treaty of Fort Laramie with the Lakota nation, Yankton Sioux, Santee Sioux and Arapaho, which guaranteed the Lakota ownership of the Black Hills, and furthered land and hunting rights in South Dakota, Wyoming, and Montana. Under the conditions of the treaty, the land was not open for settlers, and a U.S. expedition would only be allowed if it were strictly for the purpose of finding a suitable location for a military post. The Lakota specifically asked in the Treaty of Fort Laramie that the Black Hills, a land sacred to their people, not be opened up for gold prospecting. It was per these conditions that Custer and his unit the Seventh Cavalry first entered the Black Hills. Over 1,200 troopers, along with an engineer, eighty civilians, two miners, a botanist, geologist, Native American scouts Bloody Knife and Lean Bear, three newspaper correspondents, cook and a photographer accompanied Custer on the expedition.

From July 24 to August 14th 1874, Custer's company made camp on the site of present-day Custer City. While in the area he hiked atop Harney Peak and charted the area's landscape and took note of its natural resources. While surveying the land, gold was found in nearby French Creek, in present day Custer State Park. Custer sent a letter detailing the find to Fort Laramie via scout Charley Reynolds. From there the news of gold in the Black Hills was telegraphed to the press.

Suddenly a land previously untouched by settlers was flooded with gold diggers who ignored the stipulations set forth by the Treaty of Fort Laramie. In essence the discovery of gold in the Black Hills signaled the beginning of the end for the Plains Indians and also set up the stage for Custer's Last Stand. Relations between settlers and natives quickly deteriorated, and although the U.S. Military initially tried to keep miners off the region, the prospect of gold was too lucrative to ignore and the number of settlers too many for the U.S. to protect the land for the Lakota.

By 1876 a war between the Sioux and U.S. Army was in full gear, culminating in the Battle of Little Bighorn in Montana on June 25th 1876. The Native Americans led by Crazy Horse, Sitting Bull and Chief Gall, won a decisive victory over Custer's army of only 700 to the Sioux's numbers of 1800. Five of the Seventh's companies were annihilated, with Custer, two of his brothers, brother-in-law, and nephew killed in action. The battled dubbed as Custer's Last Stand,' in reality was also the last stand for the Plains Indians. Although the Sioux earned a large moral victory over Custer's unit, it was a pyrrhic victory, in that it was their last hurrah in the battle for land before the U.S. government fully took hold of the area."

"The whole thing is so sad," Merritt sighed. "For both the natives who lost their lands, and the U.S. soldiers killed in battle."

"The settling of the American west, particularly the Black Hills is filled with tragedy. We can only hope to learn from our past mistakes," Cindy replied. "Why don't we talk costume design?"

"Sounds good to me," Merritt replied with a smile.

"As an army officer, Custer sported a well-pressed uniform that included shiny cavalry boots, olive-colored corduroy trousers, a tight hussar jacket of black velveteen with silver piping on the sleeves, a sailor shirt with silver stars on the collar. Custer wore a wide-brimmed slouch hat, with his hair in long ringlets, and his signature red cravat," Cindy explained. "We have one of Custer's Jackets and a set of epaulets in this exhibit case over here. And in the adjacent display case you'll find an original rifle, which used by Custer to hunt antelope while serving at Fort Hays in Kansas."

"Do you mind if I take pictures?" Merritt requested. "It would really help to have a photograph of his actual jacket when I'm crafting the costume. And I'm sure our property master would be interested in a seeing a photograph of the gun"

"Certainly. I also have a book I'll give you about Custer and his time in the Black Hills. The book features lots of photographs and descriptions regarding the atmosphere of the camps and the clothing of Custer and his officers."

"That would be amazing! Thank you Cindy," Merritt replied graciously.

"I also suggest that you stop off by the Gordon Stockade Historical Site, just west of Stockade Lake in Custer State Park. Shortly after Custer's discovery of gold near French Creek, a party of miners from Sioux City Iowa known as the Gordon Party, settled in this region. Upon arrival they built a log fortress, to protect the party from a possible Lakota attack. During their stay the Gordon Party didn't make a profit off of gold, and shortly after their arrival they were evicted by the U.S. Cavalry for being in violation of the Treaty of Laramie. However following their eviction, a subsequent flow of fortune seekers came to the Black Hills. Because the Gordon Party played a role in the South Dakota's gold-rush history, Custer State Park formed the Gordon Stockade Advisory Committee. The park reconstructed the log stockade used by the Gordon Party and set up interpretative exhibits detailing their stay in the Black Hills. It's an interesting stop in the park."

"Thanks for the suggestion. I'll definitely check it out."

After gathering ample information on General Custer and his historical style of dress, Merritt spent time meandering through the remainder of the 1881 Courthouse Museum, which features a wide variety of exhibits. A room on Mining and Industry focuses on the history of how minerals mined in the Black Hills have bolstered the local economy and a history of Black Hills tourism, ranching and lumbering. Nearby, the General Store room showcases the town's original mercantile, where mail was collected, and a variety of items such as teakettles and neckties are sold.

In the Courthouse Main Hall, Merritt enjoyed an exhibit of hanging quilts dating back to the late 1800s to the early 1900s. Also on the ground floor, Merritt stepped foot into the original county jail, which is complete with a 'prisoner' and an exhibit on early law enforcement in Custer City.

On the museum's upper level, she encountered exhibits focused on Forestry and the history of Custer County. Visitors can also step foot into the historical Jury Room, which has rotating exhibits from the archives, Court Room and Judge's Chamber and One-Room School.

"Thanks again for all your help," Merritt told Cindy before exiting the Museum.

"It was my pleasure," Cindy smiled. "Give Bob my well wishes."

"I will," Merritt promised.

"If you're hungry for lunch I highly suggest Cattleman's. They have excellent food, and the price is just right."

Upon exiting the 1881 Courthouse Museum, Merritt took Cindy's advice to eat lunch at the Cattleman's Steakhouse where she order the half barbecue chicken with homemade fries and a side salad. The restaurant specializes in affordable family fare, and has a laidback campy atmosphere. The food was delicious and the wait staff friendly.

After lunch, Merritt walked a few blocks north to Custer's city library to do some research on Laura Ingalls Wilder. The famed *Little House on the Prairie* author spent many of her teen years into early adulthood in the town of DeSmet, located in eastern South Dakota. Her time in South Dakota is recounted in the classic children books *By the Shores of Silver Lake, The Long Winter, Little Town of the Prairie, These Happy Golden Years*, and *The First Four Years*. Each books follows Laura's life in the South Dakota prairie, detailing the hardships of homesteading contrasted by the importance of family, community and the hope of better things to come.

Laura Ingalls was born on February 7th 1867 in the Big Wood of Wisconsin. In her early childhood, the family moved west to settle on land not yet open for homesteading near Independence Kansas. This time of her life was the basis of *Little House on the Prairie*. After a few years in Kansas, the Ingalls moved to Minnesota before settling in the Dakota Territory in the fall of 1879. Charles or 'Pa' and Caroline 'Ma' Ingalls, along with daughter Mary would remain in DeSmet the rest of their lives.

Shortly before her sixteenth birthday, Laura accepted her first teaching position. Where she taught three terms in one-room schools, when not attending school herself in DeSmet. In 1885 Laura married Almanzo Wilder and quit teaching. Wilder had achieved a degree of prosperity as a homestead, given the favorable Dakota weather in the early 1880s. She agreed to help her husband's claim succeed, which lay just north of DeSmet. On December 5th 1886, Laura gave birth to Rose Wilder, who would later help her edit and promote the Little House books.

After several hard years managing the homestead, the Wilders decided to move to Mansfield Missouri to start a dairy farm. Things were slow going at first, but eventually they earned a steady income. After retiring from running the farm, Laura began writing. She wanted preserve stories of her childhood memories by putting them down on paper. In Laura's lifetime alone many things had changed. Covered wagons gave way to trains and cars. The United States added many new states including the Dakotas, Montana, Wyoming and more. Technology rapidly improved and the prairie life she'd grown up with looked to be a distant memory. Laura wanted to tell stories about early years on the prairie and how much things had changed in her lifetime alone.

Upon completion of her first manuscript, Laura asked for her daughter Rose to assist her in getting the book, which would become *Little House in the Big Woods*, published. It became an instant classic yielding subsequent books, which detail Laura's life. The books are still extremely popular and lead thousands of fans to DeSmet South Dakota each year to see where Laura lived and worked for over ten years of her life.

After finishing up at the library, Merritt stocked up on groceries. She purchased gluten-free items at the Custer City Market, a local grocer specializing in organic food. She then went shopping for laundry detergent, sodas, chips and other miscellaneous. She then made a quick shopping trip at Lynn's Dakota Mart, a medium sized grocery store servicing the needs of tourists and locals alike. There, she purchased some Tide to do her laundry, a case of Diet Cokes and 7-UP, and miscellaneous snacks requested by her roommates.

Merritt spend the rest of the evening hulled up in Alpine, finalizing her costume sketches. She felt like her designs would mirror the historical era and bring out the individual personalities of the play's characters.

Chapter 6:

"Hi Merritt," Bob and Dot greeted their associate as she walked into the Costume Shop on Wednesday morning.

"Good Afternoon," Merritt smiled before taking a seat beside her fellow costumers at the main sewing table.

"So how did your research go?" Bob inquired. "Were you able to gather enough information to sketch out some costume ideas?"

"It went great. I followed your advice and stopped by the 1881 Courthouse Museum. Cindy told me to tell you hi."

"Cindy's a sweetheart," Bob smiled.

"I was able to collect a good amount of information regarding descriptions of the characters individual dress styles from photographs and archival documents detailing the person's look, which I incorporated into each costume design."

"These designs are lovely Merritt," Dot reviewed the sketches.

"Hopefully we'll be able repurpose a few of our Costume Closet suits for President Coolidge and Peter Norbeck. I also found a really great dress pattern for Laura Ingalls Wilder that won't use much fabric, and shouldn't take too long to sew."

"We can pull most of the 7th Cavalry suits, including Custer's uniform from the Playhouse Costume Closet. We would just need to sew on period epaulets and the military insignia," Bob noted.

"Lynn Hopewell of 'The Deadwood Historical Society' has offered to loan the Custer Playhouse authentic costumes for Wild Bill, Jack McCall, Seth Bullock, Calamity Jane, and the scene's background actors for summer stage season! The costumes have previously been used for historical re-enactments around the Deadwood area."

"What a coup," Bob brimming with excitement. "Borrowing the costumes will cut down on our overall workload so we can allot more time and focus to designing in-house costumes."

"Lynn emailed me photographs of the costumes. Wild Bill's outfit consists of a buckskin gunfighter coat, pleated silk shirt, red vest, a narrow necktie, wool pants and a flat wide-brimmed hat. Not only did Wild Bill have a reputation as a sharpshooter, he was known as a sharp dresser as well. He often wore the finest shirts with the most western of jackets," Dot noted as she passed around the pictures. "Jack McCall costume will be more unkempt. He'll don a flannel shirt, paisley vest, and grey plaid pants, in an effort to make him more cowardly in appearance. Historic Deadwood hotel owner, Seth Bullock's outfit consists of a well-pressed black tweed frock coat with matching pants along with a velvet grey vest, peach striped shirt, a purple floral tie, and bowler hat. Calamity Jane's costume is very rugged, as she often wore men's cloths, and includes a buckskin suit and thin flannel under shirt. Shoes are provided with each costume."

"These costumes are fantastic," Merritt enthused. "They mimic every photograph I've ever seen of Wild Bill and Calamity Jane. The authenticity will convince the audience that they just stepped back in time to the gunslinger and gold-mining days of the Wild West."

"We can pick up the costumes from the Adams Museum in Deadwood, next Thursday, June the 3rd." Dot explained. "As for Lewis and Clark costumes, I found a really great book entitled *Tailor Made, Trail Worn: Army Life, Clothing, & Weapons of the Corps of Discovery* written by Robert J. Moore Jr. and Illustrated by Michael Haynes. According to Moore, neither Lewis nor Clark wore leather, at least not until they reached Fort Mandan, in what is now North Dakota. While straddling the Missouri River in eastern and mid-central South Dakota, both men wore officer uniforms and the Corps wore regimental uniforms. This was after all a military discovery expedition and therefore both Lewis and Clark kept a strict dress code, which was in line with the military uniform protocols. Lewis and Clark wore dark blue knee-length coats with scarlet lapels, cuffs, and standing collar, with single-breasted white vests with white buttons and flannel shirts and wool or linen breeches. Captain Lewis wore a single silver epaulette on his right shoulder and small shoulder strap outlined in silver lace on the left. Lewis wears a gentleman's sword on left side with a burgundy sash on his coat. Captain Clark wore a gold epaulet on his right shoulder, a white belt, and carried an officer's sword. Both men wore round hats with a black bearskin crest and leather cockade."

"We have round hats in the Costume Closet along an assortment of early nineteenth century pants and breeches and sashes and epaulets to pull from," Bob noted.

"I'm going to see if I can repurpose the blue and red jackets that we used in the production of *1776* a few years back. If that doesn't work, I have a pattern I can use to sew the suits from scratch," Dot replied. "What did you come up with for your set of characters Bob?"

"Crazy Horse was the hardest of the historical characters to research, as there are no known photographs of the Lakota warrior. However after speaking with our resident Ogala-Lakota tribe members Peter and Marty, I have a good idea of the style of dress worn by the warrior. Crazy Horse did not wear a war bonnet, just a single feather in his hair. He most likely wore a beaded breastplate and leather pants. A friend of Peter's, Tamara Means works as an artisan at the Native American Educational and Cultural Center at the Crazy Horse Memorial. She has agreed to loan a set of leather pants with beadwork and a beaded breastplate for the summer run."

"A handmade costume constructed by a Lakota artisan is a tribute to the warrior," Dot endorsed the decision.

"As for Sitting Bull, I called Cathy Chamberlain at the Prairie Edge Trading Company in downtown Rapid City. She offered to supply us with fabric for the Sitting Bull and the Lakota warrior costumes, which shouldn't take too long to assemble. For Mount Rushmore sculptor, Gutzon Borglum, we can pull a suit with suspenders, a fedora and boots from the Costume Closet. For Crazy Horse sculptor, Korczak Ziolkowski we can pull together a pair of jeans, a worn out shirt, faded jacket and rugged well-worn boots."

"We're off to a great start," Dot noted as the group reviewed their notes. "I say we spend the rest of the afternoon pulling what costumes and accessories we can from our Costume Closet and make a list of what items, i.e. fabric, clothing, etc...we'll need to purchase. Once we get design approval from Gully and Alistair we'll head up to Rapid City and the fabric store."

For the next four hours the trio delved through the clothing in the Costume Closet, inventorying jackets, pants, jackets, dresses and other miscellaneous accessories that could be used in the theatre production. In the end they were able to pull the wardrobe for the majority of the ensemble cast and several main characters such as Senator Norbeck and President Coolidge.

"I'll present our designs to Gully and Alistair tonight after they finish up with rehearsal," Dot offered. "The sooner they can clear our designs, the quicker we can get to work on acquiring the necessary fabric and accessories needed to sew the original costumes and to make the necessary alterations to prefabricated costumes."

"I'll brief Property Master, Ethan Daniels on today's meeting to give him a general idea of what sort of props we'll need to accompany the character costumes," Merritt stated.

"It's after six, so I say we call it a day. We'll reconvene here in the Costume Shop tomorrow morning at ten-thirty," Dot closed the meeting.

"See you then," Merritt said goodbye as she walked out the door, binder and journal in hand. It had been a long day, but an enjoyable one. She enjoyed the process of pulling each piece of clothing off the rack and assembling it one costume. The costume team was off to a good start and Merritt looked forward to the next several weeks of sewing, accessorizing and fittings.

As Merritt walked into the Alpine cabin, she was greeted by her roommates.

"Look who is back," Rebecca said with a smile.

"Hello girls. Did ya'll have a good day?"

"Good enough, considering the near death experience I had," Ginny groaned. "During the Deadwood scene sandbags started falling from the rafters, just missing me and Chet. The next thing I know the entire curtain collapses," Ginny explained, still a bit shaken up by the experience.

"Are you okay?" Merritt showed concern.

"Chet sprained his ankle, and I have a few cuts and bruises, but nothing too serious. Luckily Peter was on hand to nurse our wounds."

"Peter?" Merritt asked in surprised tone.

"Peter's our resident Medicine Man," Rebecca and Ginny explained. "He used to work as a Natural Sciences teacher on the Pine Ridge Reservation and has an EMT certification. Peter's very familiar with natural remedies from plants in the Black Hills. His medical expertise helped bandage our wounds."

"How is Chet...sprained ankles are known to fester?" Merritt inquired.

"He'll survive," Ginny none to concerned. "He begrudgingly allowed Peter to wrap his ankle. Alistair is giving Chet two days off to rest. As far as the play is concerned, his character, Wild Bill, sits down for most of the scene, so if his injury lingers, it shouldn't affect the production."

"The current dilemma is working to get curtain fixed. Unfortunately Trump was on hand to witness the entire spectacle. He told us if the curtain isn't fixed to his satisfaction in two days a formal report will be issued to the offices of the Attorney General, which could close us down for the season. "

"Do you have any clue why the curtain collapsed?" Merritt questioned.

"No idea," Ginny replied. "At the time of the incident no one was working in the rafters. It's almost as if we have a ghost or something."

"A ghost is better than a broken rafter," Emma wistful. "A ghost may be unpredictable, it's not structurally unsound."

"The stagehands will repair the curtain and make sure the rafters are safe," Merritt reassured her roommates. "I'm just glad that you're okay Ginny."

"I think chocolate's just the medicine I need. Anyone want to run over to the Mess Hall with me to indulge in ice-cream from the community freezer?"

"I think we could all use a cool treat," Rebecca replied as the girls went to the Mess Hall and tried to forget the bizarre occurrence of the curtain collapse.

Chapter 7:

On Thursday afternoon, Gully and Alistair approved of the costume designs for *Dakota*. With permission to move-forward with costume production, Merritt, Bob and Dot drove to Rapid City of Friday morning to go shopping for fabric and to pick up a few miscellaneous supplies, including the war bonnet from the Prairie Edge Trading Company.

The drive from Custer State Park to Rapid City rambles forty miles via Highway 16 through winding canyon roads, windswept grassland and granite outcroppings.

Rapid City was founded in 1876 on the banks of Rapid Creek by a group of failed miners during the Black Hills Gold Rush. To lure settlers to their town, they appropriately labeled the city as the "Gateway to the Black Hills" given its geographical location and proximity to the mining camps that scattered the area.

The city grew quickly as merchants and their families moved to the area to sell supplies to miners and pioneers. Given its location, which straddles the Great Plains and fertile Black Hills, Rapid City quickly became a regional trading hub, and center for railroads and industry. Today the town has a population of just over 60,000, making it the second largest city in South Dakota.

The costumers' first stop was the Fabric and Textile Warehouse situated in the Northgate shopping center. The store has a large selection of fabric and arts and craft materials for a fair price, making it the perfect spot to load up on costume supplies. After spending several hours in the store, debating which materials to purchase, the trio checked out and loaded their cargo in Dot's van.

They then made a quick trip to another locally owned store, "The Sew Shop," to purchase epaulets for Custer and a few additional historical fashion pieces not sold at the mainline fabric store.

"It's after five and I'm starting to get hungry," Bob noted as they pulled into a downtown parking lot adjacent to historic building housing the Prairie Edge. "Are you up for grabbing a bite to eat at the Firehouse Brewing Company next door, before we pick up the war bonnet from Cathy? She's open until nine and that way we don't leave the priceless headdress sitting in the heat while we eat."

"What about you Merritt, up for a bite to eat?" Dot asked.

"That works for me," Merritt agreed.

The Firehouse Brewing Company is housed in a historic Fire Hall dating to 1915. In 1991 the building was purchased by a group of local investors with the aim to create an urban dining experience and microbrewery to the Black Hills. They stripped the building back to its original bare brick walls and wood floors and designed the restaurants décor around the ambiance of an old-time fire hall with polish brass and fire lighting equipment decorating the walls, and a brick bar the perfect spot to try one of their homemade ales.

The atmosphere is perfect for watching sports or an after ten meal following a busy day of sightseeing; and despite the beer and alcohol, the Firehouse Brewing Company, or "FBC" is family friendly with fireman's hats for younger patrons and an affordable kids menu.

"What do you recommend?" Merritt asked Bob and Dot as she glanced over the menu.

"I'm a fan of the house gumbo, which is dubbed 'the Spontaneous Heating,'" Bob suggested. "It is a mix of sausage, clams, shrimp, chicken and homemade gravy served over a bed of rice. It's a bit spicy though, so it you don't like hot foods you might want to consider one of their delicious sandwiches."

"I prefer the Chicken Alfredo myself," Dot offered her opinion.

"Unfortunately I'm allergic to wheat so that limits some of my options, especially as far as the beer-battered treats are concerned." Merritt sighed.

"What a bummer," Dot and Bob lamented.

"It's not too bad. My mom and grandmother have it so I'm used to living with a gluten-free diet," Merritt explained before an outgoing waiter approached their table.

"Welcome to the FBC, my name is Brian and I'll be taking care of you folks today. Can I start you off with something to drink?"

"I'll have an Arnold Palmer," Dot requested.

"And I'd like a glass of your Black Hills Ale," Bob ordered.

"Good choice," Brian replied before turning his attention to Merritt. "Miss, would you like to sample one of our homemade brews."

"I would love too, but unfortunately I'm allergic to wheat so I'll abstain."

"My sister has Celiac disease as well, so I understand going gluten-free. We actually offer a gluten-free beer, called Bard's. I highly recommend it."

"I'll try a Bard's with a glass of water then."

"Can I also interest you in our homemade Artichoke Dip and toasted beer bread? I can also bring out a side of gluten-free tortilla chips on the side."

"We will definitely indulge in your Artichoke Dip," Bob replied. "We're ready to order our main meals as well."

"What can I get for you?"

"I want the Spontaneous Heating."

"Chicken Alfredo," Dot ordered.

"I think I'll opt for the Fire Marshal chicken sandwich with no bun," Merritt requested.

"I'll put your orders into the grill and I'll be back shortly with your drinks and appetizer."

A few minutes later, Brian returned with their drinks and a huge portion of the Artichoke Dip. While waiting for their meals, the trio commented on the ambiance of the brewery and also discussed their costume plans for the next few days.

"I say we start sewing the original costumes first, and then work on alterations the latter part of next week," Dot suggested.

"When will we take the actors measurements?" Merritt inquired.

"We have most of the actors' measurements on file. So we really won't have to interface with the actors until fittings begin. At that juncture we'll make note of any alterations that need to be made before opening night," Dot explained.

After a hearty meal at the FBC, the trio meandered next door to the Prairie Edge Trading Company, an emporium that features the finest in Native American Arts and Crafts, including authentic Lakota clothing, watercolor paintings, music and books.

"The Prairie Edge Trading Company has some of the finest art on display in the Black Hills. Cathy specializes in traditional Lakota clothing and beadwork," Bob noted as the group walked down the hall to Cathy's retail space.

"It's good to see you again," an attractive woman of Native American descent, smiled as she gave Bob a hug.

"Let me introduce you to my Custer costume cohorts Dot Darlington and Merritt Andrews."

"It's a pleasure," Cathy replied, as the girls shook hands. "I have the war bonnet ready for your use at the playhouse. My only condition is that you send me a pair of tickets to the opening night of *Dakota.*"

"Done," Bob promised.

After spending a few more minutes chatting with Cathy and surveying the merchandise on display, the trio headed back to Custer State Park. The drive back was stunning as they enjoyed the mountain scenery against the colorful Dakota sunset.

Chapter 8:

Merritt's work obligations filled her weekend itinerary. She began sewing the Grace Coolidge dress and cut the fabric for the Wilder dress. After attending church services on Sunday morning at the Game Lodge chapel, Merritt spent the rest of the day in the Costume Shop finishing up the principle sewing on the costumes for Mrs. Coolidge and Laura Ingalls Wilder and began sewing on epaulets to Custer's uniform. By Monday she was ready for a day of fun with Ranger Josh Ford.

"Look at you, getting all ready for your big date," Merritt's roommate's jested as she prepped for her day out with Josh.

"It's not a date," Merritt protested. "It's an outing with a fellow North Carolinian, who happens to be a qualified Custer State Park tour guide."

"Whatever you say," Ginny teased. "Either way you'll knock his socks off."

"Where are you and Josh going for your non-date anyway?" Emma pressed for details.

"Ranger Ford is giving me a tour of the park's Wildlife Loop. I'm eager to see the begging burros. I hear they are park favorite."

"The pronghorns are elegant creatures," Emma noted. "They usually hang out in the park's prairie region, which is located in southern portion of the loop."

The girls chatted a few more minutes before a knock sounded at the cabin door.

"Your date is right on time...go get him tiger," Ginny smiled as Merritt went to open the door.

"Josh, it's good to see you again," Merritt, smiled as she ushered him inside the cabin.

"I hope you're still up for a day of exploration in Custer State Park," Josh smiled.

"Most definitely," Merritt replied. She usually hated first dates, and non-dates are even harder. The tension and awkwardness usually could be cut with a knife. Yet with Josh it was different. They shared natural chemistry.

"Ahem," Ginny feigned a cough. "Aren't you going to introduce us to your parks and recreations guide?"

"Sorry," Merritt's cheeks flushed. "Josh, I'd like to introduce you to my roommates, Ginny, Emma, and Rebecca."

"You're a Custer park ranger?" Emma asked.

"I work as a curator over at the Peter Norbeck Visitor Center. I primarily handle the Junior Naturalist programs. However, I also present Evening Programs at Center Lake and Game Lodge on Tuesday and Saturday nights."

"The evening programs are a great educational tool for park visitors and Custer locals alike," Rebecca put forth. "I gained a wealth of knowledge with Peter Wiseman did his lecture on park plants last summer."

"Peter is one of our best volunteers. He knows Custer's plant species inside and out, and his evening talks on botany are some of the most popular in the park," Josh agreed.

"We'll definitely have to catch your educational talks," Merritt stated, flashing Josh a smile.

"I'm leading a program on Park Conservation tomorrow night at eight at Center Lake. You should stop by," Josh invited.

"Considering Center Lake is practically in our backyard, I think we can make it," the Alpine girls promised.

"You two have fun, just make sure to get her back by a decent hour otherwise we'll be forced to send out a search party," Becky joked as the couple left the cabin and got into Josh's Jeep.

"So Ranger Ford, what is the scoop on Custer State Park's famed Wildlife Loop?" Merritt asked as the pair headed southwest on Highway 87 to the juncture with Highway 16A and the Wildlife Loop Road.

"The Wildlife Loop is an eighteen-mile road, situated in the southern portion of the park. It traverses the park's varied topography, from its pine-speckled hills to the open grasslands, showcasing the park's most popular feature, its wildlife. Custer State Park is home to such species as Bison, Mountain Goats, Bighorn Sheep, Prairie Dogs, Pronghorns, Burros and the elusive Mountain Lion," Josh explained.

"Are there any bears in the park?"

"No, the native bear population was pushed out of this area of South Dakota by hunters years ago. It's unfortunate that bears are no longer present in the current park ecosystem, but on the upside campers don't have to worry about leaving their food during their stay at a campsite."

"It is a perk for campers, although it is shame when native populations to die out of a region."

"Luckily the likes of Peter Norbeck realized the importance of conservation and wildlife management. Custer State Park works tirelessly to ensure proper management of all park species. We monitor population numbers and any potential health risks. You'll learn more about Park Management and Conservation at my talk tomorrow at Center Lake."

"You'll going to leave me wanting more," Merritt joked.

"That's the idea," Josh smiled before changing the subject. "If you're up for lunch, I figured we could stop off by Blue Bell for a bite to eat first."

"Lunch sounds like a plan. After all what good is a wilderness adventure on an empty stomach?" Merritt replied with a smile.

"Lunch it is then," Josh grinned as they headed south on the Wildlife Loop Road towards Blue Bell, one of the four main resort areas in Custer State Park. Blue Bell is located right off the Wildlife Loop Road, in the south western region of the park, at the base of Mount Coolidge and French Creek.

Its history dates back to the 1920s, when a telephone executive for the Bell Company built a vacation home on the property. He named his western ranch "Blue Bell", the logo for the Bell Telephone Company.

Today Blue Bell is a popular choice for park visitors seeking a rustic, old-west experience with its handcrafted log cabins and campsites. Blue Bell offers western flair activities including horseback riding, chuck-wagon cookouts, hayrides into the surrounding scenic backcountry, and educational programs.

The original Blue Bell ranch lodge built in the 1920s. The laidback log lodge, recently remodeled in 2008, houses Blue Bell's Dining Room & Lounge, *Tatanka*. The restaurant is known for its down-home cooking and comfortable western atmosphere.

"Blue Bell is one of my favorite areas in the park," Josh noted as he opened the door to the *Tatanka* for Merritt. "It has a neat dude-ranch, old-west feel."

The interior décor of the main dining room consists of exposed log walls, with western art, stone fireplaces, and comfortable seating. The lounge, located to the right of the restaurant lobby, is an upscale meets down home western style saloon with a beautiful oak bar and an excellent wine and drink list.

A friendly hostess ushered the pair to a cozy high-backed wooden booth.

A few minutes later the waitress stopped by to take their orders. The diverse menu features old west hearty meals at an affordable price.

Merritt opted for the grilled chicken drizzled with cheddar cheese, caramelized onions and bacon. Josh stuck with the house special of Chicken Fried Steak. While the pair waited for their food, they discussed the day's itinerary.

"Are you up for a hike or do you want to stick to exploring the Wildlife Loop by car?" Josh sought Merritt's input.

"I'd enjoy the opportunity to explore the back country."

"The Prairie Trail is a three-mile hike of moderate difficulty located about five miles south of Blue Bell, right off the Wildlife Loop Road. The path explores the grasslands and, which makes up the southern region of the park. The trail boasts wildflowers and it's not uncommon to spot wildlife such as deer or antelope while hiking the path."

"Sounds like a great trail."

"I think you'll really like it," Josh smiled. "We'll just need to make sure we have water with us on the trail, the sun can be a bit brutal at times. After the hike we'll drive the rest of the Wildlife Loop up towards Game Lodge."

After finishing lunch around two o'clock, the pair got in Josh's Jeep and hit the road. As they left the rolling hills and canyon vistas near Blue Bell, Custer's scenery changed dramatically as it morphed into a flat windswept prairie and endless sky.

"I'm amazed by the dramatic shift in scenery within a few miles," Merritt noted as Josh parked his Jeep by the trailhead.

"It's unusual how many distinct landscapes you'll find within the borders of Custer State Park. It comes from the fact that you have two different topographical regions colliding. The Black Hills rise up, seemingly out of nowhere, from the vast Great Plains that spread across America's heartland. The end result is a mix of grassland prairie, along with mountain forests and valleys and alpine habitats, which work together to create the unique and seamless ecosystem of Custer State Park."

"Well, the mixture of topography certainly makes for a beautiful view," Merritt sighed, in awe, as the couple grabbed their water bottles and hit the trail.

The trail winds through the prairie grasslands, which define the southern sector of the park. Near the end, a portion of the parallels a small stream running through stands of mixed hardwoods.

"Do you work at Custer all year or only in the summer?" Merritt asked as they wandered a path lined by flowers, sagebrush and mix of tall grasses.

"I usually work here from early May through the end of September in Custer. The past two off-seasons I ran school group tours at the Biltmore Estate in Asheville."

"I love the Biltmore! We used to go up there every Christmas to see the decorations."

It took Josh and Merritt approximately an hour and a half to hike the complete   three-mile loop. While hiking they chatted about everything from the park to their respective interests, such as movies, music and favorite vacation spots. The more they talked, the more they found they had in common.

Mid-way through the hike, the couple encountered several Mule Deer.

"Custer State Park has populations of both Whitetail Deer and Mule Deer. Whitetail Deer are the same breed found back in North Carolina, are known for the white hair on the underside of their tails. They typically hang out in the timberlands of Custer. The Mule Deer are named for their large ears. They have black-tipped tails, and are known for their ability to bounce gracefully through the prairie and up the surrounding hills," Josh explained as the deer sprung away.

After completing their hike, Merritt and Josh returned to the Jeep and headed east on the Wildlife Loop Road. They drove a few more miles before pulling off into a turnout.

"There's a prairie dog town, off the road over here," Josh noted as he parked the car. "Prairie dogs are a keystone species in the plains and one of my personal wildlife favorites here in the park. The black-tailed prairie dog is found on the dry upland prairie and is a rodent that lives in large social groups called towns. They hang out in this area of the park and you'll find a ton of prairie dog towns near Wind Cave National Park, just south of here. Prairie dogs are highly social animals, which make a high pitched bark to communicate, and warn of possible threats."

"I adore prairie dogs," Merritt gushed. "I watched them for over an hour during my recent trip through the Badlands."

"I'll admit they're adorable," Josh smiled. "And they are a very important part of the prairie ecosystem. Ecologists, like myself, refer to prairie dogs, as a 'keystone' species as their presence is necessary for the survival of other plains species. They are the primary food source for highly endangered black-footed ferret, which is native to South Dakota, as well as the swift fox, golden eagle, and American badger. Species such as the burrowing owl, mountain plover, hares and foxes rely on abandoned prairie dog burrows for nesting areas. Even larger plains mammals such as Bison and Mule Deer benefit from the presence of the prairie dog. The nutrients in the grass are located further down in the ground, towards the root, the prairie dogs burrowing pushes the nutrient filled part of the stalk closer to the top of the soil, making it easier for the mammals get the vitamins they need with work."

"Ginny and Rebecca told me that many ranchers kill prairie dogs and consider them pests. That's horrible."

"It's a controversial issue in South Dakota. Ranchers argue that the holes from the prairie dog burrows are a risk to their cattle and horses, causing the animals to trip and to break their lands. However, ask a rancher for an example of this occurring and he'll be quick to tell you it has never happened on their property. Ranchers then claim that the prairie dogs eat all the feed for their cattle, but as I just told you, prairie dogs actually help make the grass more nutritious for the cattle. I think a lot of it is the view of the prairie dog as a pest, but in actuality prairie dogs are very helpful to sustaining the prairie and to cattle. Most ranchers are just too stubborn to admit that, and unfortunately they have a strong enough lobby to prevent the black-tailed prairie dog being listed on the endangered species list."

"I can't imagine hurting a prairie dog, they are just too cute," Merritt replied, as she watched a group of prairie dogs socializing around the burrow.

Merritt and Josh hung out by the prairie dog town for ten more minutes before getting back on the Wildlife Loop. Shortly after they got back on the road a large group of burros blocked their way.

"Hold your horses, it looks like we have a traffic jam," Josh stated as he hit the brakes. The "begging" burros approached the Jeep, nudging their head through the window.

"They're really close," Merritt commented, a little bit alarmed.

"Don't worry the burros are harmless as long as you use common sense. They are hoping for us to throw them a bit to eat. I brought some burro food in anticipation. It's in the glove compartment," Josh reassured Merritt.

"Talk about getting up close and personal," Merritt laughed, cautiously petting the animal. Josh then threw a handful of food out the window, which the white burro went after. "They seem really friendly though."

"The burros are not native to the Black Hills. They are the descendants of a herd that once hauled visitors to the top of Harney Peak. When the rides were discontinued years ago, the burros were released into the park and have since become a popular attraction. They have been dubbed the begging burros, because they hangout on the Wildlife Loop Road 'begging' for a treat from park visitors. They are the only park species that you should feed, and although you should always use caution where wildlife is concerned, the burros are really the only park species that you can interact safely with up close."

"The begging burros certainly have personality," Merritt smiled as she observed the burros finish up the last of Josh's food.

Once the burros cleared the parkway Josh and Merritt continued east on the loop past the Buffalo Corrals.

Every September, the park rounds up the entire herd of Buffalo into these corrals. The Bison are given vaccinations and tested for infections such as brucellosis. Although most of the bison are then released back into the park to roam free, a select number are held in the corrals until November to be sold at auction. This is a management technique to keep the bison from overpopulating the park. If overpopulation occurs, there wouldn't be enough natural food and habitat to support the herd over the winter. Custer keeps very good track of the individual bison and won't sell any bison at auction that haven't lived at least ten years within the park.

"I can't imagine rounding up over a thousand buffalo into those corrals. It must be quite an undertaking," Merritt commented.

"It's old hat for the park by now as they've done it for forty years," Josh replied. "Although the round-up is always exciting to watch from the stands; the rumbling of hooves and roundup calls – makes for a fun day. In fact over 11,000 people from all over the world come just to watch the buffalo rounded up into these corrals."

"It sounds like a hoot."

"It's a blast, and arguably one of the best times of the year in Custer State Park. And in addition to the roundup itself the park, in conjunction with Custer city hosts several buffalo related events including the Buffalo Roundup Arts Festival and Buffalo Wallow Chili Cook Off."

Right across from the Buffalo Corrals, Josh and Merritt noticed a group of pronghorns, running through the nearby grassland.

"Josh what type of animal is that?" Merritt pointed to a large reddish brown ungulate with white stripes, a dark face and large horns. "They look like antelopes."

"Those beautiful creatures are called Pronghorns, although they have been incorrectly called antelope given their similar build and appearance to the African antelope. Pronghorns are native to the western United States, living primarily on the open grasslands. They get their name from the bucks' large pronged horns. The females' horns are smaller and un-pronged."

"Look at them run! They are so fast and so graceful."

"Pronghorns possess remarkable endurance and agility. They are the fastest native land mammal in North America, running speeds of forty miles or faster for great distances."

"Their agility is remarkable," Merritt admired, watching as the last of the pronghorn ran out of sight.

Just past the Buffalo Corrals, the road began to shift north, with the topography becoming dotted by ponderosa pines and creeks. By the time the pair reached the Game Lodge area, at the close of the Wildlife Loop, where they found the entire bison herd was scattered around the Game Lodge campgrounds and in front of the Creekside Lodge. Merritt was also excited to see several Bighorn Sheep crossing the road near the Peter Norbeck Visitor Center.

"Look at their horns," Merritt commented, admiring the ram's namesake thick, curled horns.

"You would like a ram, given the fact it's the Tar Heel mascot and all. I'm a wolf guy myself," Josh joked.

"Custer doesn't have a native wolf population," Merritt jested back. "So I guess you'll just have to walk with a little tar on your heels."

"The Bighorn Sheep have a unique history in the park. They were originally abundant in this region, however by 1920 the sheep had become extinct in the Black Hills. The park didn't want to let the bighorn's presence be wiped out from the history of Custer State Park. They quickly reintroduced a herd of Rocky Mountain bighorn sheep into the area. Unfortunately this herd has really struggled as of late. Most of the herd was wiped out by a bout of pneumonia, contracted from unauthorized livestock brought into the park. Right now only about eighteen sheep survive in the park. We are monitoring the situation, and have vaccinated the sheep to ward off future viral illnesses, but how well they rebound is kind of hit or miss right now."

"I hope that their populations recover. They are asset to the park."

Within twenty-minutes they had returned to the Alpine Cabin.

"I had a really great day Josh," Merritt stated as Josh walked her to the cabin door. "Thanks for playing tour guide."

"I enjoyed spending time with you Merritt. I hope we can spend more time together."

"I'd love that," Merritt smiled.

"See you at my educational chat over at Center Lake tomorrow?"

"You can count on it," Merritt promised before bidding Josh goodnight. As she walked into the cabin, her roommates were waiting to hear the scoop on her day out.

"How was your date with Ranger Ford?" Emma questioned as Merritt sat on her bed.

"Fantastic. I learned so much about the park and its wildlife."

"Josh is cute and he totally digs you."

"He is cute," Merritt agreed. "Although we're just friends..."

"For now," Rebecca joked. "You'll be officially dating by this time next week."

"Why don't we grab a snack at the Mess Hall and you can dish all the dirt on your day out?" Ginny suggested.

"Sounds like a plan," Merritt replied, still on cloud nine from her guided tour of Custer's Wildlife Loop with the charming Ranger Ford.

Chapter 9:

Merritt got off to an early start Tuesday morning. She grabbed a quick breakfast with her roommates before heading to the Costume Shop to delve into a pile of sewing and alteration projects.

"Did you have a nice weekend?" Bob asked as she set her things down at her sewing table.

"I did. I explored the Wildlife Loop with a friend," Merritt gleamed at the thought of Josh. "Did you have a good holiday?"

"Dot, Dolly and I watched the Memorial Day Parade in Custer City and then went to Sylvan Lake for a picnic."

"Speaking of Dot," Merritt replied as she looked around the room. "Where is she?"

"Upstairs in the theatre taking the measurements of a few miscellaneous actors that don't have a size chart. She should be back down here within an hour," Bob explained.

For the next hour Merritt hemmed three pairs of pants. Dot returned shortly after 10:30 with a new list of measurements and a memo from Gully.

"While I was upstairs I got an updated rehearsal schedule from Gully. He has scheduled fittings from the Tuesday the 8th to the Thursday the 10th."

"That's feasible," Bob thought.

"They'll be three full dress rehearsals before opening night: Monday the 14th through Wednesday the 16th. There is also a technical rehearsal on the 13th, which one of us will need to attend, in order to observe the flow of the scene changes."

"That works," Bob and Merritt agreed.

"As you may be aware, we're going to be needed for several off-site performances."

"Emma Seeley did mention that to me. She said it was a way to bolster ticket sales," Merritt replied.

"There will be three preview nights at park campgrounds before opening night. Chet, Ginny, Jack and Leroy will perform monologues and describe their roles in the play in full costume. These dates are Friday the 11th at Stockade Lake, Saturday the 12th at Game Lodge and Sunday the 13th at Blue Bell. At least one of us should be on site for each of these performances. Dolly will also be on site to handle make-up."

"I'll take Sunday at Blue Bell," Bob volunteered.

"I'm game for Game Lodge myself," Dot requested. "If you don't mind taking on Stockade, Merritt."

"No problem," Merritt agreed.

"Also, our actors have been asked to perform select scenes from *Dakota* at Mount Rushmore on June the 23rd, right before the nightly laser show. We're also scheduled to for a theatre night set in downtown Rapid City in the City of Presidents Park on July the 14th. Mark your calendars because we'll need to be available to assist with wardrobe for both of these special events."

"I've never been to Mount Rushmore so I look forward to the 23rd," Merritt enthused.

For the next three hours, the trio worked tirelessly on a variety of costumes. They were briefly interrupted when a ruckus of shouting sounded in the hall.

"You are a manipulative jerk Trump!" Gully's voice yelled out.

"I'm your savior Gordon!" Mike Trump shouted back. "If it were up to the folks in Pierre your Playhouse wouldn't be able in business this season. The playhouse would be bulldozed over with legion of construction workers building a top-notch conference center and concession venue on site."

"So you're doing me a favor?" Gully laughed sarcastically. "That's why you keep searching for non-existent structural issues or financial problems to shut us down."

"A 500 pound curtain falling from the rafters isn't a non-existent issue Gully! It's a major hazard and insurance risk. We're lucky that no one was killed or seriously injured."

"I bet you would have liked that," Gully shot back. "A death would have been a convenient way for you to get the playhouse closed down."

"Don't be ridiculous. That would be bad publicity for the Governor," Mike rolled his eyes.

"I fixed the curtain to your satisfaction and your people proved the rafters to be structurally sound. Unless there's some other ludicrous demand you want to slap on me, this conversation is over. I've got a play to produce," Gully shot back.

"You had better follow my lead Gordon otherwise this production will go to hell."

"Mr. Trump and Mr. Gordon, I beg you to stop this bickering," Dot stepped into the hall, cutting the men off. "Fruitless arguing is disrespectful to this hallowed theatre. If you insist on shouting, I ask that you take it outside!"

"My sincere apologies Ms. Darlington, it is difficult to avoid a quarrel with a contentious man like Mr. Gordon," Trump uttered an insincere apology as he readjusted his tie.

"I'm sorry Dot," Gully interjected. "I can't communicate with a playhouse saboteur vying for a backdoor concessionaire contract."

"STOP!" Dot put her foot down. "I don't agree with Mr. Trump's tactics, but he's here and we've got to deal with him. So I suggest you focus on making *Dakota* a success Gully and not bickering with Mr. Trump."

"We'll finish this conversation later," Gully promised Mike before walking away.

"Talk about an explosive argument," Merritt noted as Dot re-entered the Costume Shop.

"If you hadn't intervened, they might have killed each other," Bob surmised.

"Mike Trump is a malicious man, but unfortunately he has the final say in playhouse matters. If we give into Trump's provocations this theatre's future will be dead in the water," Dot analyzed. "Our best option is to focus on our jobs and avoid Trump as little as possible."

"Agreed," Bob and Merritt replied before delving back into their costume projects.

At five o'clock, the costumers closed up shop. Hungry after a full day of work, Merritt, headed over to the Mess Hall to grab a quick bite to eat. After dinner she headed back over to Alpine. Her roommates were still at rehearsal, which was due to get out at seven. She took the opportunity to phone her family in North Carolina and catch up on reading.

Shortly after seven, Ginny and Rebecca returned to Alpine Cabin.

"How was rehearsal?" Merritt asked, as her roomies entered the cabin.

"The actual rehearsals went fine," Rebecca bit her lip. "It was the off stage drama that was difficult."

"Let me guess there was an argument between Mr. Gordon and Mr. Trump."

"Don't tell me that you could hear their bickering all the way down in the Costume Shop?" Rebecca asked.

"They brought their fight down to the basement. If Dot hadn't convinced them to stop, they might have wound up in the hospital or worse."

"Trump is a jerk," Ginny interjected. "Unfortunately Gully and Alistair play right into his antics. It is bait and switch every time. If we want to triumph over Trump's sabotage we need to stand our ground without stooping to his low-life tactics."

"We should get ready for Josh's ranger chat at Center Lake," Rebecca noted the time. "Emma said she would meet us there and Jim wants to come too."

At seven-thirty the girls met up with Jim, Ethan and the Barber brothers at the Norbeck cabin before walking over to nearby Center Lake.

"I really love the costume designs you Bob and Dot came up with," Ethan started up a conversation with Merritt.

"How's the prop search going?"

"I'm making headway. Would you mind picking up a few items from a shop in Deadwood for me when you go there on Thursday."

"The van will be packed with costumes, but I'm sure we could squeeze a few props in. What do you need me to pick up?"

"A small box of Wild Bill props being held a western supply store in downtown Deadwood," Ethan explained. "I would get it myself, but I'm got errands up to my neck and I'm working on building several large props and assisting with set construction all this week."

"I'd be happy to help," Merritt replied as the group reached the Center Lake amphitheatre, which is located adjacent to the lake and consists of a set of benches and a projector, which shows power point slides during the chat. Josh was already at the site setting up for the program when the group arrived.

"You showed up," Josh smiled, as he greeted Merritt.

"I wouldn't miss for the world."

"It looks like you brought a group with you."

"You deserve an audience Ranger Ford," Merritt smiled slyly.

"Hopefully I don't disappoint. It's hard to impress a group of theatre-people."

"You'll do fine," Merritt promised before heading back to the benches to take a seat with her friends.

As she waited for the show to start, Merritt noticed Celeste and Chet embroiled in an argument by the lake.

"What's going on between Chet and Celeste," Merritt whispered to Ginny.

"It doesn't look like a friendly conversation."

"Didn't they used to date?" Ethan put forth.

"That's the rumor, but I don't know the scoop," Ginny answered. "Celeste has been happily married to Alistair for years and in spite of the bad blood between her and Chet, it typically doesn't interfere with the playhouse."

Before they could discuss Chet and Celeste any further, Josh started his evening program.

"In order to preserve the natural treasures of Custer State Park for future generations it's essential to implement a sound park-management and conservation plan. At Custer State Park we have team of biologists, ecologists and foresters working tirelessly to ensure professional park management. Our efforts include forest management, wildlife management and habitat-management for over 71,000 acres of parkland.

We'll begin our discussion with a focus on wildlife management in Custer. Our top priority as conservationists is to ensure that threatened and endangered native species maintain healthy populations within the park ecosystem. We monitor wildlife populations in order to ensure that overpopulation doesn't occur. Control of numbers ensures adequate forage for all species and prevents habitat loss and competition between species. The two ways we manage populations are through limited hunting and the Buffalo Roundup and Auction. Hunting is done on a highly limited basis, not for trophy mounts, but to ensure that populations do not exceed the food resources and foraging ground available in the ecosystem," Josh explained.

For the next few minutes he detailed wildlife management and the various types of wildlife within the park at length before moving to the next management topic: forestry.

"Forestry is the art and science of managing forests and related natural resources with a focus on sustainability and preservation. Custer State Park is home to 40,000 acres of forestland. Our motto is that a 'managed forest is a healthy forest.' The park's forests serve as a diverse habitat for the vitality of the greater-ecosystem. A healthy forest is the best defense against deadly insects, disease and wildfire.

When a forest becomes overcrowded, under competitive stress, the ecosystem suffers, from the dense forest floor to the trees struggling for sunlight and water and prone to disease. The best defense against an overgrown forest is periodic, carefully managed thinning of the forest.

The principal threat facing Custer's forests is the Mountain Pine Beetle. The mountain pine beetle, or MPB, is a species of bark beetle native to the forests of western North America. It has a hard black exoskeleton and is about the size of a grain of rice. Pine beetles kill trees by boring through the tree bark into the phloem layer. Within about two weeks of a beetle attack, trees are starved to death by lack of water and nutrients, which comes through the phloem layer. After the beetle has killed the tree it turns a reddish brown. The Pine Beetle invasion has been most detrimental near Sylvan Lake and along the Needles Highway.

Stopping the pine beetle isn't easy. Trees usually don't start showing obvious signs of an attack until a year after the infestation. By then the beetles have already left the dead tree, and are possibly attacking other trees in the area. Healthy trees are able to combat the MBP by releasing resin in pitch tubes to block the beetle from entering the tree. However trees that are stressed due to overcrowding are susceptible to the beetle, and once a tree is infested the entire forest is at risk. The MBP is only eradicated if two weeks of straight negative twenty degree weather occurs in the forest. These temperature drops were common place until recent history as global warming sifts the climate to warmer winters.

In Custer we battle the MPB in several ways. First we remove infested trees and turn them into firewood or tepee-shaped critter houses. Believe it or not, dead trees emit large amounts of CO_2, which is harmful for the environment. Dead trees also prevent forest re-growth and take sunlight space away from healthier trees. As previously mentioned, we permit small amounts of logging and forest thinning to prevent overgrowth, which in turn sustains the health of the forest. This is important because healthy trees can defend themselves against the MPB. We then sell the timber to local mills, which generates $250,000 of revenue, which is funneled back into the park's conservation budget.

In addition to forest thinning we experimented with limited spraying of anti-aggregation pheromones that mimic the chemical scent given off by beetles when a tree is full of insects. This only works to a degree, but can be extremely effective in forested areas where an outbreak is just occurring. Another experimental tool in the fight against the MPB is chitosan, an eco-friendly bio-pesticide, which helps trees be stronger when attacked and more readily release resin pitch-tubes. Right now stopping the MPB is touch and go, but if it's not stopped many of our forests will be gone by the year 2020."

"That's horrible," Merritt and her friends replied, alarmed by the seriousness of the Mountain Pine Beetle infestation in park.

Ranger Ford spent the final twenty-minutes of his lecture discussing the park's management of weeds such as goldenrod, knapweed, hoary cress and poison ivy. After the program, Merritt met up with Josh.

"Excellent job Ranger Ford. I learned a lot about park management."

"I'm glad that you enjoyed the program," Josh smiled. "Is there any chance of my taking you out on another excursion in the near future?"

"What sort of excursion are we talking about here Ranger Ford?" Merritt asked with a sly smile.

"A day trip to Jewel Cave with dinner afterwards," Josh suggested.

"I think I can fit you in this coming Monday afternoon at one o'clock?"

"Monday at one is perfect. I'll call you later in the week to sort out all the details." Josh and Merritt chatted a few more minutes before she walked back to Alpine with her roommates.

"Your Mr. Ford is quite the naturalist," Emma noted as the group cut through the woods back to the cabin. "His discussion enlightened me about the science behind Custer's park management before."

"Speaking of information, do mind giving us the scoop on what you and Ranger Ford were discussing a few minutes ago?" Rebecca asked.

"He asked me to go Jewel Cave with him on Monday afternoon."

"It's only the second date and he's already taking you someplace dark and candlelit. Wow this is serious," Ginny teased.

"We're just friends," Merritt rebutted too little avail before admitting: "Well it is sort of a date."

Chapter 10:

"Deadwood, a town of deceit, gold, saloon girls, murder, corruption and visions of the gritty old west," Dot stated as the costumers made the sixty mile drive north to the historic town of Deadwood on Thursday to pick up costumes.

"My kind of town," Bob joked.

To say Deadwood is a town with a colorful history is an understatement. It's rough and tumble history is one synonymous with the Wild West, and includes a list of real-life characters such as Wild Bill Hickok, Calamity Jane, Seth Bullock and more. Deadwood's history has become part of American folklore, influencing the popular dime western novels and television shows such as HBO's *Deadwood*. Today the entire city is listed on the National Register of Historic Places.

Deadwood was established in 1876 after gold was found in a nearby canyon in the northwest corner of the Black Hills. The area was named 'Deadwood Gulch' because of all the dead trees lining the canyon walls. News of the treasure at Deadwood Gulch spread quickly and almost overnight thousands of prospectors flocked to the area fueled by greed and hopes and quick fortune.

Deadwood's mining settlement of attracted an abundance of lawless and shady characters, looking for quick riches. Gambling, saloons, dancehalls and brothels lined the streets, and it is estimated that in the first year, at least one murder occurred every day. The most infamous murder occurred when Jack McCall shot popular gunslinger and gambler Wild Bill Hickok dead. The first year of settlement also saw the epidemic of smallpox nearly wipe out the town.

By 1877, the settlement began to evolve from a primitive mining camp to a community with a local government to keep law and order. The early miners' shanties and tents gave way to wood and brick buildings. Deadwood's hopes of transitioning from mining camp to civilized community were nearly dashed when a fire in 1879 damaged the business district. The town showed resiliency and rebuilt this time in brick and stone versus lumber.

By the 1890s Deadwood had become a bustling center of business in the Black Hills and in the newly formed state of South Dakota. The railroad brought travellers and new residents, and mining continued to flourish a nearby Homestake Mine in neighboring Lead.

Deadwood's fortunes began to change when a major fire ripped through the town September of 1959, burning over 4,500 acres and destroying much of the town, though luckily many historic buildings were not affected. The catastrophic fire began a severe economic downturn for the community of Deadwood.

In the late 1980s the community petitioned for legalized gambling to be allowed in town. This would be a way to generate revenue and bring in tourists who could also enjoy the historical Deadwood. In 1989, Deadwood became the first place outside of New Jersey or Nevada in the U.S. to offer legalized gambling. The bet paid off as tourists flocked to the town to hit the tables. Although gambling sparked the town's economic resurgence, it's the history and nearby recreational activities, that keeps tourists coming back for more.

The costumers entered the city limits of Deadwood, at 10:40. Dot pulled into the parking lot of the Adam's Museum on the corner of Deadwood and Sherman streets. The Adam's Museum is the oldest museum in the Black Hills and features a wealth of information on the history of Deadwood and the Black Hills Gold Rush. The Museum was founded by Deadwood businessman and former mayor W.E. Adams in 1930 in honor of his deceased first wife and two daughters, and given as a gift to the City of Deadwood. The Museum is partnered with the nearby Adam's Historical House and Museum, a beautiful Queen-Anne manor who was built in 1892 by the Franklin family who labeled it "the grandest house west of the Mississippi." The Adams family bought the manor in 1920 and it is now the home of the Historic Preservation Commission.

"This is where we're due to meet Meg any time after one," Dot explained. "Might as well keep the car parked here since we're going to have to move it over here later on to pick of the costumes regardless."

"Makes perfect sense to me," Bob agreed as the group got out of the car.

"This town exudes the persona of the wild west," Merritt surveyed the rows of historic brick, stone and plywood buildings lining downtown streets. "Deadwood is a town with a fascinating past," Dot explained. "Gunslingers, dancehall girls, gold seekers, swindlers once roamed these streets."

"Since Merritt has never been to Deadwood, why don't we give her a tour, before picking up the costumes and props?" Bob suggested.

"I'd love nothing more," Dot smiled as the pair walked down Deadwood's sidewalks to nearby Main Street. "Let's commence our tour with Deadwood's most infamous landmark, the site where Wild Bill was shot in the back by Jack McCall. Especially since the historical events play so prominently a role in *Dakota.*"

"Lead the way," Merritt directed; eager to learn more about the infamous shooting of Wild Bill.

"Wild Bill is one of Deadwood's most famous characters. He was born James Butler Hickok in Illinois on May 27th 1857. He earned the nicknamed 'Wild Bill' during his tenure with the Union army, and the name stuck. Before arriving in Deadwood, Hickok's reputation preceded him. He had become well known as a fierce gunslinger, scout, stagecoach driver, lawman and gambler. Prior to arriving in Deadwood he had already been involved in several well-known shootouts and for being an able gambler. On March 5th 1876, he married Agnes Thatcher Lake, his long-time girlfriend. After a brief honeymoon, Wild Bill separated with her to come to Deadwood, with the plan of sending for his bride once he'd secured his finances in the town. He joined up with Charlie Utter's Wagon Train, which was bound for the Black Hills from Fort Laramie in Wyoming. It was on the Wagon Train he met Calamity Jane, who would also place her stamp in Deadwood's lore," Dot explained.

"My roommate, Ginny, is portraying Calamity Jane. She's enjoyed reading up on her biography."

"Calamity was a character in her own right. She often dressed in men's clothing and was notorious for drinking too much. She was a sharpshooter who tended to exaggerate a little, but at times could be extremely compassionate, especially when she nursed the sick during the 1876 smallpox outbreak in Deadwood."

"Is it true that she and Wild Bill were an item?"

"No. Jane may have been in love with Bill, but he was too in love with Agnes to pay her any attention," Dot gave her two cents as they approached a formidable brick and stone building, housing a popular casino. "The original Nuttal and Mann's Saloon No. 10 burned down with the fire of 1879. However, this is the original site where Wild Bill was shot. They have a small museum downstairs depicting the scene of the crime."

"Let's check it out," Merritt and Bob replied as the group entered the building, heading downstairs to a small rustic looking saloon, mimicking the original Saloon No. 10. Several realistic mannequins are seated around a table, wearing western attire with another mannequin standing up behind Wild Bill's back.

"We've come to the scene of the crime," Merritt surveyed the space.

"Here on August the 2nd 1876 one of the most notorious shootings in American history occurred," Dot replied. "Wild Bill had joined in a card game with a group of gambling buddies. Fellow gambler, Charlie Rich, was already sitting in Hickok's favorite seat, which faced the door when he arrived. Wild Bill, whose cardinal rule was never to sit with his back to the door, asked Rich to switch seats, but he refused. Begrudgingly, Wild Bill took a seat with his back to the door. During this time, Jack McCall, a drifter who had come to Deadwood to work as a miner, was sitting unnoticed at the bar drinking heavily when Hickok began playing cards.

The story goes that Jack McCall had lost heavily in a gambling game with Hickok the day before. Wild Bill generously offered to give McCall enough money to buy something to eat, and advised him not to gamble again until he could cover his losses. Although McCall took the lunch money, he was infuriated with Wild Bill for what he deemed an insult. Still angry from the heavy losses he accrued at the hand of Hickok, and the coward McCall snuck up behind him. He quickly pulled out a .45 pistol and said 'take that' before shooting Wild Bill in the back of his head. His final hand of cards fell to the table, a pair of aces and eights. This cursed hand is now known as 'dead man's hand' as those were the cards Bill had when he was murdered."

"Did they ever catch McCall?" Merritt asked.

"The trials of Jack McCall are almost as chaotic as the shooting itself. Following Wild Bill's death, McCall was instantly tried for murder. He claimed that he shot Wild Bill in revenge for killing his brother back in Abilene. The jury returned a 'not guilty' verdict.

"How could they acquit him? He was shot Wild Bill in cold bold," Merritt protested.

"Most of the town wanted him hung, but McCall was acquitted partially because of the story about his brother and mostly due to politics. In 1876, Deadwood was an illegal settlement in Lakota country, and in violation of the terms of the Treaty of Laramie. Deadwood residents wanted the town to be included in the Dakota Territory. They feared sentencing McCall to death might jeopardize that process. An acquittal would at least feign the appearance of a decent court system," Dot explained. "After he was cleared, McCall fled into Wyoming, where he began boasting of how he murdered Wild Bill and got away with it. McCall admitted that he never had a brother and had no legitimate excuse for killing Hickok. His bragging about murdering Hickok did not do well for McCall. Less than a month after the original trial, the U.S. government declared the trial in Deadwood to have no legal basis as it was in Indian Territory. McCall was arrested in Laramie Wyoming on August 29, 1876 and charged with murder. He stood trial in Yankton South Dakota, where he was found guilty and hung for murder."

"What a tragic tale."

"Alas one that has become so instilled in the history of the Old West," Bob replied.

After touring the historical site of the saloon where the coward Jack McCall shot Wild Bill, the group meandered down the Main Street, which is lined with saloons and shops, for several minutes before grabbing a bite to eat at the Bullock Hotel.

The Bullock Hotel is an elegant sandstone structure located on the corner of Wall and Main Streets. Seth Bullock who was the first sheriff in Deadwood, and his business partner Sol Star built the hotel from 1894 to 1896. The stately Victorian and Italianate style hotel is the gem of downtown Deadwood, and still serves as a center of activity with its casino and stately hotel rooms.

"This is a gorgeous building. The architecture is immaculate without being too ornate," Merritt noted as the pair approached the hotel.

"When the Hotel was repurchased in 1991, the new owners went to painstaking lengths to ensure the historical integrity of the building and its interior décor. Although slight changes were made due to structural concerns, the Bullock Hotel maintains the authenticity of the 1890s ambiance."

Oriental rugs, wooden paneling, a grand staircase, and forty-eight inch solid brass chandeliers filled the space with an ambiance of Victorian and Italianate design.

After exploring the lobby, the costumers settled into the hotel's restaurant Bully's for a hearty lunch.

"Talk about a cool atmosphere," Merritt exclaimed, stepping foot in the restaurant. Bully's named after Seth Bullock's good friend, President Teddy Roosevelt, has an intimate setting, which features a fireplace inlaid with beautiful green potter's tiles and carved woodwork. The green wallpapered walls compliment the fireplace, and large elk chandeliers drop from a tile ceiling. Emerald Green walls are adorned with period artwork.

"Bully's offers tasty entrees at an affordable price," Dot mentioned before a hostess sat the trio at a table near the fireplace."

After taking several minutes to survey the menu, Merritt opted for the chef salad, whereas Bob and Dot ordered burgers.

During lunch the group discussed their remaining workload and upcoming costume fittings.

"We've made remarkable progress. We only have a few small alterations and two or three costumes left to sew," Bob stated before taking a bite of his burger.

"As long as we don't have too many alterations to make after the initial costume fittings next week I think we'll be in ship shape for opening night," Dot added in.

The costumers finished lunch by 12:30, and started heading back to the Adam's Museum to pick up the Deadwood costumes. On the way they stopped briefly at a downtown antique store to pick up the box of props for Ethan. Once inside the store, an older gentleman in his late sixties greeted the group.

"How I help you folks today?" The gentleman asked in a friendly manner.

"We work as costumers for the Custer Playhouse. Ethan Daniels asked me to stop by on his behalf and pick up a box of props you are holding for him."

"Ethan did say you would be stopping by," the man acknowledged with a smile as he went behind the cash register to retrieve the prop box. "I'm Connor Stevens. I went to high school with Ethan's parents in Rapid City ages ago. I'm also good-friends with his aunt and uncle as well. So when he called me asking for old west faux weaponry, I was l was all too happy to oblige."

"I'm sure that these props will help the Deadwood scene come alive in *Dakota*," Merritt noted.

"I have tickets for opening night and I'm looking forward to seeing how the show comes together," Connor stated before changing the subject. "Before you go, I have something I'd like you to give Ethan. I was rummaging from some old photos from my schooldays and found a picture of his mom, Carla. I thought he might like to have it," Connor stated as he handed Merritt a faded photograph of a very attractive blonde.

"I'll be sure to give it to him," Merritt promised before the group headed back to Museum.

After loading the prop box inside the van, the costumers proceeded inside the Adams Museum to meet up with Meg.

"Dot Darlington, it has been ages!" Meg Hopewell, a tall brunette in her fifties, greeted Dot as they entered the museum.

"It's so good to see you!" Dot stated as she hugged her old friend. "Bob, you know Meg don't you?"

"It's good to see you again," Bob replied, shaking the historian's hand.

"Meg, I'd like to introduce you to the newest member of our costume staff: Merritt Andrews," Dot introduced the pair, who shook hands.

"We really appreciate the Museum loaning us these costumes," Bob showed his appreciation. "It's really cutting our workload down in half and saving money on an already tight budget."

"It is the least I could do," Meg replied. "I'm just so sick about what those politicians in Pierre are trying to do to Playhouse. Hopefully *Dakota* becomes a big hit so the state renews your lease."

"You and I both," Dot sighed.

For the next half hour the group proceeded to load up the van with the authentic Old-West costumes.

"This is the last of the costumes," Meg noted as she handed two suits to Bob.

"You've really helped us out Meg. I can't imagine all the extra time it would have taken to make these costumes by hand," Merritt put forth.

"It was my pleasure," Meg smiled.

The drive back to Custer State Park took just over an hour. The trio parked the van near the back entrance of the playhouse just after four, and began to unload the costumes and accessories.

After the entire set of Deadwood costumes had been hung up in the Shop, the group of costumers decided to spend the next two hours working on alterations and finishing up principle sewing on original designs. By seven, the costumers were ready to call it a night.

"I had a really fun day gals," Bob stated as the group brought the last of the costumes into the Shop.

"I thoroughly enjoyed the historical tour of Deadwood."

"It is a neat town," Dot agreed. "And I'm thrilled to death we were able to acquire the authentic costumes for *Dakota*."

"Why don't we meet here tomorrow around nine and dig our teeth into the remaining alterations?" Bob suggested.

"Sounds like a plan," Merritt and Bob agreed. A few minutes later the group exited the Costume Shop. As they walked into the hallway they noticed the production's Script Supervisor, Kat Warner crying in the hallway.

"Kat are you okay?" Merritt and her costume colleagues asked with concern.

"I'll be fine, I just needed to clear my head," her face beet red as she forced back tears. "Chet and I got into a huge argument. I should know better than to let him get under my skin, but he's so difficult."

"Chet's not worth your time," Bob replied firmly, handing Kat a Kleenex. "You can disregard whatever he said to you."

"I wish it was that easy," Kat sighed. "I put so much passion and energy into writing this play, that it really hurts when our headlining star tells me that '*Dakota* was the worst piece of drivel he'd ever read' and that he 'wouldn't be surprised if it bombed at the theatre box office.' He uttered a lot of other obscenities that I'd rather not repeat."

"That's nonsense," Merritt reassured Kat. "*Dakota* is an amazing play. It incorporates history in a fun and exciting way. If anything *Dakota* will be the smash we need to convince the state to renew the playhouse's lease next year."

"You really think that?" Kat asked, drying her eyes.

"Most definitely," Merritt smiled.

"*Dakota* is tops Kat, don't let anyone tell you otherwise," Bob advised. "You certainly shouldn't listen to a word Chet has to say. His opinion is null and void.

"I wish that Chet didn't get under my skin, but it is exhausting haggling with him on set. When Chet's on, he's the best actor west of Broadway, but I'm honestly beginning to wonder if Alistair should have cast him this year. Every rehearsal is a struggle and he's driving us all crazy."

"Collectively Bob and I have known Chet over twenty-five years," Dot stated. "Trust us when we say he's not worth worrying about."

After exiting the Playhouse, Merritt stopped by the Set Shop in hopes of tracking down Ethan. John Hood, the company Set Designer, told Merritt that Ethan had just left for the day and was probably in his cabin.

Following the tip, Merritt headed over to the Norbeck cabin. After a few knocks, Ethan opened the door.

"Hi Merritt," Ethan smiled as he ushered her inside his cabin.

"I'm here to drop off the props you requested from Deadwood," Merritt set the box down on a nearby bunk bed.

"You didn't have too much trouble finding the place," Ethan inquired.

"No problem at all," Merritt smiled, before pulling out the framed picture of Ethan's mom from her shoulder bag. "Oh and I almost forgot, Connor wanted me to give this to you. It's a picture of your mom."

"Thanks," Ethan's tone became slightly agitated. "Did he say where he got this picture?"

"From an old photo album, I think," Merritt, paused. "Your mom is lovely."

"She was gorgeous wasn't she?" Ethan sighed, tearing up a bit as he looked at the faded picture. "I never really knew her... you see she died when I was five years old."

"I'm sorry," Merritt showed sympathy.

"It's fine. My aunt and uncle did a great job raising me," Ethan rushed to change the subject. "Are you participating in the Harney Peak hike on Saturday? It's National Trails Day and Alistair is rounding up cast and crew to hike the peak and then hand out flyers at Sylvan Lake. He thought it would be a fun day out for the cast and crew and good publicity for the Playhouse."

"I'd love to come; that is if I finish up my sewing projects in time."

Merritt and Ethan chatted a few more minutes before she headed back to Alpine. It had been a fun, but hectic day and Merritt was ready to relax.

Chapter 11:

Merritt spent Friday morning in the Costume Shop finalizing alterations for the background actors in the 7th Cavalry and General Custer scenes. At 12:15 she took a quick break to eat a ham sandwich lunch before returning to the sewing table to assist with alterations for the newly arrived batch of Deadwood costumes. She had just finished hemming Jack McCall's suit when Bob received a cell-phone call from Peter's friend who works at the Crazy Horse Memorial.

"Tamara Means, the Native American seamstress and artisan who works at the Crazy Horse Memorial, just phoned to inform me that the pants and breastplate for Peter's costume are ready to be picked up. I'm swamped with the Mount Rushmore scene at the moment. Can you take time out of your schedule to make the trip up to Crazy Horse this afternoon Merritt?" Bob requested.

"Most definitely," Merritt agreed.

"Excellent," Bob replied, writing down a list of instructions for Merritt. "When you reach the admission gate, tell the attendant that you're from the Custer Playhouse and are picking up a set of items from Tamara Means. They will direct you from there."

"And Merritt don't feel the need to rush back. Take time to tour the Memorial while on site," Dot added in. "It's a magnificent monument."

~

The drive from the playhouse to Crazy Horse took twenty-five minutes. Merritt rolled down her windows and turned up her favorite Tom Petty record as she navigated Highway 16. With temps in the upper seventies and clear skies, it was a glorious day for a drive in the Black Hills. A background of granite mountain outcroppings protruding into the clouds paired with the foreground of swaying roadside wild flowers in, prompted the costumer to make several turnout stops for photo opts.

The Crazy Horse Memorial is an iconic emblem of South Dakota, equal in stature to neighboring Mount Rushmore. Generations have blasted and carved the art in stone as a dedication to the great Lakota warrior Crazy Horse. The monument remains a work in progress. Upon completion it will be the largest sculpture in the world.

The memorial is a tribute to Native Americans of all tribes to encourage preservation of their history and culture. In addition to the massive mountain carving of Crazy Horse, the campus has five interpretative museums.

Crazy Horse was born in the Black Hills circa 1842 into the Ogala Lakota tribe. He was a strong proponent of protecting the Lakota way of life and the traditions of his people. In this fight to preserve the ways of his people and the sacred land of the Black Hills, he grew to become a respected and feared warrior who led the fight against the U.S. Calvary at Custer's Last Stand in the Battle of Little Bighorn. He refused to sign any treaties and did not want his people to be forced onto reservations. Just over a year after the Battle of Little Big Horn, Crazy Horse was arrested and taken to Fort Robinson in Nebraska for refusal to go on the reservation. He was stabbed in back, under a flag of truce, probably by a U.S. cavalryman.

As she pulled up to the Memorial's main gate, a friendly Lakota college student in her early twenties greeted her.

"Welcome to Crazy Horse!"

"Hi, my name is Merritt Andrews. I work as a costumer for the Custer Playhouse. I'm due to pick up a set of costumes from Tamara Means, an artisan who works in Native American Cultural Center here."

"Tamara did mention that she was expecting visitors today," she replied, handing Merritt a visitor pass. "This will get you into the Memorial."

"This is my first time at Crazy Horse, so I could use some directions."

"Drive straight for a few miles until you reach the main campus and monument. You can park in any of our main lots. Once you park your car, just go in through the main museum and follow the signs to the Native American Cultural Center," the ticket agent explained. "I'll give you a copy of our brochure, which has a map of the entire Memorial along with information about the history of Crazy Horse and the carving of the mountain."

"This is perfect. Thank you."

As she neared the main parking lot, the massive mountain sculpture came into full view. She parked her car and walked through a set of double doors to the 40,000 square foot Welcome Center, which includes two theatres and a number of exhibits.

Merritt looked at her watch. It was just after three. Tamara had told Bob she could pick up the costumes anytime before five.

"I should probably tour the museum first," Merritt reasoned. "That way I don't have to worry about lugging the costumes around or be forced to leave them in the trunk of my car to be tampered by the heat."

"The next showing of the film, *Dynamite and Dreams* is going to be airing in theatre two in three minutes. The film lasts twenty-minutes and tells the story of the Crazy Horse Memorial. It is the perfect start to your tour," an announcement sounded over the loudspeakers.

Following the announcer's advice, Merritt headed to theatre two to watch the Memorial's introductory film, which is narrated by famed Lakota track runner Billy Mills. It gives a comprehensive history of the mountain carving and details attraction information. She found an empty seat on the second row just as the lights began to dim.

The origins of Crazy Horse date back to 1939 when Ogala Lakota Chief Standing Bear approached a talented young sculptor named Korczak Ziolkowski about carving a large-scale sculpture in the Black Hills to pay tribute to the Lakota nation who had long-lived in the area prior to American settlement. This sculpture was meant to compliment nearby Mount Rushmore, offering the Native American story of the land. Standing Bear told Korczak, that: "My fellow chiefs and I would like the white man to know the red man has great heroes, also." Crazy Horse was chosen because of his bravery in the fight to preserve the traditions of his people. The Paha Sapa, the area known to westerners as the Black Hills, was selected given the fact it was deemed holy to the Lakota and its rock walls and granite spires are conducive for carving.

Up to this point, Korczak had gained recognition as a sculptor and artist by winning first prize for his work PADEREWSKI: *Study of an Immortal* at the 1939 World's Fair and also for his work under Gutzon Borglum at Mount Rushmore. Korczak, intrigued by the concept of carving a mountain structure that would honor the Native Americans, he accepted the offer. However before Korczak could commence work on the project World War II broke out, thus delaying the project until 1948, when he returned to the Hills to take on Standing Bear's challenge to carve the mountain, without a sculptor's salary.

On June 3rd 1948, a dedication blast, attended by Chief Standing Bear, took just 10 tons off the mountain; just enough to ignite the dream of carving this mountain of stone.

In the beginning, Korczak started off using only chisels and hammers, slowing cutting into the mountain. He raised money for sculpting supplies by charging an admission to the monument site. He would greet tourists and give tours of his log cabin home and studio, showing them the scale model of how Crazy Horse would look when it was finally completed and inform them about the history of the Lakota people.

It was hard work, and he often battled financial hardship, injuries, and outright criticism. Although Chief Standing Bear supported the carving, many Lakota were disgusted with the project, feeling that it went against the essence of the historical Crazy Horse and would desecrate their holy Paha Sapa. However Korczak, who genuinely admired the Lakota and their heroes, continued on with the project he'd promised Standing Bear he'd fulfill.

In 1950 Korczak married Ruth, a girl eighteen years his junior, who shared his passion for the mountain carving. While Korczak worked on the carving, she raised their ten children, managed a dairy and sawmill on site, and gave tours to visitors. Following Korczak's death at age seventy-four in 1982, Ruth took helm of the Crazy Horse Memorial Foundation, and helped to expand the interpretative facilities. She and seven of the Ziolkowski children work on the monument, continuing the dream of completing the monument.

Korczak believed that if Crazy Horse was to be built, the funds should be raised not from state or federally funding, but from the interested public. As the project gained traction, more and more curious tourists stopped by to check the progress of construction, which continue to fund the carving to this day. Since 1948 millions of tons have been blasted off, with Crazy Horse's finished head revealed in 1998. Although budget and weather concerns prevent Crazy Horse from naming a final completion, the carving continues on course with all funding coming directly from entrance fees and donations. The final dimensions of the monument will be 641 feet long and 563 feet high.

After watching the informative video, Merritt headed over to the adjoining Indian Museum of North America, which is home to a collection of Native American artifacts and photograph exhibit. She then stepped outside to the Viewing Veranda to enjoy an unobstructed view of the Crazy Horse sculpture before moving on to tour Korczak's studio and original log cabin. The studio features many of Korczak's small sculptures including his award-winning bust of Paderewski.

Merritt spent an hour exploring the museum and enjoying views of the monument, before tracking down Tamara Means in the Native American Cultural Center. The Center is housed in a large stone building, adjacent to Korczak's studio, which offers interpretative programs teaching visitors about the Native American way of life. During the summer Native Americans from all over North American act as artists in residence, allowing them to create and sell their work, while interacting with visitors.

"Tamara?" Merritt inquired as she approached an attractive Native American female in her early forties, matching Bob's description.

"You must be Merritt? Bob said you would be stopping by, to pick up the Crazy Horse costume ensemble," Tamara shook Merritt's hand. "It's a pleasure to meet you."

"The pleasure's all mine."

"I have the breast plate and pants hanging up over here," Tamara stood up, walking over to a nearby rack. "I constructed all the beadwork myself, and the costume is historical, and authentically crafted."

"What magnificent craftsmanship," Merritt exclaimed, in awe of the intricate detail of the beadwork and mastery of design.

"I learned the traditional style of Lakota dressmaking from my grandmother. She grew up on the Pine Ridge Indian Reservation, just south of the Badlands. She learned developed her artistry under tutelage from her mother and grandmother. Both women were alive before western settlement of the Black Hills and passed down stories and the traditions of the Lakota people."

"I've really enjoyed learning about the Lakota and Native Americans who call this land their home."

"I commend the Dakota production for the careful attention to and accurate and tasteful display of the Lakota life on the plains."

"Your costume will certainly help the story of Crazy Horse and the Lakota come alive," Merritt smiled. "We really appreciate your making this outfit for us."

"It was no bother. I just can't wait to see Peter playing Crazy Horse. He embodies the spirit of Crazy Horse."

"Bob mentioned that you are friends with Peter."

"We grew up together. He went through a tough period by getting involved with the wrong crowd during college, but after the car accident he really pulled his life together."

"Car accident?" Merritt questioned.

"It was a long time ago. Peter had been out drinking with some buddies and made the mistake of driving. The accident left him pretty banged up. It's a miracle he survived. Ever since then Peter has stayed sober and has dedicated his life to teaching school up in Spearfish and of course working as a stock actor annually for the Custer Playhouse."

"He's an asset to the playhouse for sure. The cast and crew all rave about him."

"Except for Chet Rawlins," Tamara rolled her eyes. "He's a sly one and has treated Peter like dirt for years. I don't know how Peter puts up with him. I know I would have killed Chet by now."

"I haven't interfaced with Chet much," Merritt admitted, "Though his reputation is a bit notorious for offstage drama."

"My advice is to stay as far away from Chet Rawlins as possible. He's toxic to his core," Tamara warned.

"I'll take note of that..." Merritt bit her lip, uncomfortable with the conversation about Chet. She was aware that a lot of her fellow crewmembers couldn't stand the man, but she didn't like to bash people, even if it was deserved. "Thanks again for allowing us to borrow this beautiful costume."

"No problem," Tamara replied. "Good luck with the show. I hope it's a blockbuster."

On the way back to her car, Merritt stuffed a ten-dollar bill in one of the donation boxes near the front entrance to help fund the continued construction of the Crazy Horse Memorial and Monument.

By the time she arrived back at the Playhouse it was just after five. Merritt parked her car by the rear entrance of the theatre and headed directly to the Costume Shop with the beautifully handcrafted Lakota warrior costume.

Chapter 12:

The costume crew spend three hours on Saturday morning finishing up a number of sewing projects in preparation for cast fittings, which were due to begin on Tuesday.

They called it a day by noon in order to tackle the Harney Peak ascent via the Little Devils Tower trail with the rest of the theatre company.

Merritt change into a pair of Columbia lightweight hiking pants and her Custer Playhouse tee shirt. She threw a water bottle, tube of sunscreen, bug spray and digital camera into her backpack and headed to the Mess Hall to meet up with the group of cast and crew planning to go on the hike.

"You made it!" Merritt's roommate's greeted her.

"I pushed the sewing pedal to the metal to get out early."

"We're glad you came," Emma note, "strength in numbers."

"How long is the hike," Merritt inquired.

"It's a six mile there and back hike, ascending Harney Peak. The trail's path is fairly moderate. A spur trail, branches off from the main trail leads to a unique rock formation nicked named Little Devils Tower. We're bypassing the strenuous spur trail to continue up Harney Peak, to a picturesque vista, which offers terrific views of the nearby Cathedral Spires and the Black Hills."

"It sounds like fun. Hopefully I can get some decent snapshots to send back home," Merritt replied as Jim, Ethan, Tom and Luke entered the Mess Hall.

"Are you ready to conquer the peak?" Jim asked, stopping to give Becky a kiss on the cheek.

"As ready as we'll ever be."

"It'll be a cinch," Jim answered confidently, before turning his attention to Rebecca. "Well as long as you don't trip over the rocks and end up slathered in poison ivy."

"He's just making fun of me because I'm such a klutz," Rebecca rolled her eyes. "Last time we hiked the trail I thought I saw a snake, which turned out to be a twig. I subsequently tripped over a few tiny rocks and fell into a pile of poison ivy. I itched for weeks and couldn't be around anyone for fear of spreading the infection. If it hadn't been for Peter concocting a natural anti-itch crème I don't think I could have survived it."

"Did somebody mention my name?" Peter Wiseman asked as he entered the conversation.

"I was just recounting my battle with poison ivy last year," Rebecca groaned.

"That was quite a nasty bout you had," Peter agreed.

"It was a good thing you could help Becky out," Ethan interjected.

"I'm just glad one of my remedies actually worked," Peter joked.

"Peter I wanted to thank you for getting in touch with Tamara about sewing the pants and breastplate. I picked up your costume yesterday and it looks fantastic!" Merritt told him.

"All I did was make a phone call," Peter shrugged his shoulders. "Tamara was happy to do it. Her only condition was that I leave a stack of her cards for guests to pick up in the main lobby."

"Friends, actors, and crewmembers," Alistair's charismatic voice sounded. "I hope everyone has brought their 'A' game because in honor of National Trails Day we're going to tackle one of Custer's most beautiful hikes, Little Devils Tower. I have arranged for a bus to drive us through the beautiful Needle's Highway up to the trailhead. I ask that all of you wear your Custer Playhouse *Dakota Shirts* while hiking to help publicize the production. It's pretty steep at the top, so if you have any health concerns, you might want to sit this trip out. After the hike we have reservations at the Sylvan Lake Lodge for dinner, courtesy of dear Mr. Trump over here." Mike Trump, dressed in a well-pressed black suit did his best to feign a smile.

"That's strange," Merritt whispered to Emma. "He's been such a fiscal czar. He didn't even want to pay for our Mess Hall food in the theatre budget."

"Who knows what game he's playing?" Emma sighed. "He's probably just trying to cozy up to us, in the spirit of keeping his enemies closer."

"And speaking of Mr. Trump," Alistair continued. "He has asked that we all sign these nifty insurance wavers, just in case some sort of accident happens during our little rendezvous."

"I bet he'd like that," Emma rolled her eyes.

"My main goal is for all of you is have a safe an enjoyable trip," Trump explained, "I have a pile of waivers on the table here, along with pens. I'll collect waivers as you get on the bus."

"How about *you* sign a waiver, Mikey?" Chet shouted, limping into the Mess Hall. "Because I certainly don't believe you're looking out for our best interests."

"I can assure you my motives are just."

"I doubt that," Chet rolled his eyes. "Lucky for me, my ankle is still too wobbly from the falling curtain you orchestrated."

"Chet I really don't think this is time nor place to make false accusations," Trump replied, his tone flustered.

"It's not false. The only reason you're here this summer is to sabotage our theatre season."

"That's a blatant lie and you know it!"

"Are you calling me a liar?" Chet moved into attack mode, ready to punch out Trump.

"You're drunk, Rawlins, go home," Mike spat out. "And don't bother to come back."

"I ought to break your neck." As Chet lunged at Mike, Alistair stepped in between the two men and pushed them apart.

"Stop the bickering," Alistair directed the pair. "Chet, you've had a tough week of rehearsals. Why don't you head back to your RV and get some rest. Mike why don't you wait for us at the bus."

"I don't know how you stand him Fitzgerald. If it were up to me he would have been fired on the spot."

"Leave it to Chet to cause a ruckus," Peter sighed. "Oddly enough I actually agree with him about Mike. You've got to admit it is a little weird his buying us dinner. On the other hand, I'm not going to let a jerk like Trump interfere with a perfectly good hike."

After the dust settled a bit, the group of roughly thirty hikers signed their waivers and boarded the bus. Merritt found a window seat near the middle of the tour bus.

"The drive up to the trailhead is absolutely glorious," Alistair spoke over the loudspeaker as the bus turned right onto Highway 87. "We'll be heading north fourteen miles on the famed Needle's Highway, which is named after the unique needle-like granite formations that line the road. The road was charted mile for mile by Senator Norbeck, who scouted the parkway on foot and horseback. Norbeck wanted park visitors to experience the natural landscape, without obstruction. This massive road, cut through the land of spires and ponderosa pines was completed in 1922. The roads were built to bend with the scenery, and are therefore very curvy and at times hard to maneuver. The maximum speed limit on this road is only twenty miles per hour, and for good reason. The way the road winds and bends, even going five miles over the speed limit could cause a major accident. This road was built to showcase the scenery, not to serve as a speedway. That being said, I invite you to enjoy the sixty-minute, fourteen-mile drive up the Needles to Little Devils Tower Trailhead."

The first portion of the drive wound through fields of wildflowers with running streams, backed by thick ponderosa pines. A few miles into the drive, Merritt noticed a shady campground entitled Hole in the Wall, which is a picture stop along the highway. It features a large granite rock that has a small cave like opening.

"These roads wind feverishly. With every hairpin curve you can't even see if another car is coming towards you. I can't imagine the types of accident that could occur if someone was speeding or even worse had been drinking," Ethan mentioned to Peter, from the seat in front of Merritt and Emma.

"It would be deadly," Peter flinched, visibly uncomfortable with the thought of a car accident on the Needles.

Merritt gazed out the window in awe of the majestic scenery. After the bus drove through a large tunnel, blasted out of mountain, the needle like granite spires pierced the skyline. The Needles have been carved by years of rain, wind and heat; the end result is a masterful work of natural art.

A few miles before reaching the trailhead, Alistair asked the driver to pull off the road to allow time for the company to get out and take pictures of the Needle's Eye, a formation right off the highway that stands forty feet tall, that has an unusual slit, measuring only a few feet across. The slit takes its namesake from its resemblance to the eye of a needle.

At approximately 2:30 the bus pulled into a large turnout, situated at the base of the trailhead. Little DT is one of several paths leading to Harney Peak, the other one being the more difficult Sunday Gulch.

"Here we are Custer Players ready to tackle the highest peak east of the Rockies," Alistair addressed the cast and crew at the base of the trailhead. "Before we hit the trail, just a few housekeeping rules. Make sure you bring drink plenty of water during the hike to avoid dehydration. The air is fairly thin, so if you get out of breath just pause a few minutes before continuing on. If at any time you feel the hike is a little too much of a workout, it's no big deal; just turn around and hang out on the bus until we return. Also it's important to watch your footing. At times this trail is a little treacherous, and it's easy to trip, so just be careful. Understood?"

"Understood," the crowd of roughly thirty theatre workers replied in unison.

"That being said, let's take a hike!"

The first three-fourths mile of the trail rambled through the woods at an easy pace before forking with the left trail the strenuous spur to the Little Devils Tower formation, and the right side of the trail continuing on to Harney Peak.

"Everyone bear right at the fork in the trail," Alistair shouted back, as he led the way forward.

At the fork the scenery began to change, as the trail began to snake around colossal granite columns, and path growing steeper and steeper by each step. The altitude change made it hard to breathe at times, with the elevation increasing by 600 feet in a short period of time. However Merritt and her friends pressed on, becoming more determined than ever to reach the summit.

An hour and a half after hiking the trail, the group reached the summit of Harney Peak.

"The climb was worth the effort, this vista is stunning," Merritt stood in awe as she took in the dramatic 360 panorama of the surrounding Hills. "I feel as though I'm on top of the world!"

"Isn't it glorious?" Ginny sighed. "I never get tired of this view!"

"You can see the Cathedral Spires to the east," Emma noted, pointing to six pillars of granite standing out brilliantly, distinguishing themselves from the rest of the scenery with their dramatic resemblance to a grand cathedral. The Cathedral Spires are also home to the Limber Pine, an alpine tree known to grow on rocky outcroppings. It derives its name from its small flexible branches, which can be bent back without breaking.

Merritt snapped over a dozen pictures with her digital camera before following Ginny and Emma to the Harney Peak Fire Lookout Tower.

The Civilian Conservation Corps built the Fire Tower, which stands stoically on the summit of Harney Peak, entirely of stone in the late 1930s. It has been vacant for years, but is still open for hikers to scale its stone steps and take in the dramatic views from atop the historic tower.

"What a neat tower," Merritt commented as the girls ascended a series of cobblestone steps. "It resembles a castle among the clouds."

While enjoying the Tower views, a shrill scream sounded from below.

"Oh my god," Merritt exclaimed as she saw Celeste, who appeared to have fallen off the summit, clinging to its steep granite edge by a thread. "Hurry we've got to help her!" The girls rushed down the steep steps of the Fire Tower as Celeste continued to scream for her life. By the time the girls got down from the Fire Tower, a group of hikers, mostly theatre workers had crowded around Celeste, with Alistair, Ethan and Peter pulling her back up to safety.

"Celeste, are you okay?" Alistair questioned, shaken by how close his wife came to death.

"I was petrified," Celeste cried, still in shock from the treacherous ordeal.

"It doesn't look like she broke anything," Peter acknowledged, checking Celeste over for injuries. "What happened?"

"I was standing here admiring the scenery, when suddenly I felt a push from behind. I fell, rushing to grab hold of the mountain..."

"You think someone pushed you?" Alistair was outraged by the thought of someone trying to hurt his wife.

"I don't know," Celeste replied, confused by the chain of events leading up to the fall. "Perhaps I just tripped."

"Are you sure?" Ethan asked, "Because if you think someone pushed you?"

"No I remember it now...I just got too close to the edge and I tripped," Celeste didn't sound convinced.

"Come on dear," Alistair ushered her away from the edge. "Let's get you back to the bus."

"I've gone hiking with Celeste half a dozen times before and she's more surefooted than the rest of us. It seems implausible that she would nearly trip to her death...I wonder if someone did push her?"

"That's a good question," Emma noticed Mike Trump purposefully ignoring the incident. "It's kind of odd that Mike isn't rushing over to the scene to ensure she's okay."

"It doesn't matter to him as long as she signed an insurance waiver," Ginny replied. "As overly dramatic as Chet can be, I'm beginning to wonder if he's right, what if Mike is trying to sabotage the playhouse."

"I know he wants the playhouse to close down, but attempted murder?" Merritt debated, skeptical of Mike's involvement.

"Greed is a powerful thing. That food contract is worth millions, who knows what Mike is willing to do to secure it...even death," Emma postulated.

"Speculation is just that, speculation. Celeste says she wasn't pushed. Until we have more facts there's no reason to point fingers," Merritt replied.

"I'm just glad that she was able to cling to the ridge long enough to be rescued. Thank God that Celeste is okay," Emma and Ginny replied respectively, before the girls headed back down the mountain bound for the tour bus.

After completing the hike, the entire troupe headed over to Sylvan Lake Lodge for dinner.

Sylvan Lake is considered to be the "gem of Custer State Park." It is situated at the base of Harney Peak, amidst impressive granite rock formations and a sea of pine trees.

The Lake was created in 1881 when Theodore Reder built a dam across Sunday Gulch. The sparkling lake became part of Custer State Park in 1921 and has been one of the park's most popular tourist destinations ever since. The picturesque lake offers beaches for swimming, water sports such as kayaking and paddleboats, fishing and lots of hiking trails. The nearby Sylvan Lake General Store offers lake goers fast food, groceries and a gift shop filled with souvenirs, and hiking and camping supplies.

The nearby Sylvan Lake Lodge is set atop a cliff surrounded by forest, with views overlooking Sylvan Lake and the surrounding Black Hills. The current Lodge was completed on 1937, after fire consumed the original Victorian-style hotel in 1935. Famed architect Frank Lloyd Wright suggested the current Lodge during a visit to the Black Hills. Although Wright himself did not design the building, the architectural design follows the style of natural architectural Wright followed. The Lodge is constructed completed of natural materials found in the Black Hills and is perfectly sited to blend in with the natural setting of the area.

The bus driver let the theatre company out by the front entrance of the hotel just before seven.

"This hotel is breathtaking," Merritt commented to Ginny as the group headed inside the stone and wooden edifice.

"The Lodge is so sited to form to the land, a grand mountain hideaway," Ginny noted.

The interior of the Sylvan Lake Lodge is mix of rustic meets mountain sophistication. Hardwood floors and high wooden ceilings open up the space, with large windows drawing in natural light. The lobby is offer ample nooks to relax with a book and quiet spaces and wide porches to enjoy sweeping views of the scenery.

After waiting several minutes, the Custer Playhouse crew was seated towards the back of the restaurant. The Lodge staff had put multiple tables together to accommodate the some thirty-playhouse members eating dinner at the elegant dining room.

"This is my favorite restaurant in the park," Claudia Cosgrove mentioned to Merritt. "The interior construction and design is well thought out, with the wooden slated ceiling, large windows and top to bottom stone fireplace. Add in the fact that their food is to die for with menu options such as steaks, fish, and salads."

Within five minutes of sitting down a waitress stopped by to get their drink order. Merritt ordered a glass of red wine. About few minutes later the waitress dropped off the drinks and started taking dinner orders.

"What can I get for you Miss?" The waitress asked Merritt

"I'd like the New York Strip cooked medium with a cranberry spinach salad and a baked potato with butter please."

As the table waited for their meals, they chatted about the hike, most notably the incident with Celeste. Her fall had shaken everyone up. She had come so close to death, and so many wanted to know how a sure-footed hiker like Celeste could fall. Celeste, uncomfortable with the incident, asked the company to desist discussing it. It was too traumatic to recount over dinner.

The food arrived about twenty-five minutes after the order was taken. Merritt's steak was perfectly cooked, and deliciously tender and moist. For dessert, Mike even sprung for chocolate flourless tort cakes and vanilla ice cream.

After finishing dinner at nine, the cast and crew boarded the tour bus for the night drive back to the playhouse. Alistair suggested that the driver avoid the Needles at night, taking an alternate route, south from Sylvan Lake on Highway 89 into Custer City before heading east to the Playhouse.

"It's a dangerous road at night, and accidents are prone to happen," Alistair stated to the driver before looking at Celeste, still shaken up from her fall.

"Good call," the driver agreed.

The tour bus pulled into the playhouse parking lot just after ten. Merritt took a quick shower before heading to bed. She was tired from the hike, and had a busy day ahead of her Sunday; sewing projects galore and an afternoon jaunt to Jewel Cave with Josh.

Chapter 13:

Merritt set her alarm for seven on Monday morning. After getting dressed, she grabbed her prayer book and walked down to Center Lake for a half-hour devotional before meeting up with her roommates for a quick breakfast of eggs and hash browns.

"So what's on tap for you today Miss. Andrews?" Rebecca asked before taking a sip of orange juice.

"I'm heading into the Costume Shop for a few hours to complete a few sewing projects. Later on I'm meeting up with Josh to tour Jewel Cave."

"Dreamy Josh and Merritt touring Jewel Cave...sounds like a date made in heaven," her roommates teased.

"I'm looking forward to it," Merritt replied, her face flushed. "Jewel Cave is the second-longest cave in the world with some really neat formations."

"The Black Hills are secreted with an abundance of beautiful, mystical caves, but Jewel is my personal favorite due to its namesake jewel like formations," Emma noted.

After breakfast, Merritt spent several hours working on finishing up the majority of sewing and accessory projects at the Costume Shop before calling it a day at noon.

Merritt stopped by Alpine to grab a few supplies for the cave tour and possible hike before driving over to Game Lodge to meet up with Josh at one.

"What do you say Miss. Andrews? Ready for a little spelunking?" Josh greeted Merritt on the porch of the Peter Norbeck Visitor Center.

"Absolutely," Merritt replied, as the couple walked to Josh's Jeep.

"I ordered the tickets online for the Scenic Cave Tour. It doesn't start until four, so if you're up for it I figured we could go on a hike around the Jewel Cave area first."

"I'm always up for a hike," Merritt smiled as they got into the Jeep and drove to Jewel Cave National Monument, which is located off Highway 16, twenty-eight miles west of the Peter Norbeck Visitor Center.

"You're going to enjoy Jewel Cave," Josh promised. "It boasts over 150 miles of explored passageways, making it the second-longest cave in the world, after Mammoth Cave in Kentucky. It derives its name from the calcite, jewel-like crystals, which are abundant within the cave."

Jewel Cave lies beneath a cliff straddling Hell Canyon. In 1900, two homesteaders, brothers Frank and Albert Michaud, were exploring Hell Canyon when they noticed a tiny hole in the canyon wall, which was blasting out cold air. Suspecting they had discovered a cave, they returned to the spot with friend Charles Bush to enlarge the hole with dynamite so they could get inside the cave.

Once inside they discovered crawl ways and low-ceiling rooms coated with beautiful calcite crystals, which they described as sparkling like "jewels" in the lantern light.

Thinking the formations might have some commercial value the brothers filed a mining claim in Custer, only to find out that though the calcite crystals are beautiful they aren't worth any money. The brothers then turned their attention to turning Jewel Cave into a tourist attraction. They constructed a trail in the cave and built a lodge on the rim of Hell Canyon to attract visitors.

In the early years they didn't make a profit given the cave's isolated location. A group of locals, petitioned Washington to federally protect Jewel Cave in order to preserve the natural wonder for future generations. In 1908 President Theodore Roosevelt Jewel Cave a National Monument.

Although Jewel Cave is now known for being the second longest cave in the world until 1959, Jewel Cave was considered a very small cave with only two miles of charted passageways.

That all changed when geologist Dwight Deal enlisted the aid of two rock-climbing enthusiasts, Herb and Jan Conn to help explore the cave. The Conn's were dedicated to exploring and mapping new passages. By the late 1970s the Conn's had mapped over 64 miles of cave trail before retiring. Spelunkers continue to explore the cave, with over 150 miles of cave explored.

They arrived at the entrance to Jewel Cave just after two. After finding a parking space, Merritt and Josh briefly meandered through the Visitor Center, stopping by the Ranger's desk to pick up a brochure on cave and get some information on area hikes. The ranger suggested the Canyons Trail, a 3.5-mile loop that starts and ends at the visitor center. The loop winds through a ponderosa pine forest before descending into Lithograph and Hell Canyons, where hikers tread through a sun-baked grassland prairie. Towards the end of the trail the path ascends the canyon wall, passing the original cave entrance before winding back up at the visitor center.

"This hike really complements the cave tour," Josh stated as he and Merritt hiked down to the base of the canyon. "Although the main park attraction at Jewel Cave is underground, many visitors overlook the exterior beauty of the land above the cave during their visit. The area atop the cave is filled with unique geologic formations such as limestone cliffs, wildlife, and flora that includes over 390 species of wildflowers."

As the pair entered the canyon, the shady forest transitioned to a hot prairie and big blue sky. Butterflies danced around native wildflowers such as pasque-flower, pale-purple coneflower and wild bergamot.

About three-fourths of the way through the hike, the trail ascended the canyon wall. Josh pointed out the historic cave entrance, where the park still starts its Lantern Tour. Nearby a historic ranger cabin built by the CCC in the 1930s provides exhibits related to Jewel Cave and its history.

"That was a terrific hike," Merritt told Josh as they returned to the Visitor Center at 3:30.

"I am lucky to have you as my hiking partner Andrews," Josh smiled. "Why don't we check out the gift shop while we wait for our cave tour to start at four?"

"Excellent idea," Merritt agreed. While in the gift shop, she loaded up on a pack of twenty postcards.

"Think you got enough postcards there, Andrews?" Josh joked as she checked out.

"What can I say, I'm a postcard nut," Merritt smiled. "I collect them for my scrapbooks and I send a bunch to friends and family."

"Postcards are good," Josh replied. "My addiction is the habit of buying park biology books. My bookcase can't take many more."

"Well you are a biologist Ranger Ford," Merritt smiled, before the couple headed across the hall to meet up with the cave tour.

Just after four, a perky ranger in her early thirties with brown hair placed in a ponytail under her ranger hat greeted the tour group.

"Hello, I'm Ranger Chelsea Clark, and this is my third year working as an interpretative ranger at Jewel Cave National Monument. I'll be leading you on a scenic tour of cave. This tour is not for the faint of heart. Over the course of the hour and a half tour, we'll walk up and down 723 stair steps, along a half-mile loop. This amounts to forty flights of stairs, so if you aren't up to that much climbing I suggest you consider another cave tour, such as the Discovery Tour, which isn't so steep. The cave has a year-round temperature of forty-nine degrees, so if you have a jacket, I suggest you put it on."

"Think you can handle 723 stairs?" Josh asked Merritt.

"If I can ascend the summit of Mount Harney I think I can handle this cave tour," Merritt replied as the tour group crammed into the elevator, which goes down to the cave.

"Jewel Cave is one of the longest caves in the world at an altitude change of 637 in the cave, but it is also extremely narrow, covering a mere three-square miles. To date Jewel Cave has over 150 miles of explored passageways, and there is still a lot of cave to be explored. Each year spelunkers are allowed into the cave to explore and chart further passageways.

The number one question tourists ask is how was Jewel Cave formed? At the heart of Jewel Cave's geologic history is water. Jewel Cave wasn't carved by underground rivers like many well-known caves, but rather by the gradual dissolution of limestone by stagnant, acid-rich water," Chelsea explained as the group commenced the half-mile cavern loop. "On our tour we're going to encounter a number of unique formations, or as we cavers refer to them, speleothems and speleogens. During the course of our tour, we'll encounter formations such as the namesake jewels of Jewel Cave, boxwork, cave popcorn, flowstone, stalactites, and draperies and cave bacon," Chelsea explained as the group of twenty cavers carefully navigated the first in a series of steep steps on the scenic path.

The first formations they witnessed were stalactite and flowstone. Stalactites are pointed pendants hanging from the cave ceiling. Flowstone is a sheet like formation found on the cave walls and floor. Followed soon by the namesake jewels of the cave.

"The jewels of Jewel Cave are known scientifically as dogtooth spar and nail head spar, which are formed by calcite. An example of dogtooth spar can be found on this section of the cavern wall," Chelsea pointed to a series of shimmering crystals resembling dogs' teeth. "Nail head spar, is a calcite crystal resembling a nail, and are typically long and thin with a wide flat head."

"I can see why they named it Jewel Cave," Merritt noted to Josh. "The spar glitters in the light like the jewels of the crown."

Further up the cavern trail, Chelsea pointed to an example of boxwork, an uncommon type of cave formation, which is composed of thin blades of mineral calcite projecting from cave walls or ceilings that intersect one another at various angles; the result is a box-like or honeycomb patter.

"If you are interested in seeing another cave with boxwork in the area, I suggest a trip over to Wind Cave National Park, which is located about thirty miles south of Custer. Wind Cave is known for having the most extensive boxwork deposits in the world," Chelsea explained.

The tour finished up by 5:30, returning via elevator up to the Visitor Center.

"You gave a great tour Ranger Clark," Josh and Merritt stated to their tour guide as they exited the elevator into the Visitor Center.

"I'm glad you enjoyed it," Chelsea smiled. "Hopefully you're a little more cave savvy after your visit."

After finishing up their tour of Jewel Cave, Josh suggested they stop for dinner in Custer.

"I don't know about you, but after the Canyons Trail and cave tour, I'm famished," Josh stated. "Why don't we grab a bite to eat at the Elk Canyon Pub in downtown Custer? The foods good and the price is right."

"Fine by me," Merritt stated as they got in the Jeep and headed back to Custer.

The Elk Canyon Pub is a family restaurant serving local game and traditional American fare. Merritt and Josh were seated in a booth near the front of the restaurant. After several minutes, a waiter stopped by to take their order, with Merritt opting for a salad and Josh ordering a steak.

"I really enjoyed our day at Jewel Cave," Merritt smiled.

"I'm glad you had a good time," Josh's half grin casting a spell on Merritt. "Hopefully we can get together again soon."

"My schedule is pretty packed this week with costume fittings, rehearsals and campground shows. However I might be able to squeeze in a hike on Saturday."

"I work at the Visitor Center from twelve to eight, but am free Saturday morning."

"That works for me," Merritt smiled. "We can even do a hike in the Game Lodge area if you want."

"Saturday morning it is," Josh smiled before giving Merritt a kiss on the cheek. Whether she and Josh were a summer fling or this was the beginning of something more, Merritt, never one to seek love, had to admit she liked being with Josh.

Chapter 14:

The week leading up to Merritt's next date with Josh was jam packed with sewing projects, costume fittings and an offsite theatre performance at Stockade Lake. Despite the breakneck pace, things went fairly smoothly. Even Chet and Peter seemed to get along, and Mike Trump had kept out of the way.

On Saturday morning, Merritt woke up at six-thirty, took a quick shower, got dressed, and grabbed a bowl of cereal from the Mess Hall before heading over to the Game Lodge area to meet up with Josh at eight.

The pair had decided to spend the morning tackling the popular Lovers Leap Trail, a three-mile loop that starts behind the Coolidge General Store.

"You made it," Josh greeted Merritt in the Peter Norbeck Visitor Center parking lot.

"I weighed my options: sleeping in or waking up really early to go hiking with you. I guess I couldn't resist a walk in the woods."

"I'm glad you came," Josh smiled. "This hike is a little strenuous at times with a few creek crossing, but totally worth the views."

"I wore my waterproof hiking boots so I can weather the trail," Merritt replied as the pair crossed the street towards the trailhead.

"So how is the big theatre production coming along?" Josh asked with interest as they started up the mountain path lined with ponderosa.

"It's going great! Except for a couple of small alterations, all of the costumes are completed and ready for dress rehearsals, which start on Monday."

"How did the Stockade Lake event go?"

"It was a lot of fun! Peter did a monologue as Crazy Horse, Ginny a meet and greet as Calamity Jane, and Rebecca performed her rendition as Laura Ingalls Wilder. The best part is that Emma and her mom sold a bunch of tickets for next weekend's performances."

"That's great news," Josh enthused. "If I get off it in time I might try to check out the eight o'clock show at Game Lodge tonight."

"You'd be in for a treat. Tonight's ensemble includes Leroy Stewart as Badger Clark, Jack Webster as Peter Norbeck and Jim Carter as Calvin Coolidge."

"I'll suggest visitors who stop by the Norbeck Center to check out the free show," Josh replied.

"Are you still planning to come to *Dakota* on opening night?" Merritt asked as they path began a steep ascent up the mountain forest.

"I switched shifts with Ranger Sinclair, so I'll definitely be in attendance!"

As the couple hiked up the mountain, Josh pointed out native plant species and points of interest. Once they ascended the mountain ridgeline, they sat down near a rocky outcropping known as Lovers Leap. The vista is stunning, offering a comprehensive view of the area. Local lore dubs the spot Lovers Leap, because according to legend, it is on this outcrop that two Native American lovers leapt to their deaths when they couldn't be together in life.

After enjoying the views from the ridge, Merritt and Josh proceeded on the trail, which continued down the ridge into the Galena Creek Drainage, it was here they coincidentally ran into Peter Wiseman.

"Peter? What a surprise," Merritt and Josh greeted their mutual acquaintance.

"Howdy," Peter smiled. "Perfect weather, huh?"

"It's to die for," Merritt smiled as she noticed a large basket filled with flowers and weeds including a white lacy flower that resembled Queen Anne's lace, also known as wild carrot. "What are you up to?"

"I'm actually pulling samples of noxious weeds for a botany study with Liam Bryant at the park's wildflower management department. A few testy invasive plants have recently infested this side of Custer State Park."

"Noxious weeds are serious issue in the park," Josh agreed. "Hopefully you and Liam can figure out a way to combat the latest outbreak of weeds in this area of the park."

"Hopefully," Peter agreed. "I hope you've convinced Josh to come to a showing of *Dakota*."

"I'll be there opening night," Josh replied.

"Good man," Peter tipped his hat. The trio talked a few more minutes before heading their separate ways.

The remainder of the hike was very wet, as they descended into the core of the Galena Creek Drainage area, where there are numerous creek crossings. Many of these crossings demanded the pair trudge through deep water, without bridges of even stones to wobble across on. By trails end Merritt's legs were completely soaked from creek crossings.

"I can't believe how wet I got," Merritt stated as they finally made it back to the Coolidge General Store.

"You can blame that on me," Josh replied, equally soaked. "If it hadn't been for me telling you to walk across the loose rocks, you wouldn't have fallen into the water."

"So you forgive me?"

"Of course. The hike was still amazing. I enjoyed seeing the mix of alpine and riparian ecosystems," Merritt smiled. "I'll just remember to wear waterproof pants next time we go hiking."

"Ditto that," Josh joked, before looking at his watch. "It's just after ten. We probably still have time to grab a quick breakfast at the State Game Lodge before they close up for lunch."

"I'm game, especially if I can grab a coffee," Merritt replied as the couple walked over to the nearby lodge where they each ordered a trip to the dining room's breakfast buffet, which features fruit, eggs benedict, pancakes and more.

"I didn't notice any bison around the Game Lodge today," Merritt commented after sipping on a hot cup of coffee.

"The herd moves around quite bit. Reports have them camping out near Iron Mountain Road the past few days."

"The herd does get around then," Merritt replied before Josh changed the subject. "I know you're going to be super-busy this week, but I was hoping you might have a free afternoon on Monday the 21st? I figured we could drive down to the Hot Springs area. It's a neat historic town and worth checking out during your stay in the area."

"I'm on laundry duty Monday morning, but can do something in the afternoon."

After breakfast the couple strolled around the Game Lodge area before heading back to the Visitor Center as Josh was due in for work, and Merritt needed to head back to the Playhouse to complete costume alterations. The two parted with a quick kiss before heading in different directions.

On her way back to the Playhouse, Merritt noticed Chet and Celeste having a heated discussion in front of the Legion Lodge. Before, Merritt could pull over to make sure everything was okay, Ethan who was also on site, stepped between the pair to break up the fight.

Merritt, seeing that the fight had ended, decided it was better not to get involved in the age long feud and continued on to the playhouse; where she peacefully spent the rest of the afternoon finishing up the remaining costume alterations in preparation for the upcoming dress rehearsals.

Chapter 15:

"How did the event at Game Lodge go last night?" Merritt asked Dot as she entered the Costume Shop on Sunday morning.

"It went great! The actors put on a great performance and we had a terrific turnout. Beth said she sold about twenty tickets to tourists sticking around through next weekend, and a number of theatre programs and tee-shirts to visitors who won't be able to make the show."

After chatting a few more minutes, the costumers began working on finishing up any lingering costume alterations.

At twelve forty-five, Merritt stepped out of the Costume Shop and headed upstairs to the theatre to watch the technical rehearsal, which was due to start at one. A technical rehearsal is a rehearsal that focuses on all the technological aspects of the performance, making sure that lighting, sound and special effects work properly. For today's rehearsal, the actors would run cue lines signaling technological changes set to take place on or off stage.

Merritt took a seat on the third row in house behind Alistair, Blair and Kat. Her presence at the technical rehearsal was more a formality than anything as the costume department didn't need to have a concrete knowledge of the minute technological aspects on stage, except those related to costume changes. Still Merritt felt it important to take notes during the rehearsal and pulled out a pen and pad.

The first half hour went according to plan. Justin checked the sound levels, Lisa Thomas ensured the spotlight was functioning, and Tom and Luke tested all the lighting changes to make sure they were in sync with the production cues. John Hood and the stagehands changed sets with the appropriate lighting changes and Ethan was on hand to oversee final props were placed on stage or given to actors to make sure how they looked under the final stage lighting.

About an hour and forty-minutes into the technical rehearsal, Mike Trump quietly entered the theatre, taking a seat on the row behind Merritt. He seemed very flustered, as if he had been running around doing errands prior to coming to rehearsal. Merritt quickly forget about Mike and turned her attention back to the stage where Ginny was about to run lines with Chet, Rick, and the rest of the Deadwood actors.

"Action," Alistair directed the actors. "Starting from the cue lines."

As the lights brightened for the scene, a crackle sounded indicating a short fuse in electrical wiring for the lights. Before the cast could get out of the way, three lights had blown up falling on the stage. Screams sounded as the house went dark except for the firecracker like spark coming from lights.

"Get everyone off the stage NOW!" Gully shouted as he and the stagehands worked quickly to assist all the actors off stage.

Luke and Tom rushed down from the control booth to check the electric problem and work to stop the shorted fuse for escalating into a fire.

Worried that Ginny and the other actors on stage may be hurt Merritt along with Alistair, Blair, and Kat hurried to assist the injured.

"Ginny are you alright?" Merritt asked concerned for her roommate's wellbeing.

"Thanks to Rick," she sighed. "He pushed me out of the way before one of the lights hit me. I've got a few bruises, but other than that I'm okay."

"Thank God!" Merritt let out a sigh of relief.

"Damn it, I think I re-injured my ankle," Chet moaned from across the hall.

"I burned my hand, but other than that I'm okay," Rick noted.

"I'll get some ice and bandages," Claudia replied before heading to the Green Room to grab a pile of first aid supplies.

"How did this happen?" Gully asked Luke and Tom still in shock from the fiery blast during to the technical rehearsal. "Last I heard you had cleared the electrical wiring. You said everything was good to go."

"It was," the Barber brothers replied firmly.

"Obviously you overlooked something," Mike Trump spewed out. "And because of your negligence you could have caused this entire building to go up in smoke. It's a miracle that no one was seriously injured."

"Mr. Trump, I understand why you're upset, but I swear the wiring was perfect when I checked it earlier this morning..."

"I don't need excuses," Mike shouted. "If this isn't fixed by opening night to my satisfaction we're going to have to shut the show down production indefinitely."

"I'll take whatever measures to ensure that the electrical wiring is fixed to standard," Luke promised, still perplexed as to the root cause of the incident.

"I don't trust your shoddy cross-wire skills Barber. I'll call in a professional electrician that I can trust to see that it is fixed properly!" Trump replied.

"Your demeaning and accusatory attitude is out of line," Luke contested. "I have an electrician's license and I've never had an incident like this occur before."

"A piece of paper from a barely accredited online university doesn't give you credentials," Trump mocked.

"I'll have you know I have a degree in electrical engineering from USD and an electrical license from the top technical college in South Dakota," Luke fumed.

"Just let it go Luke. At least Mr. Trump is willing to have the lights fixed so we can continue on with production," Alistair tried to play peacemaker.

"Don't trust Trump for a minute. This whole incident has subversion written all over it with a capital S," Chet snarled at Mike.

"Are you accusing *me* of causing the fire?" Mike countered aggressively.

"Hell yes I am! This is the perfect excuse for you to shut down the theatre and get your concessionaire payoff."

"If you hadn't noticed I just volunteered to pay for the lights to be fixed so we don't have to take this incident to Pierre. I don't have to do that Chet. I have the power to shut this theatre down right now and with good reason: three lights just blew up and fell down on stage and I have the pictures to prove it."

"One thing is certain Trump, you have ulterior motives and I wouldn't be surprised if this so-called electrician you brought in will do more harm than good."

"Fine if you don't want my help, I'll call the Governor and ask him to issue an order to close the playhouse down."

"Don't do that," Gully and Alistair pleaded. "We accept your offer."

"Glad there is some rationale here. I'll call the electrician right now," Trump promised before glaring at Chet, "As for you, I'm not going to put up with this harassment much longer."

Merritt could see Chet's point. After all Mike had come into the rehearsal late, and looked very flustered. The lights had been working fine until he entered the theatre. What if he did sabotage the electrical wiring in an effort to shut down the playhouse? Then again would he be that obvious? And if Mike did mess with the electrical circuits why would he offer to get the lighting fixed? A lot of questions remained unanswered about the electrical explosion...Merritt could only hope that the incident was just an unfortunate accident and nothing more.

Chapter 16:

Despite the obstacles facing the Custer Playhouse production team, following the unexpected explosion during Sunday's technical rehearsal, the company rallied to fix lingering hazards prior to the show's opening night. Trump kept his word. A team of electricians come in first thing Monday to repair the lighting. The diagnosis was a loose fuse in the breaker box.

Tuesday's technical rehearsal went off without a hitch. Two successful dress rehearsals also took place on Tuesday and Wednesday nights.

Dakota was able to open on Thursday night to a packed house. The show went off without a hitch and the cast and crew closed to a standing ovation. Friday, Saturday and Sunday's shows also sold out. The season appeared destined for success.

"I just got the latest edition of the Rapid City Journal and *Dakota* received stellar reviews," Emma rushed into the Mess Hall on Monday morning with a handful of newspapers. "Check out Section C, Page 2."

"The headline reads: 'Dakota is a theatrical triumph,'" Ginny exclaimed as she pulled apart the paper to the theatre review, "It goes on to say: The Custer Playhouse, a Black Hills tradition since 1946, has faced adversity head on and the result is stunning. *Dakota* is an intriguing play, with a plot that follows multiple acts in the historical timeline of South Dakota. Popular historical figures such as Crazy Horse and General Custer, Wild Bill Hickok, Laura Ingalls Wilder, and Peter Norbeck and Badger Clark highlight the production with clever dialogue and moving musical numbers. The cast as a whole shines with outstanding performances led by veteran Custer actors Peter Wiseman, Chet Rawlins and Leroy Stewart. Virginia Terry offers up a quality performance as rough and tumble Calamity Jane and Rebecca Lane gives an excellent portrayal of both Laura Ingalls Wilder and Grace Coolidge. The costume designs are authentic and stand out on stage. Playhouse Musical Director Artie Scott has written several original songs, which coupled with an excellent script make *Dakota* is a must-see for locals and tourists alike..."

"You couldn't hope for better press!" Merritt exclaimed. "I'm thrilled that our awesome roommates were touted as thespians in the article."

"This article will be posted on our cabin wall of fame in honor of or two resident stars, Rebecca and Ginny," Emma agreed.

"Don't make me blush," Rebecca replied. "I'm just grateful the paper is behind the production. Hopefully the review will entice a lot of locals in the Black Hills to check out *Dakota*."

"How could they refuse a rough and tumble performance by the one and only Virginia Terry?" Ginny joked.

"Listen Ginny and I had better get over to the theatre for our cast meeting. We're going to go over this weekend's performances and discuss any changes before getting the rest of the day off," Rebecca explained. "Do you girls want to meet up around noon to go on a hike?"

"I'm pegged to help my mom in the ticket office all day," Emma replied.

"What are you up to Merritt?"

"After laundry duty I'm meeting up with Josh to go to Hot Springs."

"True love calls," Rebecca sighed.

After four nights of theatre, the costumes were due for a wash or dry-clean, especially before Wednesday night's road show at Mount Rushmore.

By one, Merritt had finished most of the laundry and Bob volunteered to finish up the rest. Merritt then headed over to the Game Lodge to meet up with Josh at one-thirty.

"Congratulations on the excellent review in the Rapid City Journal," Josh greeted Merritt in Visitor Center parking lot.

"Aw shucks you're making me blush Mr. Ford," Merritt blushed. "I really appreciate your coming on Thursday."

"The show was top notch! I'm planning to see it again in a few weeks."

"Fill me on the details of today's jaunt."

"Hot Springs is a neat town with a lot of history and natural beauty. It is located about an hour south of here at the base of Wind Cave National Park. There are lots of attractions in the Hot Springs area including its namesake warm mineral springs, distinctive architecture, and museums such as the Pioneer Museum and Mammoth Site."

En route to Hot Springs, they passed through Wind Cave National Park, which is the fourth longest cave in the world. Although they didn't have time to stop for a cave tour they enjoyed traversing the exterior scenery atop the cave, which is filled with endless prairie, and lots of wildlife such as bison, prairie dogs and pronghorns.

Hot Springs sits at the foot of the southern Black Hills on the edge of the Great Plains. In the center of the town is a natural thermally heated mineral spring known as Fall River.

After parking the Jeep, Josh and Merritt toured the Hot Springs Visitor Center, which is located in the town's train depot, which dates back to 1880. Upon entering the historic building, a friendly retiree in his early seventies greeted the couple.

"Welcome to Hot Springs. How are you doing this fine afternoon?"

"Excellent," Josh nodded. "We'd like to pick up a few brochures about area attractions and learn more about what the town has to offer."

"Hot Springs is a hot spot of activity. We were recently named a Distinctive Destination in 2009 by the National Trust for Historic Preservation. Our downtown streets are lined with thirty-five stately sandstone buildings dating back to the 1800s when the town gained national attention as a popular tourist destination for those seeking the healing warm waters of Fall River."

"The architecture is magnificent," Merritt commented, noticing several of the historic buildings as they drove into town.

"How long are you folks planning to stay in town?"

"Just a few hours...this is an afternoon excursion from our jobs at Custer State Park," Merritt replied. "I'm a costumer at the Playhouse and Josh serves as a park ranger."

"Custer's a terrific park," Dave acknowledged, pulling out a city map and highlighter. "If you're limited on time then I suggest a stroll down the Freedom Trail. The path meanders along the town's Fall River, from whose hot healing waters the town derives its name.

For history buffs, I recommend a visit to the Pioneer Museum. Run by the Fall River County Historical Society, the museum is housed in a Romanesque style sandstone edifice that dates to 1893, constructed as the town's first school. The museum features a wealth of information and exhibits on pre-history, pioneer and modern culture of the region.

You can go back to the Ice-Age at the nearby Mammoth Site, a paleontological site sitting on a sinkhole, which has preserved the fossils of at least fifty-eight Columbian and woolly mammoths. The museum stays open until eight o'clock at night during the summer."

Josh and Merritt spent several more minutes chatting with Dave about other attractions in the greater Hot Springs area, including Evan's Plunge, the city's oldest indoor water park, the Black Hills Wild Horse Sanctuary, Cascade Falls and popular local lake, the Angostura State Recreation Area.

"Thanks for all your help Dave. You've given us a lot of ideas as to how to spend our time in Hot Springs," Merritt noted before she and Josh exited the visitor's center.

They started off their stay in Hot Springs by touring the Pioneer Museum. The museum features four levels of exhibits, mostly geared towards the history of pioneers in South Dakota and their struggle to survive in the plains and Black Hills. Other exhibits are focused on the history of Hot Springs, which for thousands of years served as a watering hole for a variety of wildlife. The Sioux and Cheyenne tribes, who battled each other out for control of the healing spring, later frequented the area. In the late 1800s a group of setters began a settlement that would become the town of Hot Springs. Lavish hotels and spas were built to serve tourists looking to experience the warm mineral waters, which to this day are considered to have healing capabilities.

After spending an hour and a half exploring the Pioneer Museum, Josh and Merritt meandered down to the Freedom Trail, a paved path that follows Fall River from one end of the city to the other. At the beginning of the path, a grand waterfall tumbles over the red rock cliff straddling the path.

The path is also lined with several charming gazebos and dating back to the late 1800s. The most well-known of these gazebos is Kidney Springs, which includes a drinking fountain where walkers can sip on the warm mineral water.

"This is a charming town," Merritt commented as the couple crossed a bridge from the Freedom Trail over to North River Street.

"I thought you'd like it," Josh smiled.

The pair cooled off from the ninety degree prairie heat with chocolate milkshakes at the Blue Bison Café on North River Street before making the drive to the Mammoth Site, which is located a few minutes from downtown off Highway 18.

The Mammoth Site is the world's largest mammoth paleontological site. 26,000 years ago a cavern collapsed forming a sixty-five feet deep sinkhole. The hole quickly filled with warm artesian-fed springs, creating a popular watering hole for prehistoric wildlife such as the American camel, lions, wolves, giant short-faced bears and both the Columbia and Woolly Mammoths. Over a period of approximately 300 to 700 years, a number of animals would accidentally fall into the sinkhole after drinking water; unable to escape the animals died and over time fossilized.

For thousands of years these ancient creatures of the plains lay hidden from sight until a chance encounter by a construction worker named George Hanson occurred in 1974. While preparing the area for a new subdivision, Hanson unearthed a set of unusual bones. His son recognized one of the bones as a mammoth tooth. With news of the scientific find, donations came were procured to purchase the property and erect a museum and living palaeontology site where future excavations and studies of the area's prehistory could be conducted. The Mammoth Site was named a National Natural Landmark in 1980.

To date, the site has unearthed fossils from fifty-eight mammoths, along with a variety of other prehistoric species once native to area.

"This isn't just a museum, it's a complete dig site," Merritt noted to Josh as the pair observed the massive former sinkhole, which is situated in the center of the indoor museum and visible from a series of overlooks and walkways.

"The Museum returns select fossils to the original spot where the bones were discovered during the dig. This serves an *In-Situ* experience, allowing visitors to visualize the excavation process," Josh explained.

The Exhibit Halls feature replica skeletons of the American lion, giant short-faced bear and the pygmy mammoth. The Museum also has a collection of early North American artifacts found in the Black Hills and nearby Badlands National Park.

"No bones about it, I thoroughly enjoyed the Mammoth Site," Merritt told Josh, following their hour-long tour of the facility. "It was interested to learn more about extinct prehistoric species that once inhabited the area."

"The cool thing is that each year the paleontological teams on site excavate more fossils, furthering research and discovery about the regions ancient history," Josh followed.

With the clock pushing close to eight p.m., Merritt and Josh headed back to Custer State Park. By the time they returned to Game Lodge an hour later, dusk had vanished into total darkness.

"I enjoyed our trip to Hot Springs," Merritt smiled "It's an idyllic town with a ton of history."

"I always have fun with you," Josh replied before the pair leaned in for a kiss, their first real kiss. The kiss so effortless and felt so right, and yet it caused Merritt to blush. Josh stepped back and politely stated: "I hope I didn't cross a line..."

"You didn't. It was a nice kiss," Merritt smiled.

"It was, wasn't it?" Josh said goodnight.

Feeling as if she had just stepped off cloud nine, Merritt began her drive back to Alpine. As she neared the playhouse her focus quickly shifted from Josh to a heated argument in the playhouse parking lot.

"You lying son of a..." Peter shouted, nearly pushing Chet to the ground. "I should kill you for spreading lies about me."

"You slashed my tires Wiseman!" Chet shot back in an accusatory tone. "Don't deny it!"

"Peter, Chet, calm down," Ranger Sinclair stepped in between the two men. "Chet, when you called to report the fact that your tires were slashed, you admitted that you didn't see who did it. How can you be so certain that Peter is responsible for a crime he so adamantly denies committing?"

"Trust me, he did it," Chet snarled as he looked at Peter. "He told me just yesterday that I'm a reckless driver and that if I didn't turn in my license that he'd stop me himself."

"Did you say that Peter?" Ranger Sinclair questioned Peter, acquiring the facts in what was another explosive incident in the longstanding feud.

"Yes, but I would never slash his tires," Peter replied firmly." I only meant that the next time I saw Chet speeding I planned to call the cops."

"Have you been speeding Chet?" Ranger Sinclair asked.

"Five miles above the speed limit isn't lethal endangerment," Chet rolled his eyes.

"Fifteen miles is more like it Rawlins!" Peter shouted back. "I can't believe you'd even step foot in a car after..."

"Don't bring the accident into this," Chet fired. "It happened over twenty-years ago. Why can't you just let it go? It's in the past."

"A past with unsettled bones never disappears, it just haunts the soul and resurfaces from the grave," Peter stated firmly. "You're just too heartless to give a damn."

"Stop this fighting NOW!" Ranger Sinclair demanded. "Chet I'm sorry about your tires, but without further evidence I cannot press charges against Peter."

"He's guilty Sinclair and you need to book him," Chet demanded, alcohol oozing off his breath.

"As far as I'm concerned there could be any number of suspects, including someone not related to the playhouse. As for Peter he has an alibi."

"So he claims," Chet grumbled.

"Chet, I'm going to file an official report. In the meantime I suggest you two play nice, otherwise I'll have to bring you both down to park headquarters and possibly call in the Custer City police department to deal with your infighting. Understood?"

"I'll let this go if Peter pays to fix my tires," Chet retorted.

"If paying to fix your tires means that you'll shut up and leave me alone, fine I'll pay to fix your damn tires, but don't think for a second I'm the one who slashed them," Peter shot back.

"This is the very definition of infighting and I want it to cease this very second," Ranger Sinclair ordered. "Peter, if you want to pay for Chet's tires to be replaced that's your decision. However, you are not obligated to do so if you are innocent of the crime."

"I am innocent, although Chet's too bull-headed to see the truth."

"I can assure you that there will be a thorough investigation," Ranger Sinclair replied. "As for repairs, Chet, I called Tommy Durance and he's going to tow your car over to Custer City first thing in the morning. I'll call you with any leads regarding the crime. In the meantime, I ask that you play nice with Peter otherwise I'll have you both thrown out of the court."

"I'll play nice, but don't think for a second that I'm going to let Peter get away with murder," Chet seethed. "In my mind he's guilty until proven innocent."

"I'll get to the bottom of this," Ranger Sinclair promised. "I suggest you act civilly to one another, or else slashed tires will be the least of your concern," with that the trio parted ways.

Merritt couldn't help but eavesdrop; the argument was intense, on the verge of violence. She wondered what accident Peter was referring too. Did this supposed accident have something to do with the origin of their feud? And if Peter hadn't slashed Chet's tires who had and why? A lot of questions surrounded the incident, questions that Merritt's gut told her that they needed to be answered, even though reason told her to ignore her instincts.

Chapter 17:

On Wednesday afternoon, the Custer Playhouse cast and crew carpooled to Mount Rushmore for a special performance of scenes from *Dakota*.

The costumers carpooled, heading north towards Mount Rushmore via the stunning Iron Mountain Road. Constructed in 1933 by the Civilian Conservation Corps, the winding road offers stunning views of the Black Hills. It traverses over a series of Pigtail Bridges, and goes through a series of tunnels, which are designed to frame Mount Rushmore.

"Wow," Merritt exclaimed as she caught her first view of the stately monument, whose four stone faces jut out from the surrounding Hills.

"Impressive, isn't it?" Bob admired their first glance of the American icon, which is perfectly juxtaposed by the one lane tunnels peepholes.

Upon arriving at the Monument at three o'clock, the costumers proceeded to the Orientation Plaza to rendezvous with the rest of the Custer Company and to check in with the Park Service.

"I'm Ranger Steve Fisher," a medium built Park Ranger greeted the cast and crew as they approached the information desk. "We're thrilled to have your company perform. We've heard rave reviews at Dakota."

"We're delighted for the opportunity," Alistair acknowledged.

After getting the cast and crew checked in, Ranger Fisher led the crew into a stone building connected to the bookstore that houses park offices and conference rooms. A set of interconnected meeting rooms had been set aside for the players' pre-show costume changes, prop and gear storage.

"Regarding Audio/Video set up, we have a tech on site that will assist with tonight's performance,"

It took forty-five minutes to unload the costumes and props from the van. Ethan had hauled several boxes of Rushmore themed props, including: chisels, hammers and faux dynamite for the performance.

Luke, Tom and Justin coordinated with Rushmore's tech began the set up. The rest of the actors and crew were given a ninety-minute break to explore the Monument's highlights.

Merritt, Emma, Rebecca and Jim began their tour of the Monument in the Visitor Center with an introductory film, before touring the exhibit hall, which includes an interactive time line of Mount Rushmore's history, insight into the selection of the four presidents, the life of sculptor Gutzon Borglum and more.

One of the most recognized landmarks in the world, Mount Rushmore has become an enduring symbol of American democracy and patriotism. However the Monument began as a pipe dream that faced enormous adversity before carving its legacy in stone.

The Mount Rushmore dream dates back to 1923 when the aging South Dakota State Historical superintendent, Doane Robinson, envisioned a series of colossal memorials carved out of the South Dakota Needles, which could pay tribute to heroes of the Old West such as Lewis and Clark, Chief Red Cloud, and Buffalo Bill Cody. His hope was that the colossal sculptures would generate tourism into the Black Hills. Robinson petitioned state-wide to convince South Dakotans to back the idea. He caught the ear of Senator Peter Norbeck, who encouraged Robinson to recruit a sculptor capable of carrying out the massive assignment. Norbeck then courted fellow elected officials to help back the sculpture project; he also encouraged Robinson to recruit a sculptor capable of carrying out such a massive assignment.

In 1924, Robinson reached out to renowned sculptor and artist Gutzon Borglum, who had just finished up a similar carving project in Stone Mountain in Georgia; a monument dedicated to confederate war heroes. Always up for a challenge, Borglum accepted Robinson's offer with the condition that the monument be dedicated to American patriotism, rather than the South Dakota heroes originally proposed.

After careful consideration, Borglum selected four great presidential figures that embody the American spirit: George Washington, Thomas Jefferson, Abraham Lincoln and Theodore Roosevelt.

Borglum chose President George Washington as a historical representation an ideal leader. Washington's distinguished career as a Revolutionary War General, founding father and the nation's first president coupled with his high moral character and humble service as a citizen politician for the people is the model all subsequent public servants aim to follow.

Thomas Jefferson, the third President of the United States, was selected for writing and signing the Declaration of Independence, the document that so eloquently expressed the fundamental principles for America's right to sovereignty from British rule. The document also establishes the enduring foundations for the natural law and freedoms that guide and constitute the freedoms of "life, liberty and the pursuit of happiness," that are central to American society today.

Jefferson was also selected for the carving for his foresight to purchase the vast Louisiana Territory from the French, during his presidency. This pivotal decision more than doubled the size of the young American nation. He then sent explorers Lewis and Clark to explore the new territory, which opened the doors to western expansion.

Known as the "Great Emancipator," Abraham Lincoln's fortitude confronted the national upheaval of the bloody civil war with a focus to keep the country united and to ensure the end of slavery to ensure that all Americans could pursue the freedoms that this nation provides.

Borglum had so much esteem for Lincoln, that he named his own son after him.

The last face chosen to be memorialized in stone was President Theodore Roosevelt. Today, Teddy Roosevelt is considered to be one of our greatest leaders, however at the time the monument's proposal many objected Roosevelt's selection as the fourth face on the mountain. They felt that barely fifteen years after he left office, and only several years since his death wasn't enough time to truly judge his legacy as Commander in Chief. Borglum however wouldn't budge. He knew Teddy during his life and felt "T.R.'s" energy and passion was the epitome of the American spirit. Roosevelt had the vision to conserve American landmarks including protection of a number of national parks and monuments such as Jewel Cave and the Grand Canyon. He also oversaw projects such as the Panama Canal, which connected the waters of the Atlantic and Pacific.

Borglum's next step was to locate a mountain with a group of granite outcroppings large enough to support a massive sculpture. Per Robinson's suggestion, Borglum first visited the Needles only find their rock too brittle and the spires disproportionate for human form. In August of 1925, after Borglum finally found the perfect spot in Mount Rushmore, a craggy, pine-clad cliff named after a New York lawyer in 1885, and known to the Lakota as the "Six Grandfathers."

Although Senator Norbeck had no problem passing a bill to allow the mountain carving in the National Forest, raising money for the project became tricky. Many scrutinized the financial costs of erecting such an ambitious project. Others expressed outrage at what they deemed 'defacing' the natural grandeur of the mountain.

It wasn't until the summer of 1927 that the fate of Mount Rushmore was sealed. After spending a summer in Custer State Park and the Black Hills, President Calvin Coolidge pushed for federal spending to build the monument.

Over the next fourteen years of his life, Gutzon Borglum, along with 400 workers, dedicated his life to the carving of the Monument. It wasn't easy, as many obstacles arose such the Great Depression, lack of funding, skepticism over the project and construction delays. Borglum died in early 1941, just shy of the Monument's completion in October of 1941, which was overseen by his son Lincoln. Today the Monument attracts over two million visitors per year, squashing any doubts early critics had to the project.

"What an informative exhibit," Merritt commented to her friends as they finished the Museum tour.

"It truly attests to the American spirit," Emma replied. "Just think that in the middle of our greatest financial crisis, 400 local workers continued to fight for the sculpture's completion. Not only did the sculpture create jobs for unemployed local miners, it gave America hope for something better."

After finishing up the Museum tour, the group headed upstairs to the Grandview Terrace, a large overlook, which offers excellent views of the Monument. They snapped a handful of photos before embarking on the half-mile Presidential Trail.

The Presidential Trail is a short but enjoyable hike that offers up close views of the Monument and access to the Sculptor's Studio, the location of Gutzon Borglum's first on-site workspace.

The Presidential Trail starts off at the Grandview Terrace before heading down a series of steps to the amphitheatre. From there, the path meanders through a wooded area located at the base of the Monument. Impressive views of the heads of Washington to the far left, Jefferson, Roosevelt and Lincoln on the far right are perfectly framed.

"Did you know that out of the 450,000 tons of granite removed from the mountain, ninety-percent was carved using dynamite?" Jim noted as the group continued down the path. "Each head is sixty feet tall, roughly the size of a six story building, with each President's eyes about eleven feet wide, lips eighteen feet wide. Their noses measure twenty feet high, with the exception of Washington's nose, which measures twenty-one feet high."

"Why is Washington's larger?" Rebecca asked.

"Since Washington's position on the mountain, juts out a bit, it keeps his face in good proportion with the other Presidential faces," Jim explained.

As Merritt looked to the top of the sculpture, her thoughts traced back to scenes of Hitchcock's *North by Northwest*, where Cary Grant and Eva Marie Saint, barely avoided being thrust off the monument by the villain played by James Mason.

"I love Hitchcock, but I'm glad my stay in the Black Hills, isn't filled with murder and mayhem," Merritt thought to herself before the group made their way into the Sculptor's Studio.

The Studio houses the original 1-to-12-inch scale model of the sculpture, which means an inch of the model represented a foot on the cliff. This model was constructed by Borglum to be a guide for how the monument was to look on the mountain. The workers could figure out where to drill and blast on the mountain by find the corresponding point from the top of the figure's head and multiplying times twelve.

Within the studio, an exhibit details Borglum's concept of enclosing a "Hall of Records," within the monument. In 1938, he began carving a giant vault, intended to house records of Western civilization, of individual liberty and freedom and reasons why the monument was built. His death and the U.S.'s entry into World War II cut the plan short, however in 1998, the National Park Service completed a scaled down version of the hall.

The group returned to the main visitor complex, and the conference room promptly at five-thirty, where they enjoyed a catered dinner buffet of burgers, salad, and chocolate chip cookies.

Following dinner, the cast and crew prepped for their eight o'clock performance.

"We have ten minutes to show time," Alistair announced as he entered the makeshift dressing room. "Get in character, because it's time for us to perform the Rushmore scenes of *Dakota* in the amphitheater."

The amphitheatre is situated at the base of Mount Rushmore. It plays hosts to number events, which include ranger talks, special performances and the evening lighting ceremony of the memorial, which occurs every night promptly at nine p.m.

The performance started just after eight o'clock to an audience of 200. Gully and Alistair pitched information about the Custer Playhouse before the twenty-five minute performance took place, showcasing scenes involving the history of Mount Rushmore.

As the actors took their final bow, the crowd ignited in applause, fully satisfied by the performance.

Following the show, the cast and crew hung out in the amphitheatre until the nine o'clock lighting ceremony to talk to tourists about the play and future performances. Although many visitors wouldn't be in the area long enough to catch a show at the Playhouse, they promised to check out the theatre website and consider donating to the annual fund.

By 10:30, company had finished loading up their vehicles and started heading back to Custer State Park.

"What a fantastic performance!" Dolly commented Dot, Merritt and Bob on the drive home.

I'm glad that Merritt brought her camera. Hopefully we can post the pictures onto our website," Dot put forth.

The group pulled into the playhouse parking lot at 11:25. Exhausted for the day's activities, the costumers quickly unloaded the van, before calling it a night.

"Get some sleep," Bob advised. "We have another long day tomorrow."

Chapter 18:

Less than an hour before Thursday's show time, the Custer cast and crew scurried backstage to ensure that everything was ready before the opening curtain.

In the Costume Shop, Merritt, Bob and Dot were up to their necks in clothing and accessories, making certain that all of the actors set to appear on stage within the first half of the show were in costume and sent to make-up in a timely manner.

"I just sent Jack, AKA General Custer to Dolly for hair and make-up," Dot informed Merritt. "Why don't you go round up Chet, Leroy, and Ginny so we can get them fitted into their Deadwood attire?"

"No problem," Merritt replied before crossing the hall to the Green Room, where the actors hung out before the show.

"Where's my damn cup of tea, Celeste?" Chet shout reverberated as Merritt entered the room.

"It's still brewing," the usually calm, Celeste shot back, visibly irritated. "It will be ready within ten-minutes."

"It better be. I have to drink three cups of tea before I go on stage for a performance," the querulous actor demanded.

"How can I forget, when you so vehemently remind me prior to your every performance?" Celeste rolled her eyes.

"Ahem," Merritt cleared her throat, in hopes of dispelling the quarrel. "We're ready for the Deadwood actors in wardrobe: Ginny, Leroy and you Mr. Rawlins."

"I'll get into my costume after I've drunk my tea," Chet spoke down to Merritt. "God knows I don't want to spill the bloody concoction all over my Wild Bill suit."

"We can wait as your cue isn't for another two hours..." Merritt replied, looking at her watch.

"Chet and his stupid tea," Ginny rolled her eyes, as she and Leroy followed Merritt to the Costume Shop dressing rooms. "He nearly had a coronary when Celeste told him he'd have to wait for it."

"Let's face it, Chet may be a damn good actor, but when it comes to people skills he's poison," Leroy acknowledged.

For the next fifteen minutes, Merritt assisted Leroy and Ginny get into costume before returning to the Green Room to summon Chet.

"You damn fool Wiseman! First you slash my tires and now you force me to spill my tea all over the floor! I hadn't even tasted it yet!"

"How many times do I have to tell you that I didn't slash your tires," Peter rebutted. "As for the tea, you shouldn't drink that stuff. It's bad medicine with toxic herbs, and will probably kill you one of these days."

"The only bad medicine in this theatre is you and your whack job herbal remedies," Chet retorted.

"Would you two stop fighting?" Celeste pleaded. "Peter can you clean up this mess, while I brew Chet another pot of tea?"

"Fine, but only because you asked me to Celeste," Peter replied as he grabbed a handful of paper towels and began scrubbing up the tea.

"I hate to interrupt," Merritt interjected. "Mr. Rawlins, we're ready for you in wardrobe."

"Unfortunately Miss. Andrews, I never got the opportunity to drink the tea I was so anxiously awaiting. I don't suppose that you could spare a few more minutes?" Chet sulked.

"I, uh..." Merritt looked at her watch, trying her best to make an executive decision. She knew that to keep the rest of the actors on track for their costume changes, Chet needed to get dressed ASAP. On the other hand she wasn't particularly eager to get into a fight with him over his beloved pre-show drink. Luckily Mike Trump's surprise Green Room entry temporarily stalled her conversation with Chet.

"Ah, Custer Players," Mike Trump interrupted the conversation as he stepped into the room, standing in the vicinity of the teapot and burner. "Just the folks I wanted to see. I came to wish you all good luck before tonight's performance," Trump stated affably, leaning

"You might as well curse the ground we walk on you idiot!" Chet and several actors aired their disgust.

"Excuse me, but where I come from when you wish someone 'good luck' the polite response is to say 'thank you.'"

"Well here in the theatre that expression is the worst sort of bad luck, just short of mentioning The Scottish Play."

"What Macbeth?" Trump seemed genuinely unaware of the two major theatrical superstitions referenced.

"First you forget to say 'break a leg' and now you mention 'The Scottish Play' by its theatrical title? It's a cursed play anyone in the theatre knows that the mere mention of it is suicide. Your curses are meant to conjure doom to our season."

"Considering there's a sold out show tonight, I'd hardly say I'm cursing you. If anything I came down here and say how proud I am of your efforts thus far."

"Wishing us the opposite of 'bad luck' is bad enough, but then to mention The Scottish Play? The only way to dispel the curse you've laid on us is for you to leave the room; then knock on the door three times; wait for us to invite you back in and then read a line from Hamlet."

"You're telling me that I have to partake in some sort of hocus pocus, just to pacify a silly superstition?" Trump rolled his eyes.

"Do it," the actors demanded.

"Fine, but only because I don't feel like discussing this ridiculous topic any longer," Mike sighed. He then proceeded to exit the room, knock three times on the door before Merritt invited him back inside. "To be or not to be...are you satisfied?"

"Just try to keep your mouth shut next time you suddenly decide to pop in for pre-show salutations," Chet suggested, his tone harsh. "Better yet, don't show up at all."

"You people are impossible. I try to reach out and you spit in my face," Mike snapped. "For the record I wish you all good luck and that Macbeth steals your thunder."

The actors proceeded to wish one another "bad luck" in hopes of combating Trump's second-string of theatrical curses.

"Chet your tea still has another few minutes to brew, why don't you go on with Merritt to wardrobe?" Celeste suggested after the group of thespians felt they'd done enough cursing to dispel the bad energy left by Mr. Trump. "I'll have a cup brought to you as soon as it's ready."

"Fine," Chet sighed, following Merritt to the Costume Shop. On the way to the dressing rooms, they pair bumped into Ethan.

"Have you seen Celeste?" Ethan asked, "Alistair needs to discuss tonight's cue times with her before the opening curtain."

"She's in the Green Room," Merritt informed him. "Making Chet a pot of tea."

"Thanks, I'll look for her there then," Ethan replied before turning his attention to Chet. "Knock them dead tonight Mr. Rawlins."

"I always do," Chet grinned, before following Merritt into the dressing rooms. Ten-minutes later, after Chet was fully dressed in his Wild Bill attire, Merritt sent him next door to make-up where a fresh cup of tea was waiting for him.

"Celeste asked me to drop off your tea, Wild Bill," Ginny stated as she set a large cup of Chet's special tea on a nearby table.

"That tea of yours may work wonders Chet, but it smells like a musty mouse," Dolly stated, trying her best to ignore the nasty odor.

"Nonsense," Chet replied, before downing the concoction. "It's an ancient formula of natural herbs and tea leaves that aids in vocal relaxation and fullness of tone."

"That may be, but I honestly don't see how something that smells that bad how can it be good for you?" Dolly replied in her typical polite, yet blunt manner.

"It's the only thing other than a dash of alcohol that keeps me going."

"That bad, huh?" Ginny replied, with an expression of disgust, still reeling from the disgusting odor of the elixir.

"You are more than welcome to a cup if you'd like?" Chet offered.

"I think we'll pass." Dolly flinched at the thought of ingesting the foul smelling drink.

"More for me then," Chet grinned. "Ginny be a dear and fix me another cup will you?"

"Yes your highness," Ginny smirked running back to the Green Room to get another cup of tea.

For the next hour things backstage ran smoothly. It wasn't until about twenty-minutes before the Deadwood scene when things took a bizarre turn. Chet stumbled into the Costume Shop, his suit covered in vomit stains. His eyes, heavily dilated with saliva dripping from his mouth.

"Mr. Rawlins? Are you all right?" Merritt voiced her concern for the actor's health.

"I think the burger I ate for lunch disagreed with me," Chet stated, struggling through heavy breathing. "I just threw up in the bathroom, and unfortunately got some of the vomit on my shirt. I figured I'd ask you for another shirt, so you can get this one in the wash."

"Are you sure you're well enough to go on stage? You might have e-coli poisoning if your hamburger was undercooked," Merritt replied.

"Merritt's right, Chet, you don't want to mess around with food poisoning," Dot interjected. "Let your understudy Doug to step in for you as Wild Bill tonight and I'll take you to the hospital."

"NO! I've never missed a show and I don't plan to!" Chet protested. "I'll be fine."

"You shouldn't be so cavalier about your health Chet," Dot replied, pulling a fresh shirt from a nearby costume rack. "I really think you should go to the doctor."

"I won't bow out of a performance. It'll disappoint my audience. If I still feel sick in the morning, I'll drive over to the urgent care clinic in Custer City," Chet replied curtly.

"Fine," Dot sighed, realizing that it was futile to argue with 'Wild Bill' Rawlins.

A few minutes later Chet limped out of the Costume Shop. On the way out he nearly bumped into Bob, who was re-entering the shop after running a few quick-change stock actor costumes to the backstage dressing area.

"What's going on Rawlins? Is he drunk," Bob questioned.

"He claims that he ate a bad hamburger at lunch, but who knows? I tried to convince him to let Doug act as understudy, but he refuses."

"It's not our call to make," Bob shot back. "Although if I were Gully, I'd make sure Chet wasn't allowed on stage in his condition."

With the first half of *Dakota* wrapping up, Merritt headed over to the Green Room to signal several second half actors into wardrobe. As she entered the room, the conversation surrounded Chet and his erratic behavior.

"I swear he's drunk," Cliff Arnett stated watching the Green Room television monitor, which runs a live feed of the play, helping the cast and crew keep track of theatrical cues.

"Alcohol would certainly explain his behavior. He's fallen down three times since he stepped on stage," Jim agreed. "The funny thing is I haven't seen him sip anything other than his tea all night."

"He's been through at least ten cups of that nasty tea in the past hour," Rebecca stated..

"He could have spiked his tea with alcohol?" Hank suggested.

"Sorry to interrupt, but we're ready for you in wardrobe," Merritt interjected.

"Merritt, I didn't see you standing there," Jim replied. "I guess we were so consumed by the unusual behavior of Mr. Rawlins."

"He came into the Costume Shop about thirty-minutes ago," Merritt replied. "He'd vomited on his shirt and we helped clean him up. He said he felt sick, possibly from an undercooked hamburger at lunch. Dot and I tried to convince him to let Doug sub for him, but he refused."

"Sounds like Chet," Hank replied. "He's bull-headed."

"He looks deathly ill," Jim acknowledged, watching the monitor. At that moment Jack McCall actor Rick Summers pointed the fake gun and shot blank bullets towards Chet's back. However, Chet didn't fall back feigning death as prescribed by the script. Instead he fell to the floor, trying to crawl offstage.

"Something's wrong," Merritt whispered, as she and the Green Room watched in horror as Chet began to struggle for breath.

"Water, water...I can't breathe," Chet whispered, lying flat on the stage, pleading as he clutched his chest. "I've been poisoned. I can't breathe...I'm going to die...Help me."

Help came too late. As Leroy, Ginny, Rick, Gully, Celeste, Peter and Evan rushed to Chet's aid, the veteran Custer Playhouse actor inhaled his last breath.

Chapter 19:

"He's dead," Peter announced, checking Chet's pulse after attempting to revive him via CPR.

"Close the curtain NOW!" Gully shouted to a nearby stagehand. "And call the paramedics."

"Check his pulse again," Celeste ordered. "He can't be dead...not like this."

"He's dead Celeste. He has no pulse and he's not breathing," Peter replied.

"Keep trying to revive him then Peter," Celeste was overwrought emotion.

"Celeste, I know this is hard," Gully comforted her. "Chet's death is the last thing any of us expected tonight. As far as I knew he was good health."

"Perhaps he died from a pre-existing condition," Ethan suggested. "Did he have asthma or a heart problem?"

"He was a heavy drinker," Peter paused. "However except for a few drunk driving accidents, he never seemed to exhibit any health problems from alcohol consumption."

"What's going on? Is Chet alright?" Alistair questioned, rushing onto stage after the bizarre scene had transpired on stage.

"Chet's...he's... dead," Celeste struggled through tears.

"Dead? How?" Alistair was in a state of shock and disbelief over the death of the veteran actor.

"We don't know. The paramedics are on their way," Gully replied "In the meantime I should probably address the audience, and tell them that the rest of the show is canceled."

"That is probably best..." Alistair's voice trailed off, still confounded by the morbid turn of events. He turned his attention to Celeste. "Dear why don't you go downstairs, and wait in the Green Room while this is sorted out?"

"I cannot leave Chet," Celeste sobbed, clutching her husband's arm.   "Whatever makes you feel comfortable dear," Alistair comforted his wife, as Mike Trump stormed on stage.

"It's over. Chet Rawlins has screwed up for the last time! It is one thing to be a pompous ass and a brilliant actor, but for him to show up drunk for arguably the biggest scene in *Dakota*? And why the hell did Gully tell the audience the show is cancelled? What about the old adage 'the show must go on?' We can't afford to refund tickets? And look at him passed out on the floor...Chet Rawlins is fired, no arguments!"

"Shut up!" Celeste shouted at Mike, pointing to Chet lying lifeless on the stage. "Can't you see that he's dead?"

"Dead," Mike was stupefied by the news. "Chet Rawlins doesn't just die. He's the kind of roach that lingers. Just before the show he was cursing me out for wishing him 'good luck.'"

"He's deader than a doornail, Mike. No thanks to you and your theatrical curses," Peter replied firmly.

"This is a nightmare," Mike panicked, more concerned with the idea of refunding tickets than the death of the lead actor. "Leave it to Chet to screw up a perfectly full house."

"Could you be anymore insensitive right now?" Ginny questioned, shivering as she looked at her co-star's lifeless body. "A man is dead."

"I'm sorry he's dead. Now are you satisfied?" Mike retorted.

"You really are a jerk aren't you?" Ginny's temper stirred.

"Show some respect and stop this infighting!" Alistair demanded.

"Alistair's right," Ethan agreed. "We need to collect ourselves before the paramedics and police arrive."

"Ethan, go downstairs and apprise the rest of the cast and crew of this tragic situation."

"What's going on? Is Chet okay?" Merritt questioned Ethan as he entered the green room. "We tried to go up to the stage, but the door was locked."

"I don't quite know how to tell you this, but Chet's dead," Ethan bit his lip. "The rest of the cast and crew are upstairs waiting for the authorities now."

"Dead?" Merritt in shock, her heart sinking. "I knew he wasn't feeling well, but *dead*?"

"I knew we should have taken him to the hospital after he started complaining about food poisoning," Dot sighed. "I let it slide, because I didn't feel like arguing with him."

"Don't blame yourselves. Chet was a grown man. You couldn't force him to do anything that he didn't want to."

"Still, we could have pressured him to go to the hospital," Merritt replied. "If we had, he might not be dead right now."

"Don't play the 'what if' game," Bob advised. "In hindsight it's easy to question your actions, but Chet was stubborn and if he didn't want to go to the doctor, you couldn't make him. Even if he had gone to the doctor, who's to say that he would have survived? For all we know, Chet had an untreatable pre-existing condition."

"I can't believe that he's dead," Merritt replied, upset by the situation. "Something about it feels off..."

"It's a heartbreaking loss," Rebecca lamented. "Hopefully in the coming days we'll find out what killed him."

"I've got to get back to the stage. The authorities are on their way to the scene, and might need to question me about what happened. In the meantime, it's probably best if you all wait down here."

"Do you think, Dot and I should go with you?" Merritt suggested. "It might help for the authorities to know that Chet was complaining about food poisoning about forty minutes ago."

"I think that's a good idea Merritt," Ethan agreed. "Everyone else wait down here, until Gully or Alistair give you permission to leave."

By the time Merritt, Dot, and Ethan reached the stage the paramedics along with representatives from the Custer County police department and Custer State Park Service were on hand to investigate Chet's untimely demise. The initial verdict was that he'd died of natural causes, although an autopsy would be necessary to determine the official cause of death.

As paramedics placed Chet in a body bag and carted him off, Custer County Sheriff, Marvin Abrams, started questioning any cast and crew who could shed light on Rawlins sudden death.

Celeste spoke to Sheriff Abrams first. She briefly went over the chain of events, which transpired the past few hours.

"He didn't start acting strangely until about eight. At first he just complained of being thirsty, then his hands got wobbly and his eyes became overly dilated. Frankly I just assumed he'd mixed some whiskey in with his tea and was feeling the effects of the alcohol."

"You think Mr. Rawlins, may have been drinking tonight?" Sheriff Abrams questioned.

"Chet's always been a heavy drinker."

"I know," the Sheriff sighed. He'd had to write Chet up numerous times over the years for driving under the influence.

"Still, it is strange, Chet has never been one to risk throwing a performance by getting inebriated prior to a show. And he certainly didn't smell like a man who had been drinking whiskey."

"You mentioned that Mr. Rawlins drank tea, do you think it could have made him sick?"

"I doubt it," Celeste replied. "He's drunk that concoction prior to every show for years. The tea smells awful, but it's relatively harmless. Otherwise it would have killed him long before now."

"Do you know if Mr. Rawlins had any pre-existing health conditions that might have caused him to die so suddenly?"

"Not that I know of. Then again, Chet was never was one to talk about his health."

After speaking with Celeste, Sheriff Abrams briefly spoke with Ginny about what occurred on stage.

"In the hour before his death, he was more on edge that his usual acerbic self," Ginny admitted. "He complained of being extremely thirsty, and drank at least two, maybe three pots of his special tea."

"Do you think he added any alcohol to his tea?" The Sheriff asked.

"He acted tipsy, but I don't think he was drunken," Ginny tried to explain his behavior. "He did mention that the burger he ate at lunch disagreed with him...Chet's could be difficult I ignored the warning signs and chocked it up to his mood swings. I wish I hadn't now."

The Sheriff questioned several additional witnesses before approaching Dot and Merritt. The two costumers detailed the unusual incident

"Miss. Darlington, it's good to see you again, although I wish it had been under better circumstances."

"Likewise," Dot replied. "Sheriff Abrams, this is my costume colleague, Merritt Andrews."

"What insights can you tell me about Chet's death?"

"Twenty-minutes before Mr. Rawlins was due on stage, he stumbled into the Costume Shop and requested a clean shirt because he threw up. Of course Dot and I were concerned for Chet's health. We suggested that he allow his understudy, Doug Bates, step in on his behalf, while he sought medical attention. Chet brushed us off. I wish that Dot and I had followed our instincts and taken him to the hospital while we had the chance."

"Don't feel too guilty," the Sheriff stated. "The paramedics seem to think Chet most likely died from a chronic condition. Possibly a sudden seizure, or even a heart problem, that he never told anyone about."

"You don't think he died of food poisoning?" Dot questioned.

"Food poisoning is a possibility, but usually symptoms of E-Coli take three to seven days to manifest, not several hours after lunch. As for salmonella, it can start causing nausea and vomiting as soon as twelve hours after consumption, but usually isn't fatal," Sheriff Abrams replied before posing another question. "Where were you two when Mr. Rawlins died?"

"I was downstairs in the Costume Shop, prepping for the next set of wardrobe changes. Merritt had stepped across the hall to the Green Room to summon the next set of actors to wardrobe."

"The Green Room?"

"It's a large room where the actors hang out before going on stage. It has comfortable seating, a kitchenette, and a television monitor connected to the main theatre," Merritt replied. "When I entered the room, several of the actors were watching the live feed of *Dakota* on the monitor and commenting on how weird Chet was acting, both on and off stage. Cliff Arnett and Jim Carter said if they didn't know better that Chet was drunk."

"Do you think he could have been drinking?"

"He was known to drink whiskey off stage, although everyone agreed he didn't smell of alcohol, and the only substance he'd been drinking all night was this special tea of his."

"As much of a drunkard Chet could be outside of the theatre, he never drank alcohol before a performance. Instead he drank a made to order tea blend," Dot added in. "The whole thing is just shocking, Sheriff. I've known Chet for over twenty-years and not once did he exhibit symptoms like these."

"We won't know anything for certain until the Medical Examiner conducts an autopsy," Abrams informed. "One thing I can say for certain is that neither you nor Miss Andrews are to blame for Chet's death."

The authorities remained on site for another hour before packing up for the evening. Alistair briefly addressed the cast and crew, both on stage and in the Green Room before dismissing them for the evening.

"Chet's death is a terrible tragedy. Gully, Mike and I are going to weight our options as for whether or not to cancel the remainder of this weekend's performances. We'll have an executive decision made by tomorrow at noon. In the meantime I ask that you keep Chet in your thoughts and prayers."

After being released from the theatre, Merritt met up with her roommates to walk back to Alpine. The roommates disturbed by Chet's sudden death.

"I've watch Chet play the Wild Bill death scene at least 100 times in rehearsal and during performances. I never thought he'd really wind up dead," Ginny stated. "It's just sickening, thinking of him lying there, desperately grasping for air...and then when Peter pronounced him dead..."

"I still don't understand what happened," Merritt questioned. "He was his usual self around seven and then suddenly he started feeling sick..."

"Didn't he mention that he might have food poisoning?" Rebecca asked Merritt.

"Yes, he told Dot and me that he ate an undercooked burger at lunch. However Sheriff Abrams doesn't seem to think that killed him."

"He must have had a pre-existing heart condition or something to that effect," Emma reasoned. "Why else would he die, so unexpectedly?"

"I don't know," Merritt, sighed sensing that something was amiss.

"There's no use speculating until the reports of the autopsy come back," Rebecca advised.

Merritt noticed she had a voicemail from Josh. He had heard about Chet's death, and wanted to make sure Merritt was okay after the ordeal of losing a colleague. After phoning him back, Merritt took a quick shower, and then went to bed.

It had been a long and tragic day; a day that that none of the Custer Players would soon forget.

Chapter 20:

On Friday at noon Gully, Mike and Alistair made an official announcement that in spite of Chet's abrupt death, the remaining scheduled performances for that weekend would continue as planned.

"In the spirit of Chet's memory, we have decided NOT to cancel the rest of this weekend's performances of *Dakota*. As an actor, Chet never missed a performance and certainly wouldn't want us to on account of his death. And as heartbreaking as it is to lose such a valued member of the Custer Playhouse, the show will go on. Doug Bates, a seasoned actor in his own right, has agreed to step into the role of Wild Bill. In this time of grieving, I ask that we honor Chet's memory not through tears, but through quality theatre," Alistair stated.

The news that the show would go on, wasn't unexpected; the point of having understudies is for unexpected situations when the original actor can't perform his duties. Still, it was hard for the cast and crew to simply go on as if nothing had happened. Sure in life, Chet Rawlins could be an obnoxious jerk, and at one point or another many of the Custer Players had wished him dead, but for him to die on stage in such a painfully dramatic fashion, was more than anyone bargained for. The incident loomed over the Playhouse like a dark cloud; an unsettling omen.

Despite the awkwardness of moving forward with production so soon after Chet's death, the show did in fact go on. If anything, Chet's dramatic death had attracted more interest from crowd of curious theatre goers. Friday, Saturday and Sunday's performances of *Dakota* were sold out and there was such a high demand for the following weekend's performances that Mike suggested a Saturday matinee be added on July 3rd with an Independence Day theme.

Merritt couldn't stop thinking about Chet's death. The way he'd stumbled into the Costume Shop after throwing up, his eyes bulging and dilated... his breathing irregular. She knew that technically his death wasn't her fault, but she couldn't shake the feeling that she could have done something to prevent it. She at least wanted to know what killed him. What could trigger such a violent death? Heart problems? Seizures? Merritt, along with the entire cast and crew wanted to know what killed Chet Rawlins.

"I just spoke with Sheriff Abrams," Gully's gripped by anxiety as he addressed the cast and crew during breakfast on Tuesday morning. "He just received Chet's autopsy and toxicology reports from the Medical Examiner in Rapid City. There have been some unexpected developments in this case, and the Sheriff has requested that all members of the cast and crew report to the theatre at noon. This is a mandatory meeting. No excuses."

Just before noon, the playhouse auditorium filled up with cast and crew eager to learn what killed Chet, and what ' unexpected developments' to which, Gully referred.

Merritt and her roommates sat on the fourth row back, dead center, behind Jim, the Barber boys and Ethan. Peter, Alistair, Celeste and Mike sat on the first road. Celeste looked like she'd been crying. Mike on the other hand seemed relatively at ease considering the presence of the Sheriff, five Custer County deputy officers, and Custer State Park Superintendent Wade Harden was on site.

"I thought the Sheriff was just going to make an announcement," Ginny whispered to her friends.

"That's what I thought," Emma replied.

"Then why are there so many cops here, along with the Park Superintendent Harden?"

"We're about to find out," Merritt noted as Gully and the Sheriff took the stage.

"There is an alarming development surrounding Chet Rawlins death," Gully, visibly on edge, addressed the crowd. "Sheriff Abrams will fill you in on the details. I ask that you cooperate fully with this investigation."

"After a thorough autopsy by the Rapid City Coroner's office, we know what caused Chet Rawlins abrupt death on Thursday June the 24th. The news is deeply disturbing. The autopsy points to murder."

"Murder..." The cast and crew gasped.

"The official cause of Chet's death was consumption of the Conium plant, better known as Poison Hemlock."

The words Poison Hemlock sent chills down Merritt's spine. She remembered the deadly plant from Mr. Page's World History class at Broughton High in Raleigh N.C. The Ancient Greeks used poison hemlock for capital punishment. Their most infamous victim was Classical philosopher Socrates, who was controversially executed by drinking a toxic blend of wine laced hemlock in 399 B.C.

"We'd like to speak with each of the Custer Players individually about the case. This process will be done in alphabetical order, via your last names. I ask for your patience and honesty during this investigation."

Merritt was among the first witnesses questioned. Although she had absolutely nothing to do with Chet's death, the thought of interrogation made her uneasy.

"Please take a seat," Abrams stated as they stepped into the interrogation rooms, also known as the theatre offices. "This is my assistant, Deputy Hill."

"Sorry that we're not meeting under better circumstances," Merritt uttered a reply.

"Please detail your itinerary on the night of the murder, particularly any interactions you had with Mr. Rawlins prior to his death."

"I arrived at the theatre at four o'clock. I went straight to the costume shop. The only people I saw downstairs at that time were my fellow costumers Bob Mero and Dot Darlington, along with make-up artist Dolly Darlington," Merritt replied.

"When do the actors usually report for duty?"

"It depends. We stagger the costume fittings to sync with the actor's on stage cue times."

"What time was Chet fitted into his costume?"

"I sent for him and the rest of the Deadwood actors at 7:15, roughly two hours before he was due on stage. Chet was delayed by his ritual pre-performance cup of herbal tea." Merritt's mention of 'tea' particularly interested Sheriff Abrams and Deputy Hill.

"What can you tell us about the tea Mr. Rawlins was known to drink?"

"Chet swore by the concoction. He drank several cups before every show. He claimed it was a special elixir of herbs and tealeaves that helped relax his vocal chords."

"Do you know where he purchased the tea?"

"From England I think," Merritt bit her lip. "The stuff smelled awful, like a box of rotten potpourri. Chet is the only one who drank it."

"Are you sure that no one else drank the tea except Chet?"

"Positive," Merritt replied. "Chet would offer us a cup, but like I said, it smells really bad. No one dared touch the stuff except him."

"So you first sent for Mr. Rawlins to come to the costume shop around 7:15?"

"That's correct," Merritt replied. "Unfortunately, Celeste had been delayed in getting his tea brewed, so Chet asked if I'd send for him again in a few minutes. He still had plenty of time before his cue, so I figured a fifteen-minute delaying in dressing Mr. Rawlins wasn't that big of a deal. After seeing that the rest of the Deadwood actors were in costume and sent to make-up, I returned to the Green Room to summon Chet."

"Had Chet drunk his tea at that point?" Deputy Hill inquired.

"No," Merritt shook her head. "Just as the tea had finished brewing, Peter Wiseman accidentally knocked over the tea kettle, which caused it to spill all over the Green Room floor. Chet was peeved at Peter. The two dug into one another with a handful of accusations."

"What sort of accusations are we talking about here?" Abrams attention piqued.

"Chet blamed Peter for slashing his tires last week. Peter flatly denies any involvement, but Chet was convinced of his guilt."

"Come to think of it Ranger Sinclair did forward me a report regarding that incident," Sheriff Abrams replied. "Do you think that Peter was guilty of slashing Chet's tires?"

"I'm inclined to believe Peter...in spite of his animosity for Chet, he isn't the sort to stoop to something as vengeful as slashing tires."

"What happened next?"

"Celeste broke up the fight. She volunteered to make Chet another pot of tea if Peter would clean up the mess. During this commotion, Mike Trump, an aide to the Governor's office charged with managing playhouse revenue, entered the Green Room. He proceeded to wish us 'good luck,' which is actually a bad omen in the world of the theatre. Chet snapped at Mike, for having 'cursed the show,' and demanded that he recant his well wishes. Mike shot back, dismissing the theatrical superstitions. To ease the infighting, I cut in by insisting that Mr. Rawlins accompany to the wardrobe. Chet relented after Celeste promised to send his tea to him once it finished brewing."

"So when Chet went into wardrobe around 7:30 to 7:40 he had yet to drink his tea?"

"That's correct."

"How long did it take him to get into costume?"

"Ten to fifteen minutes? I sent him to Dolly for hair and make-up around eight, I believe."

"What was Mr. Rawlins state of health at that time?" the Sheriff pressed.

"At that point he exhibited no sights of illness. He was his usual *lively* personality. His demeanor shifted abruptly. Twenty-minutes before he was set to go on stage, Mr. Rawlins came into the Costume Shop with vomit on his shirt. It was at this point I noticed Mr. Rawlins having was having trouble breathing, and was stumbling in his step. Dot and I were concerned for his health. Chet told us that he thought that the burger he'd eaten for lunch was undercooked. Dot and I tried to convince him to let Doug Bates, his understudy, stand in for him, so he could go to the doctor, but Chet adamantly refused. In hindsight we should have forced him to go to the hospital, but Chet could be really stubborn. He wasn't the sort of man you wanted to get into an argument with."

"Would you classify Mr. Rawlins as a difficult man?" Deputy Hill asked.

"Yes, at times Chet was opinionated and cocky at times, but that is the nature of the acting beast," Merritt admitted.

"Did you ever interact with Mr. Rawlins outside of the theatre?" Hill followed up.

"I occasionally bumped into him around the park, but we didn't spend time together outside of work. Most of my days off I'm hanging out with my roommates or with Josh Ford."

"Ranger Ford?" Abrams asked, recognizing the name.

"Yes. I met him at the Peter Norbeck Visitor Center about a month ago. We're both from North Carolina and Josh offered to show me around the park."

"I have great respect for Ranger Ford," Abrams replied. "He's very knowledgeable about plants in the park. He didn't happen to mention Poison Hemlock on one of your excursions...perhaps pointed it out trailside?"

"No," Merritt was adamant in her reply.

"Death by consumption of Poison Hemlock is very rare. We have to investigate every lead to figure out how Chet ingested the toxin. That being said, you're not a suspect," Abrams' tone eased up. "Do you know if Mr. Rawlins enjoyed hiking?"

"Chet's foot was injured twice in the past month, so I don't think he was able to do anything outdoors, including hiking."

"Injured, how?"

"It's a long story, but there were a series of weird accidents in the theatre. First the curtain collapsed on Chet and the other Deadwood actors. Then during the technical rehearsal, the lights went haywire and collapsed on Chet and my roommate Ginny. Luckily no one was seriously injured, but Chet did sprain his right ankle twice."

"Did you ever find out the cause of the accidents?"

"The mishaps were chocked up to the age of the building. The crew just fixed the damage and moved on."

"It is not uncommon for people to make the deadly mistake of identifying Poison Hemlock as the eatable Wild Carrot known as Queen Anne's lace...is there any chance that Chet might have eaten Hemlock on his own, thinking it was some other type of herb?"

"I suppose that Chet could have accidentally added it to his herbal tea," Merritt's voice trailed off. The Sheriff's hypothesis was logical, but Merritt was unconvinced that even someone as cavalier as Chet would randomly consume poison hemlock.

"Do you know anyone who would have motive and means to kill Chet Rawlins?"

"Chet had his enemies, but I can't fathom anyone killing him in such a horrid fashion."

"Peter Wiseman is an herbal expert with motives against the deceased...Do you think he could be guilty of murdering his nemesis?"

"I don't think that Peter is capable of murder..." As Merritt made her reply, she remembered the day she and Josh bumped into Peter while hiking the Lovers Leap trail. Had that white lacy plant Peter been carrying around been poison hemlock? She decided not to say anything until she had the chance to speak directly with Peter and Josh.

"Thank you for your cooperation Miss Andrews," Sheriff Abrams stated as he stood up to usher Merritt out of the room. "Here's my card. If you think of additional information regarding this case please let me know."

"I will," Merritt promised before exiting the office.

The latest development surrounding the death of Chet Rawlins made Merritt sick. In the past month, Merritt had heard a number of her colleagues curse Chet's name, some even wished him dead, but did one of her fellow players go to the extreme of poisoning him with conium? The idea of a murderer in her midst scared Merritt. She prayed to God that this was some misfortunate accident void of foul play.

Over the course of the next four hours, Sheriff Abrams and Deputy Hill questioned each member of the Custer Playhouse cast and crew. Though each offered varying degrees of information, everyone testified to Chet's irascible personality.

"Mrs. Fitzgerald," Sheriff Abrams and Deputy Hill turned.

"Please call me Celeste," she requested, drying her eyes.

"What is your position with the theatre?" Deputy Hill asked.

"I'm a Call Girl, which means I'm charged with alerting actors of their entrances in time for them to appear on stage. I also signal the orchestra when the show is set to begin, and assist with scene changes."

"It sounds like a lot of work," Abrams replied.

"It's a lot of running around behind the scenes, but nothing too difficult."

"Could you please go over what happened the night Chet Rawlins died?"

"Chet arrived at the theatre around six forty-five. He appeared healthy...I didn't notice him acting out of character until a few minutes before he went on stage. Then again I was so busy with work I didn't have the time or energy to keep tabs on Chet."

"How much did you interact with Mr. Rawlins on the night of his death?"

"Chet expected me to brew him a pot of his herbal tea prior to every performance. Most nights I have it prepared by the time he arrives to the theatre, but I was running late on Thursday due to a stagehand meeting. Chet was impatient and was irritated that he had to wait for the tea."

"Did you get into an argument with Mr. Rawlins over the tea?"

"It was more of a tiff, really. At times, Chet could act out, becoming arrogant, demanding, and cruel," Celeste's face flushed as she held back tears.

"You were close with Chet," Abrams assumed. "How long did you know him?"

"Close to thirty years. We used to be engaged, but broke it off in 1992."

"What prompted the break up?"

"Chet and I were never really compatible; we were fire and ice, complete opposites..." Celeste's voice trailed off. "He smashed my heart, but Alistair put it back together. I forgave Chet for his misdeeds and I've been happily married to Alistair Fitzgerald for over a decade."

"It must have been a challenge to work side by side with a man that broke your heart and berated you until the day that he died," Sheriff Abrams prodded. "Surely you held a grudge against Mr. Rawlins?"

"My relationship with Chet has always been complicated. We argued, and fought bitter battles, but at the end of the day I cared about him. He was a friend."

"So Chet's behavior on Thursday night, didn't get under your skin?" Abrams questioned, prodding for more information.

"Yes, I was ticked off. I had a million things on my plate, and Chet complaining about that ridiculous tea exacerbated the situation. I brushed off his behavior. Chet was just being Chet. We exchanged a few terse words and then I finished fixing his tea. Unfortunately he didn't get to drink the first pot I made him."

"Why not?" Abrams asked.

"Just as I was about to serve Chet his tea, Peter Wiseman came into the Green Room, and accidentally bumped into me. The tea spilled all over the floor. Chet and Peter can't stand one another and started bickering."

"Were they fighting because Peter spilled Chet's tea, or about something else?"

"They were just arguing for arguments sake," Celeste bit her lip before sharing specifics of the argument. "Chet accused Peter of slashing his tires."

"Did Peter slash Chet's tires?" Deputy Hill followed.

"Absolutely not," Celeste replied vehemently. "Peter and Chet had their problems, but Peter would NEVER do something so vengeful."

"So this fight, Peter and Chet had over the spilt tea, how long did it last?"

"Only a few minutes. Then Mike Trump came into the Green Room."

"What's your opinion of Mr. Trump?"

"I'd be lying if I said that Mike Trump was anything other than a class-A jerk. He's here on behalf of the Governor and Attorney General to see that the state succeeds in closing down the theatre."

"Why would the state of South Dakota want to close an institution such as the Custer Playhouse?"

"Money," Celeste seethed. "Mike claims that the theatre is not profitable for the state and he's a white knight to save the day. He claims that his motives with the Playhouse are pure, but he's a rat. Mike just wants the Custer Playhouse shut down to make way for a new conference and concession center."

"What was Mr. Trump's reason for coming down to the Green Room?"

"He claimed it was to wish us 'good luck.'"

"You're skeptical of his intentions?"

"Mike never comes backstage before a show unless it is to lambaste us for something we've supposedly done wrong, and he certainly is not one to offer encouragement. Mike's decision to say 'good luck' before the show is the worst kind of curse in the theatre."

"In the theatre, 'good luck' is actually bad luck and 'break a leg' means 'good luck.'"

"If Mike came down to the Green Room to curse the show, he certainly succeeded. Only a few hours later, Chet winds up dead."

"Do you think Mike Trump had something to do with Chet's poisoning?"

"I know that Mike's a greedy bastard, but I don't know if he would resort to murder, especially via hemlock poisoning."

"How long did Mr. Trump stay in the Green Room?"

"Five minutes tops," Celeste replied. "After Mike left the room, I sent Chet to costumer Merritt Andrews, who had been waiting for him to finish his tea so he could get into costume."

"Did Mr. Rawlins drink his tea before leaving the Green Room?"

"No," Celeste replied. "After Peter spilled the first batch of tea, I had to brew another kettle. The tea is loose leaf so it takes a little longer than generic tea bags to brew. I sent Chet off to wardrobe and promised to bring him the tea as soon as it was prepared."

"What can you tell us about this special tea, Chet drank?" Abrams asked.

"Chet ordered it from a tea shop in England, I think. The tealeaves and mixed herbs come in a tin can, which I keep in a cabinet above the kitchenette in the Green Room. Everyone has access to the tea, but the only one who drinks it is Chet, because it tastes awful."

"Did the tea you prepared Chet on Thursday, look or smell different than usual?"

"You think the tea poisoned Chet?" Celeste sensed where the questioning was headed.

"We're trying to establish how Mr. Rawlins consumed the poison. Tea is one possibility," Sheriff Abrams replied. "Did he ever pick wild herbs within Custer State Park and add them to his tea?"

"I don't think so. Chet wasn't very interested in the outdoors and didn't know anything about plants," Celeste recollected.

"What about you Mrs. Fitzgerald, are you familiar with the flora of the Black Hills?"

"Until today I didn't even know that Poison Hemlock grew in the area."

"You're telling me in all honesty that you had nothing to do with Mr. Rawlins death."

"I could NEVER hurt Chet!"

"Okay, now back to Thursday night," Sheriff Abrams refocused the conversation. "When did you finally bring Chet his first cup of tea?"

"I didn't," Celeste replied. "Just before it had finished brewing, the Playhouse Property Master, Ethan Daniels alerted me to the fact that Alistair needed me upstairs. So I asked Virginia Terry to prepare Chet's cup of tea and leave it for him in the make-up room."

"Virginia Terry, she plays Calamity Jane, correct?"

"That's right," Celeste assented. "Ginny worked with Chet in the Deadwood act of *Dakota*."

"How did Virginia and Chet get along?"

"Well enough, I guess. I know a few weeks ago, Chet made Ginny cry during rehearsal. He bashed her ability as an actress, and cursed her out. Ginny was upset, but she's a pretty tough cookie and forgave Chet the next day."

"Do you think Ginny might have poisoned Chet?"

"Absolutely not," Celeste was firm in her assessment, "Ginny isn't the type to hold a grudge."

"It sounds like Mr. Rawlins had a habit of ticking people off?"

"It was quite a talent of his," Celeste agreed. "Everyone at the Playhouse endured the wrath of Rawlins from time to time."

"Thank you for your insight Mrs. Fitzgerald. We'll be in touch if we need any additional information."

Ginny entered the interrogation visibly shaken. The news of Chet's poisoning had left the headstrong actress shocked.

"How would you classify your working relationship with Mr. Rawlins?" Sheriff Abrams opened up the questioning.

"Chet was difficult to say the least, but I respected his talent as an actor."

"Did Chet ever say anything hurtful to you, something so cruel and vindictive that it made you break down in tears?"

"He infuriated me a few weeks back during rehearsal. I shed a few tears, but I got over it and forgave Chet's actions."

"In Chet's final hours, Celeste Fitzgerald mentioned that you served Mr. Rawlins his nightly cup of tea?" The question was more in line with an accusation.

"That's correct. Celeste was behind in her duties as Call Girl. Ethan Daniels had come down to alert her that she was needed upstairs, so I volunteered to take Chet his cup of tea."

"Did you add anything to the tea?"

"No, the tea was already brewed," Ginny increasingly nervous by the tone of the interrogation. "I simply poured the tea in his favorite cup and immediately served it to Chet in the Costume Shop. He gulped in down and instantly asked me to bring him another cup, which I promptly obliged him."

"What was Mr. Rawlins state of health at that point?"

"He was acting normal," Ginny gauged. "It wasn't until roughly twenty-five minutes after his first cup of tea, that Chet became fidgety. He complained of being parched and requested another pot of tea to quench his thirst. He guzzled down several pots of tea in the next hour or so. The first He threw up a few times, claiming that his lunch hadn't agreed with him. I probably should have paid him more attention, but I guess I didn't realize that he was terminally ill. It wasn't until we started running our lines on stage that I realized something was seriously wrong. Chet limped, struggling to walk and was gasping for air. His speech was slurred and nonsensical...It was horrible..." Recounting Chet's real life on stage death made Ginny feel uncomfortable, especially given the fact he'd been poisoned.

"You are a student at the University of South Dakota, correct?"

"I plan to graduate from USD with a B.A. in Theatre Arts in December of this year."

"What's your minor Miss Terry?"

"English," Ginny did not see how this information was relevant to Chet's death.

"What sorts of science classes have you taken at USD?"

"I've avoided them like the plague," Ginny admitted. "I'm not very good with science or math. I made a 'C' in biology."

"Have you ever attended a Botany talk here at Custer State Park?"

"Last summer," Ginny's voice trailed off, not liking where the sheriff's line of questioning was headed.

"At this Botany lecture, did the Ranger happen to mention the fact that poison hemlock grows abundantly in Custer State Park?"

"If you're insinuating that I poisoned Chet, then the answer is NO! I'm not a murderess," Ginny became defensive.

"That remains to be seen," The Sheriff mulled. "I do know that you gave prepared two cups of tea for the deceased, which may or may not have contained conium."

"I didn't poison him," Ginny pled her case with conviction. "I recommend that you investigate Mike Trump. He's been trying to interfere with *Dakota* from the beginning."

"That's all the questions we have for you as of now Miss. Terry. I insist that you remain in the Black Hills under further notice."

Mike Trump was the next in line to be questioned, and he was none too thrilled about it.

"I don't even understand why I'm here?" Trump shouted at the Sheriff and his Deputy. "I had nothing to do with Chet's death."

"Are you sure about that?"

"Are you accusing me of murder, because if you are I'll call the Attorney General and he'll personally vouch for my innocence?"

"Don't throw your credentials at me Trump. I'm investigating a possible homicide and so far a lot of people in this theatre think that you're behind the poisoning."

"They've been brainwashed against me. The Custer Playhouse has been having financial troubles, so earlier this year the Governor and Attorney General of South Dakota suggested that we re-access the long-term plans for the property. The playhouse is a well-known park attraction, however it costs a great deal of money to maintain, and we need to generate revenue to keep the park infrastructure up. I'm merely here to ensure this process is carried out efficiently."

"A majority of the cast and crew think that you're here to shut the playhouse down Mr. Trump and Chet's death is sabotage, to advance the closure of the theatre."

"I have gone out of my way to make *Dakota* a success. Just a few weeks ago I used personal funds to professionally rewire the lights after they faltered during a technical rehearsal. I'm here to ensure that the Playhouse makes a profit this season. A dead actor isn't good for business."

"What would you do with this land, if the Custer Playhouse were forced to vacant the premises?" Abrams inquired.

"We would move forward with plans to build a conference and concession center on the property."

"Did you get along with Mr. Rawlins?"

"I couldn't stand the man. He was an insufferable egotist. That being said, I did not kill him."

"You spoke with Mr. Rawlins in the Green Room shortly before his death."

"I was backstage as I work at the theatre," Mike replied tersely. "Is it a crime to wish the cast and crew good luck before a show?"

"Consensus is your attempt to wish them 'good luck' was in fact a curse."

"Don't get me started on those silly theatrical superstitions. They claimed I cursed them by saying 'good luck' and by mentioning 'Macbeth.' It's the last time I try to make peace backstage. If Chet was murdered, then your lead suspect should be Peter Wiseman. He and Chet loathed one another. Add in the fact that Peter is some sort of Lakota Medicine Man; I wouldn't be surprised if he knew exactly how to obtain poison hemlock, and planted it into Chet's food or that god-forsaken tea he drank. If you're a smart man Sheriff Abrams you'll take my name off your suspect list," Mike threatened.

"We don't take kindly to threats," Abrams and Hill replied before letting Mr. Trump go.

The final person the Sheriff questioned was Peter Wiseman.

"Mr. Wiseman, please take a seat," Sheriff Abrams stated as Peter entered the room. "We're hoping you might shed some light on Chet Rawlins death."

"Are you asking me if I poisoned him?" Peter retorted.

"Did you?" Abrams asked.

"Chet and I despised one another, but I didn't kill him!" Peter was firm in his reply.

"What fueled the animosity between you and Mr. Rawlins?" Deputy Hill followed.

"It's a long story," Peter sighed. "In the 1980s, Chet and I used to be drinking buddies. However in the early 1990s we were in a car accident together."

"Were either of you under the influence alcohol during the accident?"

"No," Peter hesitated before uttering his reply. "Still the accident made me wake up to the fact that I had hit rock bottom and was leading an unhealthy lifestyle. Chet, being the stubborn idiot that he was disagreed with my chastisement of his wild ways, and it cost us our friendship."

"Why did you continue to work together? Surely one of you could have found another theatre gig?"

"A common love of the Custer Playhouse," Peter assessed. "Chet had the talent to be a big New York actor, but alcohol got in the way. He loved being in Custer, but a part of him was bitter. Bitter at the mistakes he'd made, the people he'd hurt."

"Did you slash Chet Rawlins tires?"

"No, I wasn't even in the area when it happened. Although I'll admit whoever did it, did Chet a favor. He sped like a bat out of hell and needed to be off the road."

"Anyone in particular you can think of who might want to kill him?"

"Mike Trump certainly had the means and the motive."

"Ironically enough, Mike told us that you poisoned Chet," Sheriff Abrams noted.

"Mike's a jerk."

"Mike described you as 'Medicine Man,'" Abrams followed up.

"I have an expertise in natural medicines, passed down to me from my mother and grandmother. The Lakota lived for many years off the land in South Dakota. My people had to learn how to use plants for food and medicine. As a botany and natural medicine expert, I need to know the chemical make-up of plants in the Black Hills, which species are edible, which are poisonous, are beneficial and which are weeds."

"You admit then, that you have the expertise on where to find conium in Custer State Park and how to prepare it as a lethal poison?"

"Yes," Peter replied curtly. "However it doesn't take an expert to kill someone with poison hemlock. It is a widely known fact that it grows in the park, and someone could have easily added it to Chet's food or drink. The entire plant is heavily toxic and it only takes a small amount of poison hemlock to kill someone."

"I also have it on good authority that you argued with Chet just before the show, and caused his tea to spill."

"So what, I cleaned up the mess and Celeste made him another pot of that disgusting concoction he drunk."

"You did have the opportunity to douse a bit poison into the new batch of tea."

"Just because I had the opportunity doesn't mean I did it," Peter replied. "Frankly anyone could have popped hemlock juice into that tea pot, or added ground hemlock leaves to the tin can. He keeps it out all night, and has at least three cups before he goes on stage."

"So *you do know* about the tin can where he kept his tea supply?" Abrams questioned, very interested in Peter's reply.

"It's common knowledge. It's a community cabinet located in an area that both cast and crew walk in and out of all night. All the actors store their own food and drinks there," Peter replied. "I've feuded with Chet for years, if I wanted to kill him, I would have done it years ago and I certainly wouldn't have killed him with something as sinister as poison hemlock."

"The truth remains to be seen Mr. Wiseman," Sheriff Abrams stared down the suspect. "I suggest that you stay in area in case we need to follow up."

After questioning all sixty members of the Custer Playhouse cast and crew, Sheriff Abrams and his deputies unfortunately were not any closer to solving the mysterious poisoning of Chet Rawlins.

Everyone in the theatre, admitted that Chet was a jerk with many enemies that did not like his behavior offstage. It also didn't help that every potential suspect had access to Chet's tea tin, where the Sheriff's office had found that the blend of herbs and tealeaves had been soaked in poison hemlock juice, and mixed with the leaves and stem of the poison hemlock plant.

Did Chet mix the poison hemlock into his own tea, thinking it was another special ingredient to help his voice? If so, he must have added it recently, otherwise the temperamental actor would have died long before Thursday night's show from consumption of conium. Or was it something more sinister; did someone in the theatre tamper with the tea blend in the tin with the intent to poison the actor? It was a tough call, with a lot of motive and little proof.

"This is turning into a very interesting case," Sheriff Abrams told Deputy Hill as they prepped to leave the theatre. "One I hope that we can solve sooner than later."

Chapter 21:

Poison Hemlock and murder, the bizarre development in the death of actor Chet Rawlins left Merritt both disturbed and puzzled. Merritt wanted answers.

Following her questioning, the costumer tracked down Josh, who was on duty at the Peter Norbeck Visitor Center. Merritt wanted to tell him the latest news surrounding Chet's death and also to obtain some information regarding poison hemlock. She figured the more she knew about the poison that killed Chet, the better her chances of figuring out whom, if anyone had murdered him.

"Merritt, what a pleasant surprise," Josh smiled as she entered the Visitor Center.

"Josh, I'm so glad to see you!"

"Are you okay?" Josh asked, sensing the stress in his girlfriend's voice.

"I just found out that Chet Rawlins was poisoned!"

"Suzy his autopsy results are being released today, but Chet being poisoned, that's shocking?" Josh replied in disbelief.

"I just spent twenty-five minutes being questioned by the Custer County Sheriff's department. Sheriff Abrams revealed that Chet died from poison hemlock."

"Poison hemlock," Josh was taken aback. "Does Sheriff Abrams know how Chet consumed the hemlock?"

"He didn't say, but after the Q&A session I had with him, I'm guessing that somehow the poison hemlock was added to Chet's tea. Whether or not he mixed it in on his own accord or it was planted to murder him I don't know."

"You're saying that there's a possibility that Chet was murdered?"

"It looks that way," Merritt sighed.

"Who would kill him? Especially using poison hemlock? It's so random."

"I know that Chet has his enemies at the theatre, but the thought of someone poisoning him is vile."

"You must be a wreck," Josh sympathized. "It's unsettling to think that you might be working alongside a killer."

"Way to make me feel better Ranger Ford," Merritt rolled her eyes.

"I'm sorry."

"It's okay. I'm just rattled by this whole thing."

"What can I do to help?"

"Can you provide me with background information on the conium plant? If I know more about the plant, it might help me figure out whether or not Chet was murdered," Merritt explained. "Not to mention the fact I want to know what the plant looks like so I don't accidentally ingest during my next meal."

"I'd be happy to tell you what I know about poison hemlock," Josh replied. "Just give me a minute, okay?"

"I'll wait here," Merritt promised as Josh returned to the Visitor Center information desk to pull a file folder related to conium maculatum; better known as poison hemlock.

"Ranger Sinclair says I can take off early. Why don't we head over to the Creekside Lodge, so we can talk?" Josh suggested.

Once at the Creekside Lodge, they sat down a table in the lobby and began discussing the ins and outs of poison hemlock.

"Poison hemlock is an herbaceous biennial, known scientifically as conium maculatum. It is a member of the Apiaceae family, the same species of plants to which the parsley, fennel, parsnip and carrot belong. Poison hemlock grows to be six-to-ten feet in height, and has an erect hollow stem, with distinct ridges. The bottom half of the stem is purple or red in tint. The leaves are shiny, green, lacy and triangular in appearance, spanning anywhere from twelve inches long to four inches wide. Its flowers are small, white and lacy, and grouped in umbels with five-notched petals."

"Poison hemlock is a direct relative of my two favorite salad items: carrots and celery?" Merritt asked, a little disturbed by the prospect.

"The plants are cousins, yes, but neither carrots nor celery contain any levels of toxicity. Poison hemlock contains several toxic alkaloids; the most potent of these is coiine. It is a neurotoxin, which causes the central nervous system I humans and livestock to go haywire. Ingestion in any quantity can result in respiratory collapse and death by asphyxiation."

"What are the warning signs that someone has hemlock poisoning?" Merritt asked, trying to match Chet's symptoms with those related to consuming the toxic parsnip.

"The symptoms of hemlock poisoning usually begin with numbing in the feet, excess salivation, vomiting, heavily dilated eyes, and trouble breathing. In the end, the cause of death is ascending paralysis and respiratory failure."

"Chet exhibited a lot of those symptoms, but never in a million years did I think he had poisoned with hemlock," Merritt lamented. "Chet brushed off his condition as a mild case of food poisoning. I wish that I could have gotten him to a doctor before he died."

"Unless someone knows that they ingested poison hemlock, it's easy to assume they just have the flu or food poisoning. Time is of the essence in surviving hemlock poisoning. Doctors treat conium consumption by putting the patient on a respirator, which keeps the patient breathing to prevent asphyxia doesn't kick in. In many cases the patient dies even with medical attention."

"At the risk of sounding morbid, but how long does it take after someone's consumed poison hemlock to die?"

"It depends," Josh replied. "The less you consume the longer the effects take to manifest. If a person were to consume say five petals or a couple of leaves on the plant, death could come as swiftly as a few hours."

"Sheriff Abrams seemed to indicate that Chet consumed the poison through his tea. Chet had his first cup of tea at almost eight and died an hour and hour later."

"Chet must have consumed a hefty dose of hemlock in a short period of time to die so suddenly."

"It sounds like a painful way to die."

"If someone did poison Chet, they would have to really hate his guts to kill him in such a cruel fashion."

"I just really hope that this turns out to be nothing more than a tragic accident. The idea that one of my fellow cast members is a cold-blooded killer is disconcerting."

"I don't like the scenario of a murderer on the loose. I worry about your safety," Josh voiced his concern. "I hope that Sheriff Abrams is going to have patrol officers on the theatre complex to ensure that no one else is murdered."

"CSP is on lockdown, so chances of another murder occurring on site are slim," Merritt rationalized. "I still can't get over the fact that poison hemlock even grows in this park. I thought it was native to Europe, not North America."

"The plant is indigenous to Europe, but was brought to North America by colonists for use as a decorative plant. The unassuming lethal weed is delicate in appearance, resembling non-toxic wild carrot, commonly referred to as Queen Anne's lace."

"The only garden hemlock belongs in is Rappaccini's," Merritt referenced the toxic garden trap told by her favorite author Nathaniel Hawthorne.

"Poison hemlock is an aggressive invasive species naturally distributing itself throughout North America. In Custer State Park, hemlock is considered a noxious weed, displacing critical native species that sustain park ecosystems. It is commonly found near streams, ditches, on the side of the road, and along hiking trails, flowering in late spring and early summer. It is a killer plant in every regard," Josh explained, showing Merritt a several photographs of hemlock.

Merritt recognized the plant that Peter was carrying on the day of the Lovers Leap hike. Could Peter's hatred of Chet lead him to poison his rival? Merritt decided she wanted to learn more about the plant before she implicated him.

"You mentioned hemlock's resemblance to Queen Anne's lace, how can you tell the difference between the two?"

"Hemlock stems are smooth and have purple and red streaks in the lower part, whereas the stems of Queen Anne's lace are hairy and devoid of a purplish red tint. Hemlock reeks of a pungent odor akin to a musty mouse. Queen Anne's lace on the other hand, has a pleasant scent, which smells like carrot."

"Do you remember when we hiked Lovers Leap and ran into Peter?"

"He was working on collecting noxious weeds."

"I'm fairly positive that the weed that Peter was carrying was poison hemlock," Merritt stated.

"If you're insinuating that Peter had something to do with Chet's death," Josh protested the notion.

"I have immense respect for Peter's character and hope that he is innocent. That being said I cannot ignore the facts. Peter abhorred Chet. Given his extensive knowledge of botanical medicine and the fact we witnessed him collecting hemlock, is highly suspect.

"Did you mention that you saw Peter with poison hemlock to Sheriff Abrams?"

"Not yet. I wanted to talk with you first to confirm Peter was carrying hemlock. I also wanted to allow Peter the chance to give me an explanation for having the hemlock in the first place."

"To be honest, I don't recall which plants Peter had on him that day," Josh admitted. "I can reach out to the weed management team with whom Peter is working to see if he was charged with removing poison hemlock?"

"I'd appreciate that," Merritt smiled.

"You must be pretty hungry after all that drama. Can I treat you to a non-poisonous meal?"

"I appreciate the offer, but all this talk of death and hemlock has left me queasy," Merritt admitted. "Will you take a rain check?"

"Name the time and the place and I'll be there," Josh promised.

The couple enjoyed a leisurely walk along the Creekside Trail before parting ways.

Upon arriving back at the playhouse, Merritt tracked down Peter, who was in his cabin, involved in the heat of an argument with Celeste. She could hear the shouting as stepped on the porch.

"Did you poison Chet, Peter?" Celeste demanded an answer.

"If I had wanted to kill Chet, I would have done it ages ago," Peter rebuffed.

"I want to believe you Peter," Celeste was conflicted, "but you were there when I was preparing the tea. You caused the first teapot to spill."

"I told you that was an accident," Peter avowed. "I despised Chet for what he put you through. He never should have asked you to cover for his sins ...He deserved to die, but I didn't kill him."

"I don't want to talk about that, not now, not ever," Celeste shot back.

"I wouldn't blame you if you had doused his tea. He abused you emotionally for years," Peter whispered, gauging her emotions. "If you did kill Chet, I promise I won't tell the Sheriff."

"Don't accuse me of murder," Celeste cried out. "I hated Chet for what he did to me, but a part of me still loved him. I'd never hurt him."

"You didn't kill that snake and neither did I," Peter recognized. "The question is which of Chet's many enemies hated him enough to do the deed."

After some debate, Merritt knocked on the cabin door.

"Merritt...," Peter a bit startled ushered her inside. Celeste looked on, her eyes red from crying.

"I apologize if I'm interrupting," Merritt stepped into the cabin.

"I was just leaving," Celeste stated abruptly exiting the premises. "I hope I didn't cause her to leave," Merritt stated, feeling a little awkward having walked into a heated discussion.

"No worries," Peter smiled. "We'd finished our conversation. What can I do you for Miss Andrews?"

"I regret having to broach this subject, but a few weeks ago when Josh and I bumped into you on the Lover's Leap trail you claimed to be uprooting noxious weeds...the basket was full of poison hemlock."

"I won't lie. It was conium in the basket," Peter conceded. "I can assure you that I wasn't collecting the plant with the intention of poisoning Chet. Conium maculatum is an invasive species, a noxious plant, in Custer State Park. I saw a patch of it and wanted to remove it before it had the chance to reseed later in the summer. I gave the poison hemlock to Liam Bryant to be disposed of."

"I assumed it was a coincidence, but given the latest developments I wanted to be sure."

"Did you mention this to Sheriff Abrams?" Peter asked.

"No. I wanted to hear your side of the story before I implicated you in Chet's murder."

"I appreciate that," Peter smiled. "I recommend share this information with the Sheriff, otherwise he could use this to ramp up suspicions of my guilt if it comes to like at a later date. I'm innocent of this crime and know that the truth will out eventually."

"Any suspicions on who poisoned Chet" Merritt sought Peter's opinion.

"He had a lot of enemies; Celeste didn't do it, I know that for sure. My best guess is Mike Trump."

"Perhaps," Merritt replied, not quite convinced with Peter's hypothesis. Sure Mike is a jerk, but why would he resort to murder when he had the power to close down the playhouse without discretion.

Upon finishing her conversation with Peter, Merritt returned to Alpine. When she entered the cabin, she found Ginny in tears, and Emma and Rebecca trying to comfort her.

"Ginny, what's wrong?" Merritt rushed to her side.

"They think I did it. They think that I poisoned Chet!"

"Who thinks that?"

"Sheriff Abrams," Ginny yelped. "He thinks I added the poison to Chet's tea."

"That's ridiculous!"

"Is it? The Sheriff has every reason to suspect me. I served Chet his tea tainted with poison hemlock. Not to mention a week ago I wished him dead during rehearsal. You've got to believe that I'm innocent," Ginny was hysterical.

"Of course you're innocent," Her Alpine roommates consoled Ginny.

"I want to go home, but Sheriff Abrams says I have to stay here, in case they require further interrogation."

"He told everyone that," Rebecca shrugged it off.

"Sheriff Abrams asked me point blank if I poisoned Chet's tea."

"My dad's a lawyer," Rebecca stated. "If charges are brought against you, he'll get you off. You're innocent."

"It's an investigation Ginny. They have to ask those questions. You told them that you didn't poison Chet, and I'm certain that they believe you," Merritt gave her two cents.

"I hope so," Ginny replied through tears. "I'm scared. We could be the next victims of the playhouse killer. Just being here makes me sick."

"We need to focus on figuring out who did this so that justice can be served and we can move on with our lives."

"Merritt's right, the show must go on," Emma held. "Although *Dakota* is likely to be canceled until Chet's mysterious death is solved. It makes you wonder if Mike Trump is behind this."

"It wouldn't surprise me," Rebecca replied. "We certainly can't make a profit off the show with a murder investigation going on."

"Why don't we get out of here, drive up to Rapid City and go shopping?" Ginny requested drying her eyes. "I just really can't stand being at the Playhouse right now."

A few minutes later they got into Merritt's car and drove fifty minutes north to the Mount Rushmore Mall in Rapid City, hoping to forget about poison hemlock for a while.
Unfortunately murder isn't something you just brush off with a shopping bag in your hand.

Chapter 22:

It didn't take long for the media to catch wind of Chet's autopsy results. On Wednesday morning the Rapid City Journal ran a cover story on Chet's poisoning entitled "Death by Hemlock."

The latest act in the mysterious death of veteran Custer Playhouse actor, Chet Rawlins is playing out much like a scene out from a Greek tragedy. The Rapid City Medical Examiner's office confirmed late last night that Mr. Rawlins died from consumption of Poison Hemlock, scientifically known as conium maculatum. Poison Hemlock is notorious for its role in the execution of famed Greek philosopher Socrates. Mr. Rawlins died on Thursday night, while performing on stage in the popular Custer Playhouse production of Dakota. The Custer County Sheriff's office issued a statement saying that: "they are still investigating how Mr. Rawlins consumed the poison, and are treating the case as suspicious." So the question remains: was Mr. Rawlins murdered, betrayed by a theatrical colleague or did he take his own life by accidentally eating the unassuming killer plant: poison hemlock? Only time will tell. A decision as to whether performances of 'Dakota,' will be made by noon on Thursday.

If the article wasn't enough to stir up a controversy, by noon several local television affiliates were camped on the Playhouse lawn broadcasting live, in order to follow all the latest developments in what they deemed a 'toxic case of murder.'

"Can you believe this media spectacle?" Ginny peered through the blinds. The roommates had been holed in the Alpine cabin the better part of the day, evading the reporters. "You'd think the journalists would be more respectful of Chet's life, than skulking around for a story."

"You can't blame them for being here," Rebecca admitted. "It's not every day that a well-known actor dies on stage by hemlock poisoning. It's something out of Agatha Christie."

"The problem is that this is real life, not some fantasy death sequence," Ginny heaved a sigh, under duress that she was a key suspect in Chet's murder.

"My mom and I have been trying to conjure up publicity for the Playhouse for months," Emma sighed. "I just wish it hadn't come at the expense of Chet's life."

"I'm convinced that whoever poisoned Chet, was behind the curtain collapse and wiring problems during the technical rehearsal," Merritt hypothesized.

"Someone like Mike Trump you mean?" Emma presumed.

"Trump is a bully, but I'm skeptical that he's a murderer. He could have shut the theatre down the minute the technical issues occurred, but instead he paid to have the lighting fixed." Merritt replied. "I think it was someone else, someone who had a very strong vendetta against Chet. Think about it, both accidents occurred when Chet was on stage. He was nearly killed both times."

"Along with a handful of additional cast and crew, including myself," Ginny recalled.

"Precisely," Merritt continued. "The goal was for Chet to die during a stage accident, where murder wouldn't be suspected. When the accidents failed to kill Chet, then the murderer opted for a more sinister death trap. By poisoning Chet's tea, a tea that only he drank, it was a sure-fire way to ensure the actor perished."

"I hate to say this, but I suspect Peter of Chet's murder. He is a genius with medicinal plants and would have known exactly how to prepare the hemlock, and enough about Chet's habit to add it into his tea," Ginny theorized.

"I admire Peter, but I cannot turn a blind eye to the fact that he had the means and motive for murder," Emma analyzed.

"Peter is an obvious suspect, but my gut tells me that he's innocent," Merritt held.

"You caught Peter red handed with a basket of poison hemlock when you were hiking with Ranger Ford. That is highly suspicious," Emma rebutted.

"It is coincidence," Merritt defended. "Peter was collecting noxious weeds for the Park Service."

"So he claims..."

"It doesn't take an expert to kill someone with poison hemlock. The entire plant is toxic, and it wouldn't have taken a plant expert to poison someone with it. Everyone knows Chet's tea routine. They could have snuck into the Green Room and easily added the hemlock into the tea without anyone noticing."

"Merritt does have a point," Rebecca conceded. "Souvenir shops throughout the park sell guidebooks detailing Custer's plants. The culprit could have no background in chemistry."

"Let's track down Tom and Luke to ask if they noticed anything odd on the day of the curtain collapse or before the botched Tech Rehearsal," Merritt stated.

"The sooner we find out whom, if anyone poisoned Chet the quicker this nightmare will be over!" Ginny followed suit.

"If you two are going to play Nancy Drew, we'll tag along too," Emma and Rebecca insisted.

The sleuths eluded the television cameras long enough to reach the Norbeck cabin, where they found Tom, Luke, Jim and Ethan.

"With all the television cameras, I'm surprised that you girls made it here in one piece," Jim stated as he ushered them into the cabin.

"We wanted to obtain your insights regarding the curtain collapse and botched Tech Rehearsal."

"Both incidences were catastrophic failures."

"The question is was the cause of these bizarre events accidental due to malfunctions with aging theater equipment or carefully constructed schemes to cause injury and death?" Merritt put forth.

"I've said all along that Mike Trump was behind these so-called accidents. The curtain and pulley system were in top shape...as for the technical rehearsal, the wiring was in perfect order...nothing in the theater circuits should have caused that fuse to ignite. The breakers didn't even trip," Luke gave his two cents.

"With a building this old, the electricity is bound to go haywire from time to time – are you positive that the system simply didn't overload? It takes a lot of power to light up *Dakota*. The breakers going off could have sparked a fuse and thus ignited the fire."

"I'll admit that lighting and sound can be taxing on the circuits, but this wasn't a mere malfunction. Even the electrician from Rapid City couldn't find a root cause to the explosion."

"It's a bit coincidental that the explosion and curtain collapse both occurred during the Deadwood scene," Ginny shivered, realizing the danger she'd been in.

"Did you notice anyone else in the area when you were looking over the electrical circuits and breaker box?"

"It was just Ethan, Luke and I."

"What about Mike Trump, did you see him?" Ginny inquired.

"Mike wasn't around, but that doesn't mean he didn't play a role in the accidents," Luke asserted.

"Do any of the stagehands have knowledge of the Playhouse's electrical circuits?" Merritt followed up.

"No, just Tom and myself..."

"What about Spotlight Operator Lisa Thomas?" Rebecca tried to cover all bases.

"Lisa strictly works in the Spotlight booth and never messes with any of the electrical issues in the theatre," Tom responded.

"I'm sorry we couldn't be of more help," Luke replied.

"Before we go," Merritt stated, turning her attention to Ethan, "I wanted to ask you about the night of the murder."

"I'm not sure I can be of much help," Ethan shrugged. "I only saw Chet very briefly when I bumped into you two in the hall, remember?"

"I remember. However, as Chet was in the Costume Shop, his tea was being prepared in the Green Room. Celeste was making it, but she had to leave."

"Ginny volunteered to finish preparing it for Chet...Why is this relevant?"

"The Sheriff considers me a suspect since I served Chet his tea," Ginny admitted. "It would help if you noticed anyone put something in the tea kettle when I wasn't looking."

"I'm sorry Ginny, but I didn't notice anything," Ethan replied.

"Just great," Ginny sighed. "I'm going to jail for a crime I didn't commit."

"Don't be overly dramatic," Ethan reassured Ginny. "Whoever poisoned Chet probably added the hemlock to his tealeaves not directly into his tea cup."

"What makes you say that?" Ginny asked.

"An intuition I have after talking with the Sheriff," Ethan explained. "He kept asking me about the tea tin and who had access to it. Considering everyone had easy access to the tea tin, they'll have a hard time proving guilt beyond a reasonable doubt."

"Ethan's right," Jim told Ginny. "All the evidence they have is circumstantial. And at this point we can't be certain that Chet was murdered. There is the offshoot chance that he accidentally added the poison hemlock leaves to his tea, thinking that they were a natural herb or something."

"I hope you're right, because I really don't want to become part of the next Dateline Investigates."

"We should probably slip out, while the television crews are on break," Merritt stated, after glancing out the window. "Thanks again for the information."

"We'll let you know if we remember anything else," the boys replied before the girls headed out the door. Their next stop was Ponderosa, where they met up with Stagehand Claudia Cosgrove.

"Howdy neighbors?" Claudia greeted her neighbors as she opened her cabin door.

"We're playing detectives," Emma replied. "Merritt has a working theory that whoever killed Chet was also behind the curtain collapse and the explosive tech rehearsal."

"It certainly makes sense. I've been suspicious of sabotage and ill intent ever since the incidents occurred."

"Why do you say that?" Merritt questioned.

"The Custer Playhouse uses a fly system, an elaborate system of ropes, counterweights, pulleys, sandbags, and additional devices to enable the crew to quickly move components on stage during a production, such as lights, set pieces, and curtains. Our stage has several curtains with the largest being the Grand Drape."

"The front curtain that separates the audience and actors before a show," Merritt asked.

"The Grand Drape is controlled by a series of ropes and sandbags. What caused the curtain and sandbags to collapse were the fact that several of the ropes looked to have been intentionally cut to cause the curtain, and sandbags to fall."

"Isn't there a possibility that over time, the rope eroded and finally gave way?" Merritt postulated.

"I don't buy that assumption," Claudia continued. "Back in March, Gully and several stagehands, fixed the fly system to ensure it was up to code to avoid having the Playhouse listed as unsafe by the state of South Dakota. Why would the ropes, which are relatively new, suddenly break?"

"Did you notice anyone suspicious backstage the day of the curtain collapse?" Merritt asked.

"No," Claudia replied. "Most of the stagehands were assisting John Hood in the Scene Shop. The only people backstage were me, Gully, and Ethan."

"Did you notice anything strange that might indicate that someone was hijacking the lights during the tech rehearsal?"

"No, I wish I did," Claudia sighed. "If Mike Trump hadn't been so eager to help in resolving the issues, I would have pegged him for saboteur."

"What about Chet's poisoning? Any thoughts into who wanted him dead?" Ginny asked.

"A zillion people," Claudia smirked. "Chet was a jerk. I didn't kill him, but after seeing the way he's treated a number of people at this theatre it doesn't surprise me that someone murdered him."

"We had better get going," Ginny stated. "Thanks for your time Claudia."

"No problem and good luck with your investigation."

"I'm convinced that someone staged the curtain collapse and electrical malfunction," Ginny noted.

"Unfortunately we're not any closer as to figuring out who was behind it," Emma sighed.

"We'll keep digging," Merritt held. "Eventually something will turn up."

Taking a break from their investigation, the roommates decided to drive into Custer City to purchase groceries. With a playhouse killer on the loose, they were leery to eat anything from the playhouse mess hall.

"Canned goods will be my diet from now on," Ginny declared. "At least I know that I'm the only one who handled the food since it left the factory. That way no one can add any sort of toxin to my food supply."

"The thought of accidentally eating poison hemlock is enough to drive anyone to starvation."

While at the grocery store, the girls bumped into Mike Trump. He was behind them in line, talking loudly on his cell-phone. Merritt noticed he had a large tube of anti-itch and poison ivy medicine in his hand.

"I told you that I have things under control," Mike spoke into the receiver. "Of course I didn't kill Chet."

As Merritt eavesdropped on the conversation, she wondered if Mike was telling the truth.

Chapter 23:

Gully and Alistair called a meeting at eleven o'clock on Thursday to discuss the status of *Dakota* in light of Chet's poisoning.

"After lengthy discussions, the Custer Playhouse board and Sheriff Abrams have decided to proceed with scheduled performances as planned. This is under the condition that the Sheriff and his deputies remain on site for every performance until the case of Chet's untimely poisoning has been resolved. He has also asked me to reiterate the fact that none of you are to leave the greater Black Hills area until further notice. I'll see you all tonight at the show."

It was obvious from Gully's tone, that he wasn't comfortable with the keeping the curtains up in the midst of this crisis. The revelation that Chet had been poisoned and most likely murdered during a performance of *Dakota* was unsettling for all involved. Sheriff Abrams insistence that the show must go on was aimed at keeping the cast and crew in one location during the homicide investigation, and also because he wanted to watch Mike Trump's movements. If Trump had killed Chet in an effort to stall production, the Sheriff figured Mike would attempt to do something else to sabotage the production, in which they could bait him. The Sheriff also wanted to monitor Peter, Celeste and Ginny; his other top suspects.

"Now that we know that Chet died an unnatural death, it doesn't feel right for the show to go on," Ginny voiced her disapproval.

"I never thought I'd say this, but I wish the performances this weekend had been canceled," Emma frustrated. "It's just too much of a gamble allowing the show to continue with a possible murderer amongst us."

"Sheriff Abrams is hoping that he can bait and trap whoever was behind Chet's murder by keeping watch during production," Merritt rationalized. "It'll be less likely that the culprit will flee the scene of the crime, when *Dakota* is still in production."

"How can we function normally with the knowledge that a killer is on the loose," Rebecca lamented. "I personally don't know how I can act on stage with murder on my mind."

"The best thing that we can do is to focus on why we love the playhouse and try to forget the tragic events that have happened here as of late," Merritt did her best to make light of a difficult situation.

"I wonder how Doug Bates feels about stepping into Chet's shoes, it's a burden to carry," Rebecca pondered.

"If I didn't know Doug better, I'd point the finger at him," Ginny asserted. "What bigger motive is there to kill someone in the theatre than to step into a role they coveted? However, Doug is a reluctant actor, who prefers background roles to the limelight. This will be a nightmare for him."

After the announcement, Merritt headed down to the Costume Shop to meet up with Bob and Dot; neither of whom was particularly thrilled to continue production now that Chet's death had be deemed a possible homicide. In spite of this, the trio of costumers gathered their composure and focused on the task ahead of them. They had a lot of work to do in order to prepare for that night's performance of *Dakota*.

At four o'clock the costumers broke for an hour and a half dinner break. Merritt decided to return to Alpine, where she fixed a bowl of soup with crackers. After finishing up hemlock-free meal, Merritt checked her cell-phone voicemail. She had ten messages, all of which were from her frantic parents, who had heard about Chet's death by poison hemlock.

"What's this business of someone having been murdered at the Custer Playhouse? Your father and I read an article in the paper this morning saying that Chet Rawlins had been murdered with poison hemlock? I thought you said Mr. Rawlins died of accidental food poisoning? You didn't tell me that his death was a homicide! Merritt you need to call us back right this minute and tell us what is going on! I don't like the idea of you working out there all by yourself with a homicidal maniac on the loose! If I don't hear from you soon then I'm going to book a flight to South Dakota and bring you home myself."

As close as Merritt is to her parents, she had been reluctant to share the news of Chet's murdered, because it would cause them to worry about their daughter. Unfortunately she couldn't hide the truth from her parents any longer as the story had been covered by her hometown news station, WRAL, in the national news segment of the noon news.

Merritt dialed her parent's home phone number. After three rings, her mom picked up.

"Thank God! I have been trying to call you all day! Why didn't you answer your cell phone?"

"I left my phone in my dorm while I was at work," Merritt explained, sensing that it was going to take more than a few subtle apologies to smooth this crisis over with her mom.

"It doesn't matter now," Lynn Andrews, replied, "I'm just glad that you finally called me back. I've been worried sick about you ever since your father and I heard that one of your co-workers had been murdered! You told me that he died from accidental food poisoning."

"Well technically he did die of food poisoning," Merritt replied. "His food was poisoned."

"Don't be smart with me Merritt Andrews," her mother shot back. "You know darn well that death by poison hemlock isn't the same thing as dying of salmonella or e coli."

"I'm sorry I didn't tell you sooner. I only found out about the poison hemlock on Tuesday, and I didn't want to worry you until I found out more information about the case."

"Too late, I am worried. Your father and I want you to drive back to North Carolina tomorrow. My daughter is NOT going to continue living in the midst a killer."

"I think you're being a little over dramatic..." Merritt rebutted.

"A man you worked with has died from poison hemlock and there's a murderer on the loose, and you tell me that I'm being over dramatic for wanting you to come home, alive?"

"Over dramatic was the wrong phrasing," Merritt tried to save face. "It's just that you're jumping to the wrong conclusions. For one the Sheriff isn't even sure that someone added the poison hemlock to Chet's tea. You see, um, poison hemlock looks a lot like the herb Queen Anne's lace and there's a theory that Chet accidentally consumed the poison on his own, by mistake."

"There is also the strong possibility that one of your fellow cast and crew purposefully poisoned Mr. Rawlins."

"I understand why you're worried, but I'm fine. I've bought canned food to ensure I won't die from poisoning and the Sherriff's staff is patrolling the playhouse 24/7."

"Thanks for your reassurances," her mother replied in a sarcastic tone.

"And my friend Ranger Ford has promised to protect me from toxic substances."

"I don't like it. I want you home."

"Even if I wanted to come home I can't. *Dakota* is still in production. We have a show tonight. I can't leave my co-workers in a lurch by quitting before my contract is up."

"Better to quit now than wind up the next victim."

"The Sheriff needs everyone to stay until Chet's death is resolved."

"Are you telling me that the Sheriff considers you a suspect?"

"Of course not, he just needs everyone to remain in the area just in case he has to ask us more questions."

"Fine, you can stay, but I want daily updates regarding your well-being and itinerary," Lynn conceded.

"I'll call you every day," Merritt promised. She was grateful for her mother's concern. Most would run away the minute a colleague was murdered to protect their own safety. Still, Merritt didn't want to leave Custer State Park, not without seeing that Chet's case was solved.

"Otherwise I'll be on a flight to South Dakota, and won't leave until the Sheriff in charge of the investigation says that my daughter can come back to the Tar Heel state."

After ending the tumultuous conversation with her mom, Merritt returned to the Playhouse. The mood of the theatre cast and crew was somber, and tainted with paranoia. Suspicion filled the air, particularly hovering over Peter Wiseman and Mike Trump.

"I know the events of the past week have been tragic and trying, but I ask that for the sake of Chet's memory that we give our best performance possible," Alistair addressed the Custer Players before the show. "In addition, I ask that you please accommodate Sheriff Abrams officers to ensure a safe performance."

Sheriff Abrams had enlisted the help of some twenty Custer County deputies and Custer State Park rangers, including Josh.

"Josh, I didn't expect to see you here," Merritt smiled. It was nice to see a friendly face.

"I begged the Sheriff to allow me to help out so I can keep an eye on you. The thought of you working with a killer, makes me uneasy."

"I just hope this performance goes off without a hitch," Merritt responded, touched that Josh was so concerned about her.

"Everything will go fine," Josh reassured her. "I'll make sure of it."

"You better," Merritt smiled before returning to the Costume Shop.

The curtain opened just after eight. The house was packed to the brim. Many patrons had been lured to the theatre out of curiosity, hoping to witness the next leg in what was the state's biggest news story, the poisoning of Chet Rawlins.

Luckily for the cast and crew, the drama of *Dakota* was contained to the play itself. Everything ran smoothly and thankfully there were no unforeseen deaths. Merritt just hoped things would stay that way.

Chapter 24:

After a successful performance run on Friday and Saturday, the cast and crew were given Sunday, the 4th of July, off in honor of Independence Day. The holiday was a welcome relief for Merritt and her roommates under the duress of the investigation.

They spent their free time hanging out at Sylvan Lake. Then they headed over to Custer City for the fireworks celebration and free concert. Where they met up with Josh, Jim, Justin, Ethan, Tom, and Luke.

"How was Sylvan Lake?" Josh greeted Merritt, when they met up at the county fairgrounds.

"It was very relaxing," She smiled. "Did you have good day at the Visitor's Center?"

"I'd much rather have spent the day with you."

"We're together now for the big fireworks show; that's all that matters," Merritt clutched Josh's hand.

"So how was your day out?" Rebecca asked Jim about his day fishing with Ethan, Luke, Tom and Justin on Grace Coolidge Creek.

"We caught a lot of fish, only to be eaten alive by the mosquitoes."

The group of friends set up their fold out chairs and coolers not too far from the stage, and chatted for half an hour before the concert started up at eight o'clock. The musical act was a local bluegrass quartet called *Mountain Fiddle* who played a selection of patriotic themed music. By ten darkness fell, and a twenty-five minute fireworks spectacular lit up the sky.

As the grand finale wrapped up, Merritt and Josh gave each other a quick kiss.

"I had a fun time tonight," Merritt told Josh in the parking lot.

"Me too," Josh grinned. "If you're free tomorrow, maybe we can get together and go on a hike?"

"I'll call you first thing in the morning to solidify our plans," Merritt replied, as she and her roommates piled into her Civic and drove back to the Custer Playhouse.

When they pulled into the Playhouse dorm parking lot Mike Trump and Peter Wiseman were firing insults.

"We all know that you poisoned Chet, so for the sake of the Playhouse why don't you just fess up?" Mike shouted accusations at Peter.

"I'm not going to confess to a crime I didn't commit," Peter snapped back. "Especially not to save your skin."

"My skin?" Mike his expression dumbfounded. "Are you insinuating that I killed Chet?"

"I'm not insinuating anything," Peter retorted. "I'm flat out accusing you of spiking Chet's tea with poison hemlock."

"Me? You're the shaman who despised him. I'm just a guy trying to help keep the Playhouse afloat. What motivation would I have in killing our top actor? That's bad business," Mike countered.

"No it's good business for you, Mike, because you thought that by murdering Chet with a notorious toxin such as poison hemlock, the Sheriff would shut the theatre down as soon as the coroner's report was released. Too bad your plan didn't work out, and Sheriff Abrams isn't stupid enough to fall for your scheme."

"Even if I did want to shut the Playhouse down, I certainly wouldn't have to resort to murder to accomplish the task. Goodness knows there were enough structural issues in the first month of production for me to have shut down production long ago," Mike seethed. "Yet for some idiotic reason I believed that a sixty-plus year tradition deserved one last chance."

"You don't give a damn about our tradition. You only see one thing, Mike, and that is money. You saw that our early success hindered your chances of closing us down at the end of the season, so you poisoned Chet. Only, in light of Chet's death, the Playhouse is making more money than ever. That ticks you off Trump."

"The only person who is ticking me off is you," Mike replied. "On Tuesday I'm going to speak with Sheriff Abrams about incarcerating you in the Custer County Jail so this business about Chet's death can finally be put to rest."

"I invite you to try, but considering that I didn't kill Chet and all the evidence against me is circumstantial, your case against me will evaporate," Peter put his foot down as Mike walked away.

"Great," Ginny sighed as the girls got out of the car. "The latest in the Chet Rawlins murder debate."

"Just what we didn't need to hear," Emma rolled her eyes. "An argument between the two leading suspects."

"Unfortunately until Sheriff Abrams solves the case, this isn't going away," Rebecca stated as the girls entered Alpine. "I just hope there are no more *Dakota* casualties until the case is solved."

"Me too," Merritt replied.

After washing up, the Alpine girls went to bed just after midnight. Merritt quickly fell asleep, but her sleep was marred by a series of terrifying nightmares related to the murder investigation. In the last of these fitful dreams, Merritt was forced to drink poison hemlock unknowingly and died an agonizing death. She spent her final moments desperately trying to find her killer and force him to confess. Just as she was about to see the killer's face, Merritt woke up. She was drenched in sweat and panting for air.

"Thank God that was just a dream," Merritt let out a sigh of relief as she sat up. She glanced at her bedside clock. The time read three o'clock. The rest of her roommates were still dead asleep.

Restless and on edge after a terrifying dream, Merritt pulled on a pair of jeans and walked outside to use the restroom and get some fresh air.

It was a brisk fifty degrees outside. In the mountains, the temperature drops severely once the sun disappears into the horizon. The night was eerily still, yet Merritt had the inexplicable feeling as if she were being watched. As she entered the bathroom she frantically kicked in every stall, just to make sure she was alone.

"I must be going crazy," Merritt thought to herself as she washed her hands, trying to shake off her anxiety. A few minutes later, however her senses were put on high alert again.

Stepping outside, she heard the sound of footsteps nearby. She scrambled to turn on her flashlight to see whom, if anyone was there.

"Darn it, my flashlight battery just died on me," Merritt froze, trying her best to track the sound of the footsteps in the dark. As the steps edged closer, she could hear heavy breathing as well.

"Who's there?" Merritt shouted out, quickly realizing that if there was a predator on the loose alerting him to her presence probably wasn't the smartest move.

After calling out, the air went still again, yet Merritt still felt as if someone was lurking in the shadows. Afraid for her life, she decided to take a gamble and run back to Alpine and lock the door as quickly as possible. However, just as she neared the cabin, Merritt crashed directly into, a six-foot man dressed in black. She screamed in panic, certain she was destined to meet death at the hands of a mask stranger, before realizing whom it was.

"Merritt?" Ethan Daniels questioned, surprised by her presence.

"Ethan," Merritt let out a sigh of relief. "You scared me half to death."

"I'm sorry," Ethan apologized. "I didn't even know anyone else was outside."

"It's okay, you just took me by surprise," Merritt replied. "You look as if you're about to go on a hike wearing your jeans, flannel shirt and boots. What are you doing out here anyway?"

"I had to use the bathroom," Ethan explained. "It's cold out here, so I just pulled on the pair the clothes closest to my bunk to stay warm. What about you? Why are you up so late?"

"I had a nightmare and needed some fresh air," Merritt explained.

"What kind of nightmare?" Ethan questioned.

"I dreamt that a fellow Custer Player poisoned my food with poison hemlock, and I died just as I was about to face my murderer."

"I don't think you need to worry about being poisoned Merritt. Who would have it in for you?" Ethan tried unsuccessfully to reassure her.

"I hope not. I can't think of a more painful way to die than consuming poison hemlock."

"You won't get poisoned, I'm sure of it."

Merritt and Ethan said their "goodnights," and headed back to their respective cabins, where the rest of the Alpine girls were still sleeping soundly. After lying awake in her bed for about twenty-minutes, Merritt finally dozed off, and slept peacefully the rest of the night.

Chapter 25:

On Monday morning around seven, Merritt and her roommates were awakened by a shrill scream on the lawn.

"Help," the female voice yelled out.

Still in their pajamas, Merritt and her roommates rushed outside to see what was going on. They found Celeste, frantically knocking on doors, begging for assistance.

"What's wrong?"

"It's Peter," she gasped, barely able to make out a reply.

"What about Peter?" Merritt asked, sensing something was dreadfully wrong.

"He's, he's...he's dead," Celeste stammered. "Peter's dead. He's been murdered."

"Dead?" The Alpine roommates replied in shock. "Are you sure?"

"Yes," she replied in tears. "A few minutes ago I stopped by his cabin to drop off some paperwork. When he didn't answer his door, I let myself in. Once inside, I smelled a pungent odor that made my mouth swell up. It was as if something had been burning. I didn't think much of it at first, Peter's cabin has a fireplace and he's always burning medicinal herbs, especially sage. However when I saw him lying on the bed, not breathing, his body covered in pimple-like blisters...I immediately checked his pulse; his heart wasn't beating. It was then that I knew he was dead." As Celeste finished her statement, she completely broke down, overwhelmed that she'd uncovered the dead body of her friend.

"We need to call 911, ASAP," Merritt stated, trying her best to stay calm, in spite of the deadly circumstances. Although inside the news of another playhouse death weighed heavily on her.

"I'll make the call," Rebecca volunteered. "The rest of you wait here with Celeste."

"We heard screaming," the Ponderosa boys stated, as they stepped outside of their cabin. "What's going on?"

"Peter's dead," Celeste yelped. "He's been murdered."

"Murdered?" Tom asked, stunned by the news.

"Celeste found him dead in his cabin this morning," Merritt explained. "Rebecca just went to phone the authorities."

"Any idea how he died?" Luke asked, disturbed by the news of Peter's death and potential murder.

"All I know is that he has blisters all over his body and bloodshot eyes," Celeste winced at the thought of Peter's dead corpse.

"Did he have any allergies that might have caused an outbreak of hives and respiratory failure? Peanuts or fish, for instance?" Jim inquired in an attempt to diagnose what might have caused such a deadly reaction.

"Not that I know of," Celeste distant in her response.

"I just spoke with Sheriff Abrams," Rebecca stated, re-joining the conversation. "He's on his way. In the meantime he asks that we don't do anything to contaminate the scene of death, and wait for his arrival in front of the Mess Hall."

"Someone should alert Gully and Alistair to what's happened," Ethan suggested.

"Please tell Ali to get here as quickly as possible," Celeste requested. "He's in the Playhouse ticket office with Mrs. Seeley."

"I'll go fetch them," Emma volunteered. "If the Sheriff gets here before I return, let him know where I went."

"We will," the group replied before heading over to the Mess Hall.

Within ten minutes, Sheriff Abrams and his team of deputies arrived on the scene. They started off their investigation by examining Peter's body to verify that he was in fact, dead.

"He's dead all right," Sheriff Abrams confirmed as he and his men entered the cabin to find Peter's corpse lying motionless on his bed, heavily blistered, and his mouth wide open as if his body had gasped for air in his final moments of life. "Judging from the smell in here, coupled with the blisters on Wiseman's body, I'm fairly certain that the deceased died from some sort of smoke inhalation; most likely due to burning poison ivy leaves."

"If that's the case we need to get out of here ASAP," Deputy Hill replied. "The plant's toxic urushiol sap might still be in the air, and most likely skill on Peter's skin."

"I agree with Deputy Hill. Inhalation of smoke burned from poison ivy can cause lungs and air passages to blister. No one is allowed in here without a mask and gloves," Sheriff Abrams stated, ushering his group of officers out of the cramped cabin. "In the meantime, Carl and Nathan I want you to set up crime tape and barriers around the inner, outer and exterior perimeters. Dave and Sid, go suit up, and start the interior investigation. Make note of any potential clues, in and around Peter's cabin. Log any evidence and photograph every part of the scene of the crime, but don't move anything until after the Medical Examiner arrives. Understood?"

"Hill, you stay here, and keep an eye on the crime scene while I question the Custer Players," Sheriff Abrams directed before heading over to the Mess Hall where a number of the cast and crew were gathered, anxiously awaiting news on Peter's death.

"Sheriff Abrams, what's going on?" Gully and Alistair questioned the Custer County lawman, the minute he walked through the door.

"Mr. Wiseman is dead. That's all I can tell you until the Medical Examiner arrives in roughly an hour," the Sheriff replied. "In the meantime, I'd like to question members of your cast and crew about the incident."

Sheriff Abrams individually questioned select members of the cast and crew regarding Peter's murder in the Mess Hall kitchen. He started off by speaking with chief witness Celeste, who had been the first person to report Peter's death.

"Mrs. Fitzgerald, I understand that you're extremely upset by Peter's death," Sheriff Abrams prefaced. "However, considering you were the first known person at the scene of death, I need you to assist me in answering a few questions."

"I'll do anything, if it means bringing Peter's killer to justice," Celeste's face red from crying.

"So it's your belief that Peter was murdered?" Abrams asked.

"Of course he was murdered," Celeste stated with conviction. "You saw his body. He was poisoned just like Chet. How else do you explain a perfectly healthy man suddenly dying in his sleep, with blisters all over his body?"

"I can't answer that question until I have the Medical Examiner's report. I'll admit that Peter's death is suspicious, but there's still a possibility that he died of natural causes," the Sheriff replied, still trying to read Celeste's emotions. Even though he believed she was innocent of wrongdoing, she had the means and possible motive to kill both men and couldn't be ruled out as a suspect.

"There is nothing natural about the way Peter died," Celeste held fast. "Someone poisoned Chet and now they've murdered Peter."

"Who would have the motive to commit the crimes?" Sheriff Abrams followed up.

"Chet had lots of enemies, but Peter? I can't think of anyone who would do this to him, except for..." Celeste's voice trailed off.

"Except for whom Mrs. Fitzgerald?" Abrams pressed.

"Mike Trump. Peter was convinced that Mike killed Chet and was trying to sabotage the Custer Playhouse, in order to receive a lucrative concessionaire payoff if the Playhouse were forced to vacate the property. "

"What about your husband, Mr. Fitzgerald. How did he feel about both Chet and Peter?" The Sheriff asked, realizing that Celeste's tumultuous history with Rawlins and close friendship with Wiseman might be fuel enough for jealousy killings.

"Sure Ali was annoyed with Chet from time to time, but he valued his talent and friendship. As for Peter, he served as Alistair's best man at our wedding. The two were great friends. He is just as devastated by the news of his death as I am."

"So you don't believe your husband to have been jealous of your relationships with both Peter and Chet?"

"Absolutely not!" Celeste averred. "Alistair knows how much I love him. Not to mention that he is far too busy managing a playhouse to be concerned with something as trivial jealousy over my friendships with Chet and Peter."

"When is the last time that you saw Peter alive?"

"Last night, around six. He stopped by to wish us a 'Happy 4th' and to lend us his DVD of *1776*."

"How long did he stay at your cabin?"

"Ten minutes," Celeste replied.

"Did he say where he was heading?"

"No, only that he had some errands to run."

"How was Peter feeling at that time?" Sheriff Abrams inquired.

"He didn't complain about feeling ill," Celeste recalled.

"Did he mention that he may have possibly inhaled smoke from burned poison ivy?"

"I can guarantee you that Peter never burned, digested, or touched poison ivy. At his park lectures, he always warned park visitors to avoid the toxic plant. He was well aware that burning poison ivy can cause blistering of the lungs," Celeste replied, suddenly realizing where this was going. "Did Peter die from poison ivy inhalation?"

"I don't know anything for sure right now Mrs. Fitzgerald," Sheriff Abrams replied. "It's just a working scenario that I'm sharing with you because if Peter did die from poison ivy inhalation, there's a good chance that you might have contracted the plant's toxin urushiol when you checked his pulse. I think it's important that you get checked out by our medic after our interview. Poison ivy isn't something to take lightly."

"If your theory is right Sheriff Abrams and Peter did die of inhaling smoke from a burning pile of poison ivy, then there is no doubt that he was murdered."

"Celeste, do you know what time Peter usually went to bed?"

"It depended on his schedule."

"Do you know if Peter slept with the bedside window, open or closed?"

"Yes, he slept with the window open. These cabins get stuffy."

"Was Peter a sound sleeper?"

"I don't really know," Celeste admitted. "I will say that the one time we went camping together. There was a huge thunderstorm and he was the only one in the tent that didn't wake up."

"Do you think he would wake up if someone entered the cabin after he fell asleep?"

"I'm not sure."

"Before I let you go Mrs. Fitzgerald, I need to know where you were, between the hours of six-fifteen last night to the time that you found Peter's body this morning."

"As I mentioned earlier, I spent the night with Alistair in our cabin. After watching a few movies, we went to bed around midnight," Celeste replied. "This morning we woke up early and went to meet Beth Seeley for an early morning business breakfast in the theatre ticket office just after six."

"What was the purpose of the meeting?"

"We were going over the weekend's ticket sales and reviewing the payroll records. It was then I noticed that Peter hadn't picked up his last pay check, so decided to drop it off by his cabin before I headed out to do some errands in Rapid City."

"What happened when you got to the cabin?"

"I knocked several times on his door to no avail," Celeste explained. When he didn't answer, I figured he was either still asleep, or had already left for his morning walk down to Center Lake. His door was open so I let myself in, so I could drop off his check on his desk. Upon entering the cabin I instantly I smelled a nasty odor of burnt smoke. I didn't think too much of it at first. Peter was known to burn a lot of herbs and incense. It wasn't until I saw Peter's lifeless body that I knew he was dead." Celeste, unable to hold her composure, burst into tears.

"I think that's all the information I need from you right now, Mrs. Fitzgerald," Abrams stated. "Why don't you have your husband take you to the doctor to ensure that you didn't contract poison ivy," Sheriff Abrams suggested. "Just make sure to tell Alistair that I'd like to get his statement as soon as possible, and to contact my office at his earliest convenience."

After speaking with Celeste, Sheriff Abrams called Merritt to the kitchen to question her about Peter's death.

"When did you learn of Mr. Wiseman's death?"

"This morning," Merritt replied. "Just after seven, my roommates and I were awakened to a loud set of screams outside our cabin. We rushed to see what was wrong, and found Celeste, obviously distressed, begging for help. It was then that she told us that she had found Peter dead in his cabin a few minutes earlier. Rebecca Lane, then phoned 911, and Emma Seeley went to notify Alistair, Gully and her mom Beth Seeley about what had happened. We then waited in Mess Hall for your arrival."

"So you and your roommates didn't go inspect Peter's body, to confirm Mrs. Fitzgerald's statement that he was dead?"

"No, Celeste was virulent in her claims that Peter had died. She said that she checked his pulse and to made sure he wasn't breathing. We figured it would be better to stay away from the crime scene in order to avoid contamination."

"It sounds as if you believe Peter's death was a murder."

"I'm not fool enough to assume anything, particularly his cause of death," Merritt paused. "That being said, given the circumstances of Chet's untimely demise by poison hemlock, I find it too coincidental that Peter would simply die of natural causes. If Peter was murdered, then it's my guess that whoever killed Chet, probably killed Peter as well."

"That's a logical conclusion Miss. Andrews," the Sheriff replied. "Now assuming that it's the right conclusion, who do you believe committed the crimes?"

"Whoever it was certainly had a vendetta against both Peter and Chet, which narrows down the list of potential suspects."

"How so?" Abrams questioned, intrigued by Merritt's theory.

"Considering that most people disliked Chet, but adored Peter, common sense tells me that your probable suspect is Mike Trump." Merritt offered her theory begrudgingly. She knew that Mike was the obvious suspect, given the monetary gain he'd receive, if the playhouse failed. He despised Chet and Peter and argued with both men shortly before they died. In spite of the mounting circumstantial evidence weighing against Mike, Merritt's gut instinct told her that he was innocent of murders.

"You seem hesitant in your assumption."

"My gut feeling is that Mike Trump is innocent of murder. However I can't ignore the fact that he had means and motive to kill both men," Merritt explained. "I saw Mike fighting with Peter last night when I got home from the fireworks at the Custer City fairgrounds."

"What time was this?"

"Around eleven o'clock."

"And you're sure that it was Mike fighting with Peter?"

"I'm positive," Merritt confirmed.

"What were they arguing about?" Abrams inquired.

"They were throwing around accusations. Mike demanded that Peter turn himself in for murdering Chet. Peter shot back and said that he was innocent of the crime and he wouldn't be a scapegoat for Mike's have murdered Chet. They argued for about five minutes before going their separate ways."

"Did anything indicate in the argument indicate to you that Mike might consider murdering Peter?"

"No, it just sounded like a basic argument," Merritt recalled. "I didn't think much of it until now."

"Can you give me a timeline of your itinerary after witnessing the argument until this morning when you found out that Peter was dead?"

"My roommates and I were exhausted after the Independence Day activities, so we went straight to bed," Merritt replied. "Unfortunately I had a fitful sleep. I woke up from a nightmare around three o'clock. I decided to get up for a few minutes and go outside to use the bathroom."

"Did you notice anything suspicious, or see anyone else when you were outside?"

"I saw Ethan Daniels," Merritt answered. "He had just used the bathroom and was heading back to his cabin the same time as I was. Other than that I didn't see anything suspicious"

"Did you notice any smoke coming from Peter Wiseman's cabin?"

"No, I did not," Merritt, replied

"Were your roommates in the cabin when you woke up?"

"Yes, Ginny, Rebecca and Emma were in their beds sleeping soundly."

"What was your personal opinion of Peter Wiseman?" Sheriff Abrams asked, in an effort to gage whether or not Merritt might have had motives against the late actor.

"He was a great guy," she replied honestly.

"How familiar are you with Poison Ivy?" Abrams inquired.

"Familiar enough to avoid it at all costs," Merritt, stated, unsure what poison ivy had to do with Peter's sudden death.

"Are you aware of poison ivy's toxic nature if the plant is burned?"

"I had no clue," Merritt cringed. "It sounds like a horrible way to die."

"Inhalation of poison ivy smoke is excruciating," Abrams replied. "And unfortunately it's a working theory my department has on what caused Peter's death. That being said, do you have ideas on whom, if anyone might be responsible for Peter's death by poison ivy inhalation?"

"Actually, I did see a crewmember purchasing some poison ivy medication at the Dakota Mart, in Custer City, a few days ago..." Merritt's voice trailed off.

"A name would be helpful, Miss Andrews," The Sheriff pressed.

"It was Mike Trump," she sighed. "He was ahead of me in line. I just happened to notice the clerk scanning the anti-itch and poison ivy creams, as I set my food on the counter."

"Did Mr. Trump explain why he was purchasing the medication?"

"No. I didn't talk to him," Merritt answered. "He was on his phone the entire time, talking to someone about a business deal."

"Your assistance has been most helpful Miss Andrews," Sheriff Abrams stated as he completed the interview. "I'll let you know if I have any further questions."

Chapter 26:

The Rapid City Medical Examiner, Doctor George Adams, arrived on the scene just before nine o'clock.

"So what's the verdict, George? How did Mr. Wiseman die?" Sheriff Adams asked the M.E.

"My first impression is that the victim died from inhaling smoke from a burned poison ivy plant," the Coroner answered. "Judging from the blisters visible on his skin, and on his mouth and throat, I'm guessing that he inhaled a large concentration of the plant's toxic sap urushiol in a very short amount of time. This caused him to suffocate to death."

"When do you think the victim inhaled the toxin?" Sheriff Abrams followed up.

"Mr. Wiseman inhaled the urushiol last night, possibly for several hours while he slept."

"How?" Sheriff Abrams inquired. "The fireplace was clean and from the looks of it, the victim slept with his window open."

"I noticed a large pile of burnt poison ivy leaves on the ground right underneath the victim's bedroom window," Doctor Adams stated. "One can assume that the poison ivy was burned in that spot to ensure that the toxic smoke would blow into the cabin through the bedside window. As more smoke filled the cabin, the more toxic urushiol saturated the air supply. Inhaling this much urushiol in such a short period of time caused the victim's airways to constrict along with blistering of the skin, mouth, throat, esophagus and lungs. He either died from suffocation, or the blisters on his lungs burst, forcing him to drown in his own bodily liquids," Dr. Adams explained.

"It seems hard to imagine the body sleeping through that much trauma?" Sheriff Abrams questioned. "Wouldn't the smell of smoke wake him up?"

"I saw a bottle of sleeping pills right by the victim's bed. Depending on how strong the dosage, the victim may have been in too deep a sleep to wake up."

"In your professional opinion, do you think that there's any way the victim's death was accidental?" Abrams.

"Absolutely not," Dr. Adams accessed. "In order for the poison ivy to do this much damage so quickly, more and more leaves would have to have been added to the fire after it initially started. Someone had to be monitoring the smoke for a portion of the time Peter was breathing it in. Your men and I noticed a set of recent footprints in the mud; indicating that a man, wearing size ten boots was present in the area late last night. Not to mention the fact that Deputy Hill stated that he found a set of protective gloves a few feet from where the poison ivy was burned."

"Another homicide at the Custer Playhouse," Sheriff Abrams sighed. "Until Peter's death, he was my lead suspect in Chet's murder. If only I'd listened to him when avowed his innocence, I could have prevented his murder."

"Don't blame yourself. The entire Black Hills thought Peter might have been involved in Chet's death. I guess the question is now, who had motive and means to kill both men?"

"Sheriff," Deputy Hill rushed over to his superior. "We were searching the extended perimeter, and found this just behind the victim's cabin. It was found adjacent to a pair of latex gloves and goggles." Hill held up a clear Ziploc bag containing a wallet. "It's Mike Trump's sir."

"I want the gloves and goggles sent to the lab for DNA and fingerprint testing," the Sheriff directed. "Deputy Hill, get started on acquiring a search warrant for Mike Trump's cabin, along with the rest of the Playhouse facilities."

"Yes sir," Hill replied.

"In the meantime, I'm going to have a conversation with Mr. Trump about where he was last night," Abrams replied, sensing he had found the Playhouse murderer.

Sheriff Abrams grabbed the plastic bag containing Mike's wallet, and walked across the dorm quad to Mike Trump's single occupancy cabin, McGovern. After a dozen knocks, the state's theatre czar belligerently answered his front door.

"Sheriff Abrams, I was wondering when I'd have the displeasure of speaking with you," Mike stated, ushering the lawman inside. "I know you're short on time, so let's make this simple. I didn't kill Peter. I went to bed last night around midnight and didn't wake up until Gully Gordon knocked on my door to alert me to Mr. Wiseman's sudden death around 7:30. Now that you've gotten you're information I'll politely ask that you leave my cabin."

"It's not going to be that easy to get rid of me Mr. Trump," Sheriff Abrams stated, not intimidated by Mike's hostile manner. "You see I have murder to investigate, a murder I believe that you're involved with."

"I'm innocent. That's all you need to know," Mike replied curtly.

"I suggest that you answer my questions here, otherwise you'll be forced to answer them down at the station." Abrams threatened. "Now I heard you had an argument with Peter last night. I'd like you to tell me what the feud was about?"

"I told Peter he needed to confess to killing Chet, so that the rest of us could get on with our lives," Mike replied. "He accused me of being the guilty of murder, which I flatly denied and we parted ways."

"Where did this argument occur?"

"On the quad."

"So you didn't argue in the vicinity of Peter's cabin?"

"Nope," Mike replied with conviction "Look, the fact that we fought doesn't mean that I killed him."

"So you claim," The Sheriff replied, convinced that Mike was the guilty party. "Mr. Trump, how much do you know about poison ivy?"

"Is this a botany test Sheriff or investigation?" Mike asked sarcastically.

"It's highly a relevant question, so I suggest you answer it."

"Leaves of three, let it be," Mike replied. "Leaves, berries and vine toxic to the touch and blister the lungs to a silent hush. That's what I know about poison ivy."

"So you do know that when the plant is burned it releases a toxin, which can damage the lungs, and even cause death."

"Of course," Mike replied. "My granddad was a farmer, he always made sure never to burn poison ivy as a removal method. He bought a goat instead."

"Have you accidentally come into contact with the plant, recently?" The Sheriff followed up.

"No," Mike lied.

"Are you sure about that, because my sources tell me that you were purchasing a lot of anti-itch cream and poison ivy medicine in Custer City a few days ago?"

"Come to think about it, yes, I did have a poison ivy infection. I walked into a patch of it around Center Lake. It cleared up once I bought the medicine."

"How long did you have the rash then?"

"A few days," Mike replied, inadvertently scratching his right ankle.

"That's odd as a poison ivy skin infection usually persists for weeks, even with medication."

"What can I say, the medicine worked wonders?" Mike shrugged the Sheriff's comment off.

"My bet is that you are still battling the infection. You don't want me to know about it, because you received the rash while gathering poison ivy leaves in the woods. You proceeded to burn those leaves under Peter Wiseman's window last night and to ensure that he died a gruesome death."

"That's outrageous! What motive would I have?"

"The same motive you had for killing Chet; you want the Custer Playhouse shut down so you can profit from a lucrative concessionaire deal."

"You're crazy Sheriff! I don't have to resort to murder to shut this place down. And if I had killed Chet, why would I murder the best scapegoat in town for his death?"

"That is unless Peter uncovered some new information to implicate you and you murdered him to shut him up."

"I didn't murder Chet and I certainly didn't kill Peter," Mike countered.

"The jury's still out on that Mr. Trump. For now don't you tell me where you were last night, between your argument with Peter and when his body was found around seven this morning?"

"I was asleep in my cabin the entire time."

"Mr. Trump when is the last time that you used your wallet?"

"My wallet? What does my wallet have to do with anything?" Mike asked, confused by the question.

"Answer the question Mr. Trump," Sheriff Abrams replied, losing patience with Mike's attitude.

"I had it last night around eight when I went out to dinner at the Legion Lodge, why?"

"We found your wallet while investigating the crime scene," Sheriff Abrams replied bluntly. "Mind telling me how it got there?"

"I have no clue," Mike began searching the pockets of the pants he had on the day before to ensure that his wallet was actually missing. The empty pockets confirmed his fear: his wallet was gone. "Someone must have stolen my wallet and planted it near the crime scene, in an effort to frame me."

"Do you know what I think? I think you that you inadvertently dropped your wallet while you were suffocating Mr. Wiseman to death by burning toxic poison ivy."

"If I was burning poison ivy, I'd be in the hospital or dead by now," Trump argued.

"Not if you were using a gas mask," the Sheriff dismissed.

"I refuse to be railroaded," Trump fired back.

"I am just trying to get some information Mr. Trump."

"No, Sheriff, you're accusing me of a crime that I didn't commit. I'm not saying another word until my lawyer is present."

"You can wait for him at the station. Mike Trump you now are under arrest on suspicion of the murders of Chet Rawlins and Peter Wiseman. You have a right to remain silent. Anything you say can and will be used against you in a court of law. You have the right to speak to an attorney. If you cannot afford an attorney, one will be appointed to you. Do you understand these rights as they have been read to you?"

"Finding my wallet at the scene of the crime doesn't mean that I'm guilty," Mike protested.

"If you're innocent your name will be cleared. In the meantime I'd feel a lot better if you were placed in temporary custody until an arraignment can occur."

"You're going to get fired for this witch hunt against me," Mike warned.

"My job is secure," Abrams rebuffed. "Right now you and I are going to the station, by force if necessary."

"Go ahead and cuff me," Trump sneered. "According to you I'm a dangerous serial killing sociopath."

"Sheriff what's going on?" Gully asked, as he saw Abrams walking Trump across the theatre quad in handcuffs.

"I can't comment on that right now Mr. Gordon. Deputy Hill will finish the rest of the questioning and on-site investigation today. Consult with him for further information."

"I'm being falsely accused of murder Gordon," Mike shouted out. "Beware while I rot in jail, the murderer is on the loose."

By the time Mike in the Sheriff's patrol car, a majority of the cast and crew had migrated to lawn to find out what was going on.

"They just arrested Mike?" Rebecca exclaimed.

"It doesn't surprise me," Ginny thought. "He's the only logical suspect."

"I hope they didn't jump the gun on arresting him," Merritt sighed, still not convinced that Trump was the killer.

"You don't honestly think that Mike is innocent? We saw him arguing with Peter last night and we saw him purchasing poison ivy medication at the Dakota Mart," Emma contended.

"I don't care for Trump's tactics, but I don't like the idea of an innocent man, no matter how despicable, sitting in a jail cell for something they didn't do. What evidence do they have against him?"

"They found his wallet at the crime scene," Ethan added in.

"Are you sure?" Merritt replied, unaware that information had been released.

"I overheard Deputy Hill mentioning it to one of the fellow officers." "According to the Medical Examiner, Peter died of poison ivy inhalation. I didn't even know that the plant's toxin was poisonous if inhaled," Ginny stated.

"It's a horrible way to die," Ethan followed. "Then again I've never had to worry too much about it. I'm one of those lucky folks who's not allergic to the plant's toxin urushiol."

"Not allergic to poison ivy?" the group questioned. "How can you NOT be allergic to poison ivy?"

"Apparently fifteen to thirty percent of the population is immune to the plant's toxic allergen."

"I wish that I was immune to poison ivy," Rebecca envious. "It's a hellish infection. I despise Mike for killing Peter that way."

After talking with her friends about the latest Custer Playhouse death, Merritt phoned Josh. She was eager to meet up for their date, since the thought of hanging around the crime scene the rest of the day made her uncomfortable.

"I was just about to call you about meeting up for the day," Josh's upbeat tone indicated that he was unaware of Peter's death.

"Something terrible has happened. Peter Wiseman was murdered last night."

"Murdered?" Josh was startled by the news. "Do you know how he was killed?"

"Poison ivy inhalation," Merritt stammered. "Sheriff Abrams has arrested Mike Trump for the murders of both Peter and Chet."

"I know that Mike Trump is an antagonistic jerk, but a murderer?" Josh questioned. "I guess the concessionaire contract offered him was too enticing to pass up, so much so that Mike murdered Peter and Chet in the hope of nabbing it."

"Politicians are prone to deception, but murder seems an extreme, even for a jerk like Mike," Merritt said. "I'm probably shooting a dead horse, but would you be willing to assist me in doing case research? If my instincts are correct, and Mike is innocent, then most likely the murderer either had a personal vendetta against both men, or killed Peter because he had information to put the killer behind bars."

"I'll be glad to help."

"Can you meet me in front of the Visitor's Center in twenty-minutes?"

"I'll be there."

Chapter 27:

Josh waited for Merritt on the steps of the Peter Norbeck Visitor Center when she arrived just before eleven. They started off their investigation, by first speaking with Ranger Sinclair, who had known both Chet and Peter for more than twenty-five years.

"Howdy guys," Suzy greeted the pair as they entered Visitor Center. "I didn't expect to see you in today, Josh. Isn't it your day off?"

"It is, but something has come up," Josh replied. "Something both Merritt and I were hoping you might be able to help us with."

"Does that something have to do with Peter Wiseman's death?" Suzy sighed.

"You heard the tragic news," Merritt responded.

"Sheriff Abrams called Superintendent Harden to alert the Park Service about the death, and to ask for ranger assistance in securing the crime scene from Center Lake campers and recreational users," Ranger Sinclair replied, upset by the news. "I only know details of the investigation because Sheriff Abrams called me fifteen-minutes ago to ask me a few questions about the case, since I was good friends with Peter. He also informed me that he had arrested Mike Trump on suspicion of murdering both Chet and Peter," Suzy explained. "It's Mike's nature to be unscrupulous and money hungry, but I never thought he'd stoop to murder, just to nab a concessionaire deal. I guess greed sent him over the edge."

"I'm not convinced that Mike Trump is guilty of killing both Chet and Peter. There were no guarantees that murdering both men would result in the closure of the playhouse and the concessionaire deal. Mike could have closed us down after several botched rehearsals, and chose not to."

"Sheriff Abrams told me that he was confident that Mike Trump is culpable of double homicide. He claimed that his office had acquired sufficient evidence to charge Mike with murder."

"I won't deny that there is ample circumstantial evidence tying Mike to the murders," Merritt conceded. "That being said, my intuition tells me that Mike is innocent and the killer is still stalking the playhouse grounds."

"You can't deny instinct," Ranger Sinclair agreed. "Although you're going to need hard evidence to get Mike out of the mess he's in."

"I know I could be wrong," Merritt admitted. "I don't even really like Mike Trump, but wouldn't wish a false conviction on my worst enemy."

"I understand," Suzy smiled. "Just tell me what I can do to help."

"I was hoping to ask you a few questions about Peter and Chet."

"Come into the office and we'll discuss the case there," Suzy acquiesced, as the group headed into a nearby administrative office. "So what did you want to know?"

"Any insights into Chet and Peter's history would be helpful," Merritt hoped to uncover a definite connection between the murders.

"It was long and complicated," Suzy sighed. "When I first met the pair back in the late 1980s, they were hell-raising that lived life fast and hard. They spent most of their free time guzzling down whiskey and tequila at local bars and driving recklessly on park roads. I can't tell you how many times I ticketed Peter for speeding and driving under the influence."

"Did he lose his license?" Merritt asked.

"Unfortunately, Peter and Chet never lost their licenses, in spite of their madcap irresponsible driving habits. People didn't take drunk driving as seriously then as they do today. Add in the fact both men were friends with local law enforcement, it was easier to give them a ride home and ignore the offense. Luckily today we enforce the laws regarding speeding and driving under the influence with much more scrutiny than we did twenty years ago."

"Hairpin turns, wildlife, alcohol and speeding are certainly a deadly combination in Custer State Park," Josh agreed.

"My fellow costumer, Dot Darlington mentioned that Chet and Peter had a falling out in the early 1990s? She said the origin of their feud was alcohol related, is this true?" Merritt asked Suzy.

"It one was one of the factors, yes," Ranger Sinclair replied. "However the feud mostly started after they were in a car accident together."

"What happened?"

"In the summer of 1991, Peter, Chet and Celeste were involved in a traumatic accident in the Park, on the Needles Highway around Hole in the Wall."

"The picnic area and geologic site?" Merritt asked.

"Correct," Suzy confirmed. "As you know that entire Needles Highway is very curvy and it's hard to see around every corner, especially at night. On that particular night, Celeste, Chet and Peter had been driving back to the Playhouse from a party at Sylvan Lake. The driving conditions were abysmal. It was pitch black with a heavy drizzling, leaving the roads slick and treacherous. As they made their way around the curve at Hole in the Wall, a bison ran into the road. Celeste, who was driving the car veered into the other lane, unaware of the oncoming traffic coming around the curve simultaneously. She had a head on collision with the other car."

"That's horrible," Merritt exclaimed. "Was anyone hurt?"

"Sadly, the young couple driving the other vehicle was killed instantly," Suzy lamented. "Peter, Celeste and Chet survived, but barely. After that tragedy Chet and Peter's friendship quickly deteriorated."

"Was alcohol involved?" Merritt inquired.

"Chet and Peter had both been drinking, but Celeste was sober," Suzy attested. "It was tragic accident."

"What a horrible ordeal," Merritt sympathized.

"Even though Celeste was not at fault, she did not handle the aftermath of the accident well. She felt guilt for the victims' deaths."

"I would feel the same way."

"During the course of their relationship, Chet had been verbally abusive towards Celeste. His abuse only escalated after the accident. Peter, cared deeply for Celeste like a sister, grew weary of Chet's behavior. He stood up for Celeste, and that made Chet angry. Chet hated being told how to act, and was livid when Celeste broke off their engagement," Suzy explained. "Peter endured a long stint in rehabilitation after the accident. It was then he gave up drinking and gets his life together. He's been sober ever since. Chet temporarily sobered up a few years later after he was fired from a Broadway production when he showed up drunk. Chet's alcoholism ruined his chance of a big career. It made him bitter. He allowed that inward bitterness to turn into raging resentment against Peter."

"Do you think Celeste might have resented Chet or Peter enough to kill them?" Merritt asked. The idea of Celeste as a killer seemed farfetched, but given her history with both men and the fact she'd been present when Chet was poisoned and found Peter's body, it was a theory she couldn't over look.

"Celeste doesn't have a murderous bone in her body," Suzy stated with certainty. "Although she hated Chet for what he put her through, a part of her will always love him. As for Peter, he was her best friend and the only person who was there for her after the accident. I know she's devastated by Peter's death."

"How did Alistair feel regarding his wife's close ties to Chet and Peter?"

"Alistair knows that Celeste loves him, and certainly wouldn't murder Chet and Peter in a jealous rage. If that were the case he would have done the bloody deed years ago."

"If Mike Trump is innocent, then it seems logical that whoever committed the crimes either had a personal vendetta against both of the deceased, or they had motives against Chet and only killed Peter because he had information that could implicate the killer."

"That's a sound conclusion," Ranger Sinclair agreed.

"Can you think of anyone in particular who might have motive against both men?" Merritt asked.

"I can think of a lot of people who had it in for Chet, but I don't know anyone who would have it in for Peter too," Suzy thought.

"I know that you were investigating the case regarding Chet's tires being slashed, a few days before he died. Did you ever garner any leads as to who was behind it?" Merritt inquired.

"I never made any inroads into the investigation. There were no witnesses. Peter and Mike both had alibis, putting them away from the crime scene."

"Do think there's a possibility that whoever is the murderer slashed the tires as a pre-emptive warning to Chet?" Merritt followed up.

"That's what I assumed when Chet died," Suzy agreed. "However Mike's alibi was airtight the night of the incident. So if he is guilty, it's my assumption that either Mike hired someone to slash Chet's tires to ensure that he wouldn't be implicated, or it was an unrelated incident."

"One more question before I go. Do you happen to remember the last names of the young couple killed in the accident?"

"Yates, I believe," Suzy replied.

"I appreciate your help Suzy," Merritt thanked the Ranger. "Hopefully with a little more digging, I'll be able to lay this hunch of mine to rest."

"Let me know if I can be of any additional assistance," Ranger Sinclair smiled as Josh and Merritt exited the Visitor Center.

"So Detective Andrews, what's the verdict? Do you still attest to Mike's innocence?"

"There is reasonable doubt regarding Mike's involvement," Merritt admitted. "So I say that we keep digging."

"The question is where does the sleuth trail lead us next?"

"Let's go over to the Creekside Lodge? We can search the Internet for any clues, especially regarding the car accident Celeste, Peter and Chet were involved in back in 1991."

"You don't think that someone related to the family is behind the murders?" Josh asked, surprised by Merritt's hunch.

"I don't think so," Merritt replied. "However, I do want to learn more about the impetus of Chet and Peter's feud."

"The Creekside Lodge it is then," Josh replied, leading the couple across the street to the nearby lodge.

Merritt plugged in her Mac laptop and connected to the wireless Internet. She started off her search by keying in "Chet Rawlins, Peter Wiseman accident 1991." The search inquiry brought up several website results, which linked to articles on the 1991 accident.

"Here is an archived articled on the accident from the Custer County Chronicle," Merritt stated as she opened the article link, to find a half page write-up on the tragic accident.

Friday July 12, 1991, Custer County: Two are dead and three are injured after a deadly collision on Highway 87 around the Hole in the Wall picnic area on Wednesday July the 10th at midnight. The two-car crash occurred on a notorious hairpin curve on the Needles Highway, as driver, Celeste Wood veered into the other lane after nearly hitting a bison, not realizing there was any oncoming traffic. Mr. and Mrs. William Yates of Rapid City were killed instantly. Celeste Wood, along with passengers, popular local actors Chet Rawlins and Peter Wiseman were rushed to the hospital. The Custer County Sheriff confirmed that alcohol wasn't involved and has ruled this case a no-fault accident. "The conditions for driving that night were abhorrent," Sheriff McKenzie stated in a press release. "Rain, fog, slick roads, wildlife and blind curves are a deadly mix. My prayers go out to the victims and their families.

Relatives of the deceased, told law enforcement that the Yates' were vacationing in the area, while family members babysat their five-year old son. "We are deeply saddened by the loss of our son and daughter-in-law. He was a wonderful person who loved his family dearly. I will miss him, but I am more concerned about the son he left behind, who will grow up without a father and a mother," Greg Yates told our paper. As for the injured, they are listed in stable condition at an area hospital. We will update this story as more details come to light...

"What a tragic accident," Josh sighed. "It's a miracle that Celeste, Chet and Peter even survived."

"The Yates' son would be twenty-four now," Merritt replied. "I wonder if he still lives in the area."

"We can try to find out," Josh replied. "I'll go grab a phonebook from the receptionist desk. If nothing else we can start phoning Yates' in the area."

"Good idea," Merritt agreed. "In the meantime, I'm going to keep surfing the web to see if I can find out any more about Mr. and Mrs. Yates' son, and the accident itself."

While Josh searched for a copy of a regional phone book, Merritt clicked on a link to an archived webpage with Mrs. Yates' obituary. As the page loaded, she was shocked by what she saw.

"That's Ethan's mom!" Merritt exclaimed, instantly recognizing the women in the black and white still. Could it be that Ethan was the surviving son of Mr. and Mrs. Yates? If so, why is his surname Daniels? Merritt decided to read the obituary in order to acquire more information.

Carla Daniels Yates, 30, died along with her husband William Yates in a tragic car accident on the Needles Highway in Custer State Park on July 10, 1991. Carla was born on June 21st 1963, in Rapid City to Frank and Amy Johnson. She met her husband, William, during their tenure at Rapid City High School. After tying the knot, they moved to Vermillion, where they both attended the University of South Dakota. Carla graduated with an honors degree in Business. After graduation, the couple moved back to Rapid City where they had a son, William Ethan Yates. While William Sr. worked as an area accountant, Carla dedicated her time to being a mom and volunteering in the community. She was known in life for her sweet personality, and positive attitude.

She is survived by: her son, William "Ethan" Yates, sister, Katherine J. Daniels and brother-in-law Tommy Daniels, Mother, Amy Johnson, and Father-in-law and Mother-in-law, Greg and Sandy Yates.

The funerals of Mrs. Yates will be held along with her husband's at the Good Will Church of Christ in Rapid City on Thursday July 18th at noon.

"Ethan *is* the son of the couple killed in the accident," Merritt realized. "He must have been adopted by his aunt and uncle, and that's why he goes by the last name Daniels instead of Yates!"

"I found a phone book."

"I just found out that Ethan Daniels is the son of the Carla and William Yates," Merritt exclaimed. "The same couple that died in the collision with Celeste, Chet and Peter."

"The same Ethan who hung out with us at the fireworks celebration?" Josh questioned, surprised by the news.

"One in the same," Merritt assented.

"Did Ethan ever mention anything about the accident to you?"

"Never. He just said his parents died when he was young and that his aunt and uncle adopted him," Merritt replied. "And I'm pretty sure that Celeste, Chet and Peter had no clue about Ethan's identity."

"Why would they recognize him, unless Ethan revealed his identity? He was only five when the accident occurred and has a different last name than his biological parents." Josh analyzed.

"Ethan didn't want anyone to know his identity. That was the point," Merritt finally putting the pieces of Chet and Peter's murder together. "Ethan grew up without his parents because of that accident. My guess is that he wanted to infiltrate the Playhouse, acting like an unassuming crewmember, when in fact his motives were to seek revenge on those who caused his parents death."

"If that's the case, then why didn't he kill Celeste first? She was driving the car."

"I think that he tried to kill Celeste, when the cast and crew hiked Harney Peak on June 5th. Celeste nearly fell off the cliff. At first she claimed that she had been pushed, but when pressed about the issue she said she might have slipped."

"And it's your hypothesis that Ethan pushed her?"

"Ethan was in the vicinity when Celeste nearly plunged to her death," Merritt replied. "I also ran into him around three o'clock this morning when I had to use the restroom."

"Did he say why he was out of bed at that hour?" Josh asked.

"He claimed he needed to use the bathroom. We chatted a few minutes and then I saw him go back into his cabin. I naturally assumed that he went back to bed, but what if Ethan just pretended to go back to bed only to step back outside to kill Peter?"

"Aren't you jumping to conclusions? I realize that Ethan's secrecy about his parentage is suspicious, but he might have concealed his identity because the accident was a part of his past that he wanted to forget," Josh reconciled, still trying to wrap his head around the fact that a seemingly laid-back guy like Ethan could be responsible for such heinous acts of revenge.

"It is difficult to picture Ethan as a killer, but he had the motive and opportunity. If he is guilty, Celeste might be his next victim."

"Ethan's tragic connection with the victims certainly casts doubt on Mike Trump," Josh agreed. "I'll phone Sheriff Abrams to arrange a meeting. In the meantime see if you can get a hold of Celeste? She deserves to know what's going on, in case, Ethan does attempt to kill her."

Merritt pulled out her cell-phone to phone Celeste. It went straight to voicemail.

"This is Merritt Andrews from the playhouse. I know it's been a rough day, but I have something important to tell you about the case. Call me back as soon as possible, and in the meantime stay clear of Ethan Daniels." Merritt then attempted Alistair's cell, to no avail.

"Any luck getting in touch with Celeste?"

"No, they must still be at doctor's office," Merritt sighed. "Did you get in touch with Sheriff Abrams?"

"Abrams was tied up, but I spoke with Deputy Hill. He says to come down to the station to make a statement."

When they arrived at the Custer County Sheriff's Station approximately fifteen minutes later, Deputy Hill greeted them.

"Ranger Ford," the Deputy stated. "Sheriff Abrams is tied up on a phone call, but as soon he's finished he'll come out to speak with you and Miss Andrews."

"That's fine. We don't mind waiting," Merritt and Josh replied, sitting down in a set of nearby chairs.

About twenty-minutes later, Sheriff Abrams emerged from his office.

"My colleague tells me that you have new information regarding the playhouse murders?"

"I think that you have the wrong man in jail Sheriff Abrams," Merritt stated bluntly.

"Why do you presume that?" Sheriff Abrams' tone was irritable. He was not in the mood to have an amateur detective prying into the case.

"Ethan Daniels, the prop master has an axe to grind with both of the victims."

"An axe to grind doesn't equal double homicide?" the Sheriff rebuffed.

"In July 1991, Celeste, Chet and Peter were involved in a two-car collision on the Needles Highway near Hole in the Wall, in Custer State Park."

"I'm familiar with that accident. I was serving as Deputy Sheriff when it occurred," Abrams replied.

"Then you are aware that a young couple by the name of Yates died in the collision?"

"I don't see how this relates to the murders of Chet and Peter?"

"Josh and I did a little research and it turns out that Ethan Daniels is the son of Carla and William Yates, the victims who died in that crash. He only changed his last name from Yates to Daniels after his maternal aunt Katherine and her husband Tommy legally adopted him after the death of his parents."

"Ethan's parentage hardly constitutes the label of killer."

"The fact that Ethan's parent's died in a catastrophic car accident that Chet, Celeste and Peter managed to walk away is cause to spur him to vengeance. As playhouse property master, Ethan had ample opportunity to douse Chet's tea with poison hemlock. In addition to which I ran into him at three o'clock this morning, hours before Celeste found Peter dead."

"Yes, but you told me earlier today that you saw Mr. Daniels go back inside his cabin after you bumped into him?" The Sheriff followed up.

"I did see Ethan go back into his cabin, but that doesn't mean that he didn't step back outside to murder Peter, once he knew I was out of the way," Merritt postulated.

"Or Mr. Daniels could have just gone back to bed as you originally thought."

"I wish I could believe that," Merritt wrestled with the reality that her friend may have committed two monstrous crimes. "Unfortunately my instincts tell me that Ethan is responsible for killing Chet and Peter. And if he has the opportunity, I believe that he'll finish his vendetta by murdering Celeste Fitzgerald as well."

"He already tried to push Celeste off a cliff a few weeks ago," Josh chimed in.

"What do you mean he 'tried to push Celeste off a cliff'?" Abrams questioned, the first he'd heard of incident.

"A few weeks back, a large group of cast and crew embarked on a hike atop Harney Peak. At the summit, Celeste nearly fell to her death. After being rescued, she claimed that she was pushed," Merritt replied.

"I don't remember this being reported to area law enforcement," Abrams replied.

"It wasn't," Merritt admitted. "She later recanted her statement that she was pushed. And since no one claimed to have witnessed the initial fall, it was ruled an accident."

"Yet you still think that Ethan pushed her?" Abrams asked.

"He was in close proximity to Celeste when the incident occurred," Merritt replied.

"Without a viable witness, attesting to the fact Ethan pushed Mrs. Fitzgerald, your statement is pure speculation."

"Ethan has been secretive about his identity all summer," Merritt argued. "I think that his sole purpose for working at the Custer Playhouse is to seek revenge on the three people he blames for causing the accident, which killed his parents back in 1991: Chet, Peter and Celeste."

"Mr. Daniels might have chosen not to reveal his connection to the accident, in order to avoid bringing up bad memories," Abrams argued, still convinced that Mike was the guilty party.

"Look I know that you want to lock Mike Trump up for two life sentences after hearing that he purchased poison ivy medication, and the fact that you found his wallet on the lawn near Peter's cabin, but that's circumstantial evidence at best. Mike may be a greedy jerk, but I don't think he had motive enough to kill Chet and Peter, not when he had enough authority to shut down the Custer Playhouse and nab the concessionaire deal without resorting to murder."

"How do you know about the wallet? That's classified information." Sheriff Abrams was alarmed by Merritt's comment.

"Ethan told me, along with at least ten other people that Mike's wallet was found on the scene, right after he was arrested. He also made a point of mentioning the fact that he's not allergic to poison ivy," Merritt replied.

"How did Ethan find out about Mike's wallet?" Abrams asked, beginning to suspect that Merritt might be on to something.

"He claimed that he overheard Deputy Hill mentioning it to a fellow officer," Merritt replied. "If you ask me, Ethan knew that Mike's wallet was found at the crime scene because he planted it there."

"If that's the case, Ethan would have had to swipe Mike's wallet after he got home from the fireworks last night around eleven, which would have been difficult to accomplish."

"It's a plausible theory though," Merritt held her ground. "I think you owe it to this investigation to at least examine the possibility of Ethan's involvement. If I'm wrong and Mike is guilty, then so be it."

"I'll admit that Ethan has motive, and he certainly had the opportunity to murder both men," Sheriff Abrams conceded. "I'll tell you what. I'll have the lab results back from the forensic evidence acquired at the crime scene tomorrow by noon. If it turns out that none of the fingerprints match-up with Mike Trump, I'll release him, and realign my focus on Ethan. In the meantime, I'll do a little digging to see what I can find out about Mr. Daniels. I'll also have an officer keep an eye out on Mrs. Fitzgerald, just in case Ethan does try to hurt her."

"Fair enough," Merritt agreed.

"In the meantime, I suggest that you try don't mention this theory to anyone else, except Celeste, Josh and myself. Otherwise it might tip Ethan off to the fact that he's a person of interest in this case."

"Fine," Merritt and Josh jointly agreed. "However you have got to promise us that you at least investigate Ethan as a suspect."

"You have my word," Abrams promised. "Now let's see if we can get a hold of Mrs. Fitzgerald."

For the next ten minutes, Sheriff Abrams attempted phoning both Alistair and Celeste's cell-phones before Alistair finally picked up.

"This is Sheriff Abrams. Did your wife check out okay with the doctor?"

"Psychically, she'll be fine," Alistair replied. "On the emotional end, she's still a wreck over Peter's death."

"I know that your wife is upset right now, but there's been a new development in the murder investigation and I need you both to come down to the station as soon as possible."

"Does this have anything to do with the frantic voicemail we received from Merritt Andrews regarding Ethan Daniels?" Alistair inquired.

"I'd rather not discuss the details over the phone," Sheriff Abrams replied. "Just get here as soon as you can."

"We're on our way," Alistair promised before hanging up.

Thirty minutes later, Alistair and Celeste arrived at the Custer County Sheriff's Station.

"We got here as soon as possible," Alistair stated as he and Celeste walked into the station lounge. "What's going on?"

"I want to speak with you both about a possible new suspect in the playhouse murder investigation," Sheriff Abrams replied.

"I thought that you arrested Mike Trump for the murders?" Alistair questioned in a confused tone.

"We did," Sheriff Abrams replied. "And as of right now, Trump is still our primary suspect, however Miss Andrews presented me with some new information, leading me to believe there is a chance that Ethan Daniels might be guilty of the crimes."

"What motive would Ethan have for killing Chet and Peter?" Celeste questioned.

"Merritt and Josh did a little digging and it turns out that Ethan is the son of Carla and William Yates," Sheriff Abrams replied.

"The couple I killed in the car accident?" Celeste asked, unsettled by the news.

"That's correct," Abrams replied.

"Are you sure? Ethan never mentioned that he was the Yates' son," Alistair questioned.

"I'm positive," Abrams confirmed. "His last name was changed from Yates to Daniels after he was legally adopted by his aunt and uncle."

"It all makes sense now," Celeste whispered, her face turning a pale white. "He blames us for the accident that killed his parents."

"It's a working theory," Abrams replied. "However we need to acquire more evidence, in order Mr. Daniels as a suspect. In the meantime I'm going to assign a security detail for you, Mrs. Fitzgerald, just in case Ethan attempts to harm you. And given the ongoing nature of this investigation, I ask that you refrain from discussing any of this with Ethan. The second that he knows we're onto his true identity, the more likely he is to cover up any outstanding evidence."

"We'll do whatever you ask," Alistair promised.

"Ethan has every right to kill me for what we did to his parents," Celeste muttered through tears. "I told Chet and Peter that we couldn't hide the truth forever...you don't just run down two innocent people and walk away without having to pay a price."

"It was an accident, Celeste plain and simple. A tragedy, yes, but certainly not your fault," Sheriff Abrams reassured her.

"You don't understand," Celeste shouted. "I can't lie anymore."

"Lie about what?" The group questioned.

"I wasn't driving the car the night that Ethan's parents were killed, Chet was!" Celeste declared. "He was drunk, at least double the legal limit. So was Peter. I was sober when we left the party at Sylvan Lake, because I was pregnant. I tried to convince Chet and Peter to allow me to drive, but Chet promised me that he was perfectly capable of handling the road. Chet started swerving when we hit Hole in the Wall. A few minutes later he'd crashed into the Yates's car. After we knew that Carla and William were dead, Chet insisted I switch places with him. He said that he would have to go to prison if I didn't cover for him and Peter backed him up. I loved him so much then that I agreed to lie. Chet, Peter and I made a pact, swearing never to tell the truth about what really happened that night. And it was easy to lie, at least at first. The authorities believed our story. It was plausible enough, and Chet had friends in high places. No one pressed me, because I'd miscarried because of the accident. Later on I tried to convince Chet to come clean about what really happened, but he refused. We broke up after that. I've carried this burden of guilt ever since that night, wishing I had done things differently."

"Celeste why didn't you tell me," Alistair asked, holding his wife's hand. "You shouldn't have had to go through that alone."

"I should have," Celeste wept. "I just didn't want to risk losing you. I'll understand if you don't forgive me for this, Ali."

"Not forgive you? That's impossible," Alistair replied. "I love you Celeste."

"I love you too, Ali," Celeste replied before turning her attention to Sheriff Abrams. "Are you going to arrest me for lying Sheriff?"

"Although I don't condone your actions, I think you've paid your debt in carrying the guilt of knowing Chet got away with murder all these years."

"If Ethan is guilty, then I feel responsible for his decision to murder Chet and Peter. If I'd told the truth back in 1991, forcing Chet to face judgment for driving under the influence, Ethan might have had the closure he needed to move on from his parents' death..." Celeste sighed.

"If it does turn out that Ethan is guilty, he has no one to blame for murdering Chet and Peter, except himself. I don't care how bad a hand that you are dealt, in this life; you don't try to make it right by doing harm to those who wronged you. Vengeance is a terrible thing in human hands. I hope for Ethan's sake than he's innocent of the crimes," Sheriff Abrams stated firmly.

"I wish I felt that way," Celeste sighed, still plagued with feelings of guilt over the accident.

"You've had a rough day, Mrs. Fitzgerald," the Sheriff replied. "Why don't you and your husband check into a hotel here in town in order to avoid bumping into Ethan? I'll post one of my men outside."

"Good idea," Alistair agreed.

"As soon as I get the results back from the crime lab, we'll plan our next step," Abrams stated before the group parted ways. "In the meantime, just try to stay clear of Ethan."

"Sounds like a plan," the group jointly agreed.

"It looks like your sleuthing has paid off," Josh told Merritt as they left the Sheriff's station.

"It will only pay off once the real killer is behind bars, and even then the whole thing is a tragedy."

"Revenge isn't sweet, especially if it takes away your freedom to live," Josh agreed.

"Do you mind if we take a drive? I'd like to get away from the murderous mayhem for a few hours?" Merritt asked. "I really don't think I can stomach going back to the crime scene, not knowing that Ethan is the probable killer."

"We could drive up to Hill City," Josh suggested. "Grab a bite to eat at the Alpine Inn if you're hungry?"

"As appetizing as the steak at the Alpine Inn sounds, murder makes me lose my appetite. However a shopping trip in Hill City will at least calm my nerves," Merritt replied, as the couple got into Josh's Jeep.

It had been a long and toxic day. Merritt could only hope that by tomorrow she'd have definite answers regarding Ethan's guilt and this murderous act would be concluded.

Chapter 28:

Merritt woke up at eight o'clock on Tuesday morning, after an unsettled sleep.

After getting dressed, she headed over to the Mess Hall with her roommates for a quick breakfast. She quickly lost her appetite when Ethan Daniels sat down at the table beside her.

"I still can't get over the fact that Peter was murdered yesterday," Ginny stated.

"It's horrible," Emma replied. "I'm just glad they solved the case before Mike could kill again."

"Yeah," Merritt sighed, trying her best to keep quiet over the fact the real murderer was possibly sitting with them. "I talked to Sheriff Abrams and he said that Mike's arraignment is tomorrow morning."

"Do you still think that Mike's innocent, Merritt?" Ethan inquired.

"No, I guess not," Merritt lied. "There is a lot of evidence against him."

After breakfast, Merritt headed over to the Game Lodge area to hang out with Josh until they received news from the Sheriff's office regarding the lab reports around noon.

"Miss Andrews, I just got the lab report back, and it seems that your instincts about Mike's innocence were correct. The fingerprints and DNA found at the crime scene don't match-up with Mike's prints. In fact, there is no evidence that Mike was even on the scene other than his wallet."

"I guess that make's Ethan suspect number one," Merritt sighed.

"You could say that. However, I don't plan to release Mike right away. I need him to stay in jail, just for another few hours until I have a chance to wrap things up with Ethan," Abrams explained.

"Over the phone you said that you have a plan to nab him," Merritt replied. "How?"

"Usually I would bring him in for questioning, and let the evidence convict him, but given the nature of this case, I have a better plan for nabbing Ethan as our possible killer. Unfortunately it's contingent on Celeste playing the role of actress."

"What exactly do want my wife to do?" Alistair questioned, concerned for Celeste's safety.

"If Ethan is on a killing spree fueled by the car then his next victim is going to be Celeste. I want to set a trap where we can attempt to catch Ethan at own game."

"You want to use my wife as bait to lure Ethan? That's ludicrous! She could get killed!"

"Ethan might try to kill her, but I'll be there to stop him. And when we do, we'll have verification that he is our killer," Sheriff Abrams replied. "And while we lure Ethan away from the Playhouse, another unit of my men will do a warranted search of Ethan's cabin."

"It sounds risky," Merritt replied, not wanting Celeste to be placed in unnecessary danger. "Still it's probably the most effective way to prove or disprove Ethan's involvement."

"What do you say Celeste? Are you up for this?" Abrams asked.

"I don't know," Celeste sighed. "I'm conflicted. I know that if Ethan is guilty of murdering Chet and Peter he needs to be arrested, but I'm not sure I want to be the one to do it. I'm already partially responsible for his parents' death, an event that put him on a path of revenge..."

"Celeste, I told you yesterday and I'll tell you again today that you are NOT responsible for Ethan's decision to avenge his parents' death. He is not a vigilante righting a wrong. You never right a wrong with a wrong. Have compassion on Ethan, fine, but you know firsthand that letting someone go free for a crime committed will only to more agony. At least if Mr. Daniels faces his crimes now, then he'll have a chance for redemption and forgiveness," Sheriff Abrams stated.

"What do you want me to do?" Celeste asked, still hesitant about setting up Ethan.

"I need you to phone Ethan around six to tell him that you know the truth about his identity and that you need to talk to him in person about the murders of Chet and Peter. Ask him to me you at the Hole in the Wall."

"Then what?"

"Presuming he comes to the site, you'll tell him that you are sorry for what happened to his parents. The rest will play out from there. If he is guilty, Ethan will most likely admit his guilt, thinking he'll be able to kill you before you can turn him in. Of course we'll be hiding in the woods, ready to pounce if and when he does anything to harm you," the Sheriff explained.

"I know that Ethan is solely responsible for the crimes he committed, but I still don't know if I can trap him into a life sentence or more for what he did," Celeste replied.

"I promise that if you assist us Mrs. Fitzgerald I will personally make sure that Ethan is treated fairly by my department and will get a minimal sentencing in concordance with the law. The death penalty will be off the table."

"You promise that you'll make sure Ethan gets a fair trial and no death penalty?"

"You have my word," Sheriff Abrams reassured her.

"Okay," Celeste sighed. "I'll do it."

"Celeste you can't do this! It's too dangerous!" Alistair rebutted.

"I'll be fine Ali," Celeste replied firmly. "Sheriff Abrams and his men will be there if Ethan tries to hurt me."

"Fine, but only because I know once you've made up your mind about something there's no use changing it," Alistair sighed.

"Now that everyone's on board, we need to spend the next few hours strategizing," Sheriff Abrams stated.

~

A few hours later, Celeste, Alistair, Merritt, Josh, Sheriff Abrams and his team of deputies headed drove over to the Hole in the Wall picnic area to set everything up for the operation. At six-fifteen, Sheriff Abrams gave the go ahead for Celeste to phone Ethan and request that he meet her at the sight.

"It is show time," Sheriff Abrams stated, looking at his watch. "Are you still up for this Celeste?"

"I'm ready," she replied.

"Okay, here's a cell-phone, which you can use to call Ethan. All you have to do is dial 7, and the phone will automatically connect with his number."

"Here goes nothing," Celeste replied, before dialing Ethan's number. After a few rings, Daniels picked up.

"Hello," Ethan's voice sounded over the line.

"Ethan, this is Celeste Fitzgerald. I know that you've been lying about your true identity," she proclaimed.

"Celeste, what are you talking about?" Ethan played dumb.

"I know that you're the son of Carla and William Yates, the young couple that died tragically in an accident that Chet, Peter and I were involved in back in 1991." For a second Ethan was speechless as Celeste made her reply.

"Yes, I'm the son of Carla and William Yates, the car that you rammed into accidentally nineteen years ago," Ethan replied, his tone changing from one of confidence to fear. "I never told you because I didn't see the point of bringing up a bad memory."

"We need to talk as soon as possible," Celeste demanded. "Meet me at the Hole in Wall campground in half an hour, otherwise I'll phone Sheriff Abrams and tell him that you killed Chet and Peter."

"I'm on my way," Ethan replied curtly before hanging up the phone.

"He's headed over here right now," Celeste sighed, still a bit nervous over her impending confrontation with Daniels.

"Celeste, I know that this is stressful, but just go through the motions that we practiced this afternoon and you'll be fine," Abrams replied. "Deputy Hill is tracking Ethan and will alert us the second he leaves the Playhouse. A CSI unit is also ready to search Ethan's cabin as soon as he leaves. In the meantime, everyone start getting into your positions, and make sure the cameras are rolling so we catch this on tape."

Thirty minutes after Celeste spoke with Ethan, he sped into the Hole in the Wall parking lot, barely missing Celeste as he parked his car.

"You have some nerve calling me here," Ethan shouted, as he approached Celeste. "After what you did to my parents almost at this exact spot nineteen years ago."

"I'm very sorry for what happened to your parents Ethan," Celeste replied sincerely. "I think about that accident every day and wish to God that things could have gone differently."

"You wish that you didn't run them down, after barely missing a bison? Or you feel like hell because you allowed Chet Rawlins to drive drunk, murder my parents with reckless driving, and then you covered for him so he wouldn't have to pay for his crimes?" Ethan questioned, his face bright red from a furious anger towards Celeste.

"What are you talking about? I was driving the car that night," Celeste lied.

"Don't lie to me, Celeste!" Ethan shot back. "I know that you weren't driving the car that night, Chet was. I heard you discussing it with Peter and Chet that day at Legion Lodge, when I had to break up your fight. Up to that point, I was angry about my parent's death, but I wasn't ready to kill. I just wanted to remind the three of you of how lucky you were to walk away from that accident when two wonderful people died. However when I realized that the three of you murdered my parents through a web of lies and drunken recklessness, I knew that I had to take action. I couldn't just let the three of you get away with murder."

"So you admit to killing Chet and Peter?" Celeste questioned through tears.

"Yes I killed both of the scumbags as a service to society. Chet never learned his lesson from that accident. He still sped like a demon and was hateful and cruel to everyone around him. Peter was too much of a wimp to turn Chet in, for fear that it might get you in trouble for lying about what happened."

"I tried to convince them to tell the truth, but I couldn't Ethan. I feel terrible for what happened. It was a horrible tragedy. However murder was not the right way to solve this. Your revenge will cause you to lose your freedom; it'll be like a sack of rotten potatoes on your back dragging you down. Now you're going to have to go to jail for the crimes you committed," Celeste replied compassionately towards Ethan.

"I'm not going to jail," Ethan cocky.

"Mike Trump is. The bastard deserves it after he tried to screw over the Custer Playhouse."

"You can't convince Sheriff Abrams that Mike Trump is guilty with no hard evidence against him?" Celeste asked.

"Maybe not, but I think the circumstantial evidence implicating Mike will hold up for now. For instance, the fact Trump has poison ivy. I burned poison ivy underneath Peter's window until the urushiol-laden smoke killed him. And it was a godsend when I happened to find Mike's wallet on the ground by the McGovern cabin. I picked up the wallet and conveniently placed it outside Peter's cabin for the authorities to find. As for Chet's death, Mike was present when Chet's tea was brewing. The authorities will assume that he added the hemlock to the mixture, when it fact I had already mixed poison hemlock into Chet's tea leaves the night before. They certainly won't trace the murder back to me..." Ethan boasted, pulling out a knife. "Not once I'm through killing you and making it look like suicide."

"You're a fool if you think you can get away with this!" Celeste shouted to ensure Sheriff Abrams and his deputies could hear her. "The Sheriff will figure out your identity and your motives and you'll have to go to jail for life. You'll live an angry, resentful existence, full of guilt over the choices you made. Unless you confess and try to redeem yourself."

"You're one to talk about redemption, Celeste. If you hadn't lied to cover up a crime that Chet committed, then I wouldn't have been forced to kill all three of you."

"You have every right to hate me Ethan, but in the end killing me won't make you feel better. It'll make things worse. I'm willing to do whatever I can to help you, but you have to come forward and admit what you've done."

"I'd rather spend a lifetime in jail than see you walk away from this place alive," Ethan replied sadistically, ready to plunge the knife into Celeste's chest.

"Put the gun down Ethan," Sheriff Daniels ordered, sneaking up behind Daniels. "Otherwise I'll shoot."

"Shoot me, I'd rather die than allow Celeste to go unpunished," Ethan replied.

"Ethan, I know that you're upset, but this isn't the way to handle your anger," Merritt took a gamble, stepping into the conversation. "However as satisfying as killing Celeste may feel now, you'll regret it later. Just like I know you will regret the fact that you poisoned Chet and murdered Peter later on."

"Merritt? What are you doing here?" Ethan questioned.

"I'm the one who figured out that you were the murderer. I wish that my instincts hadn't be right. You're a nice guy, but you chose a terrible path, a path driven by revenge that you'll never be free of, not unless you face the consequences of the crime."

"The only crime is the fact Celeste, Peter and Chet murdered my parents and walked away without so much as a traffic ticket."

"What happened to your parents is tragic, and I'm sorry that justice wasn't served. I'm mostly sorry that you had to grow up without your parents. However avenging their deaths with murder is the last thing I know that your parents, Carla and William Yates would have wanted you to do."

"How do you know what they would want me to do?" Ethan sneered.

"I know that they were good people, people who loved their son and wanted him to live a happy life in spite of their death. Not to be haunted by their deaths, chained by a life of revenge and hatred," Merritt replied.

"I did what needed to be done. Justice has been served," Ethan cried.

"You're wrong," Merritt replied firmly. "Justice is never served by murdering two people. The only thing you've gained is the fact that you now have blood on your hands, and will have to go to jail for pursuing your feelings of revenge. I don't care how much you've been wronged, revenge is never the right path. You turn the other cheek and learn to move on, not for the sake of the people who wronged you, but for the simple fact you can't live a sane life carrying all that hatred on your shoulders. It'll blackened your heart, until your good nature is dead."

"You may be right, Merritt," Ethan admitted. "I may regret the fact that I resorted to murder, but Celeste, Chet and Peter pushed me to it."

"Unfortunately the only person responsible for your actions is you Ethan. The actions of Celeste, Chet and Peter may have made you angry, but they didn't put a gun to your head and force you to commit these crimes. You had a choice to walk away, yet you chose vengeance over forgiveness and it was deadly choice. Now you'll have to live with the consequences," Merritt sighed, saddened by the situation.

"Ethan Daniels, I'm arresting you for the murders of Chet Rawlins and Peter Wiseman," Sheriff Abrams stated as he took the knife from Ethan, and cuffed him. "You have the right to remain silent. Anything you say can and will be used against you in a court of law. You have the right to speak to an attorney. If you cannot afford an attorney, one will be appointed to you. Do you understand these rights as they have been read to you?"

"I do," Ethan replied smugly. "And for the record, I'm guilty."

With that, Ethan was walked down to a nearby turnout, where the Sheriff's car had been parked, hidden from view.

"If it hadn't been for you this case may gone unsolved and Celeste could have become the next victim. Thank you for your help Merritt," Alistair stated.

"I just wish it never came to this," Merritt replied. As nice as it was to know that the killer had been captured, she couldn't help but feel depressed. "Ethan had everything going for him and he threw it away for revenge. Now he'll have to spend years, if not life in jail."

"The whole thing is a tragedy," Josh agreed.

A few minutes later Josh drove Merritt, Alistair and Celeste back to the Custer Playhouse where Deputy Hill's unit of officers was searching Ethan's cabin.

"Merritt, thank God you're back," Ginny stated. "You won't believe what happened! The Sheriff's men are searching the Norbeck cabin. They suspect that Ethan actually killed Chet and Peter, and that Mike Trump is innocent."

"I know," Merritt replied with a sigh.

"How could you possibly know that?" Emma asked.

"It's a long story," Merritt replied, before spending the next half hour recounting the events leading up to Ethan's arrest.

"You figured that out and didn't tell us?" Ginny asked, a bit annoyed by her roommate's secrecy.

"The Sheriff wanted us to keep quiet until he could conclusively prove that Ethan was guilty."

"I can't believe it," Luke Barber replied. "I've known Ethan since childhood. He never once mentioned anything about that car accident."

"He only said that he was adopted by his aunt and uncle because his parent's died when he was young," Tom added in. "I just don't get it, we were best friends. How could he deceive us like this?"

"And to think what his poor aunt and uncle are going through right now. They loved Ethan like a son and have always done everything they could to ensure his happiness. This is how he pays them back?" Luke shook his head.

"The whole scenario is sad. Chet and Peter dead and Ethan in jail...it's so senseless that this even had to happen," Merritt stated. "I just hope the Playhouse will be able to move on from the tragedy and continue our run of *Dakota.*"

"The show will go on," the group promised. "Even if it kills us."

Chapter 29:

During the arraignment, a few days after Ethan's arrest, he plead guilty to two counts of murder one. In the terms of the plea deal, the D.A. and Sheriff Abrams agreed to reduce the sentence from life to twenty-five years, contingent on good behavior.

As for the Custer Playhouse, Sheriff Abrams gave the go ahead for *Dakota* to continue as planned for the rest of the summer season. In spite of the adversity the cast and crew faced in the wake of the murders the production continued to be a smash hit. By summer's end the theatre had made an enormous profit, such that Mike Trump personally offered the Custer Playhouse a new ten-year lease come September.

Merritt and Josh continued to grow closer over the summer, becoming an official item by late July. Unfortunately their budding romance made it all that harder when it came time for Merritt to pack up her bags and head back east when the theatre season wrapped up in late August.

"So what's next for top crime sleuth and costume designer, Merritt Andrews?" Josh asked as Merritt loaded up her Civic for the return trip to North Carolina.

"The plan is to head back home for a week or two before moving to Charleston South Carolina for a few months to work as a costume designer with my good friend Julia Manigault at the newly restored Dock Street Theatre," Merritt replied. "Although I'd gladly stay out west if it meant the chance of being closer to you."

"I think you should go to Charleston," Josh encouraged her. "It's not like I'll be that far away."

"I thought that you were working for South Dakota Fish and Wildlife this fall and winter?"

"Change of plans," Josh smiled. "I've been offered a job in Wilmington N.C. working as a biologist for marine wildlife organization who are working to stop the effects of the Gulf Oil Spill off the eastern seaboard."

"Wilmington's only a few hours from Charleston," Merritt replied, excited that she would be in close proximity to Josh in the coming months.

"It's certainly close enough for us to meet up on the weekends," Josh said, kissing Merritt's cheek.

In spite of the murder and mayhem that had plagued Merritt's Custer State Park adventures, the summer had been fulfilling. She'd fallen in love with the scenery of the Black Hills, not to mention Ranger Ford, and had met lifetime friends in Ginny, Emma and Rebecca. She just hoped that her theatre gig in Charleston wouldn't be tainted with murder...

Traveling to the Black Hills:

The Black Hills is truly a pristine paradise, filled with wonder and natural diversity from the dancing prairie floor, vast and wide open, to jagged spires, monuments in stone, colorful Badlands to the colorful history, epic geology, spelunking caverns and more. It is a top notch family destination, beckoning the heart of every traveller to explore.

In planning your journey to the Black Hills and Custer State Park there are a wide variety of resources. I recommend starting with the following sites:

Travel South Dakota:
http://www.travelsd.com

Custer State Park:

http://gfp.sd.gov/state-parks/directory/custer/ - Here you can download the Tatanka and get camping and hiking information.

http://www.custerresorts.com – the go to source for all things Custer State Park

Custer City, SD: http://www.custersd.com

Mount Rushmore: http://www.nps.gov/moru/

Crazy Horse Memorial: http://www.crazyhorsememorial.org

Wind Cave National Park: http://www.nps.gov/wica

Jewel Cave National Park: http://www.nps.gov/jeca/

Hot Springs, SD: http://www.hotsprings-sd.com/

Rapid City, SD: http://www.visitrapidcity.com

Merritt's Day Trip Picks:

In Custer State Park:

- The Needles Highway –
- Sylvan Lake – enjoy the views of this serene mountain lake, while climbing on granite spires in the shadow of Harney Peak – the tallest mountain east of the Rockies and west of the European Alps! Enjoy lunch in the refinement and natural elegance of the Sylvan Lake Lodge. Bring your swim suits and trunks, the lake is the perfect spot to cool off from the South Dakota summer heat.
- Wildlife Loop – This eighteen mile scenic drive showcases the ever-changing converging prairie and mountain landscape. You'll be sure to encounter Bison. The park's herd is 1300 bison, also known as 'buffalo.' Remember to keep your distance. Bison weigh over two tons and run thirty miles an hour. Every September the park visitors can witness the herd as it is corralled in amazing 'Buffalo Round-Up.' The Wildlife Loop is also home to prairie dogs, elk, mule deer, pronghorn, bighorn sheep and the friendly begging burros. Hike the Prairie Trail, before stopping for a bite to eat at Blue Bell.
- Iron Mountain Road
- Game Lodge Area: Visit the Peter Norbeck Center; Hike the Creekside Trail, then dine at the State Game Lodge, also known as the 'Summer White House.' Tour the home of South Dakota Poet Laureate Badger Clark
- Center Lake and the Black Hills Playhouse: enjoy a day swimming and picnicking on the shores of Center Lake and a cookout. When the sun sets you can 'head yonder' to the nearby historic Black Hills Playhouse for one of their many riveting summer performances.

- Legion Lake: Eat a hearty breakfast at the Legion Lake Lodge, before embarking on the Legion Lake Loop Trail. Spend the afternoon swimming in the crystal waters. Cap of the day with a scoop of ice-cream, while watching the sunset.

Regional Excursions:

- Custer City, SD – the gateway to Custer State Park. This lively town has an eclectic mix of gift shops, grocery stores, restaurants and historical sites. Catch up on Black Hills History in the Historic 1881 Courthouse.
- Mount Rushmore National Memorial: No trip to South Dakota is complete without a visit to Mount Rushmore, where "America's History is Alive in Stone." Tour the Lincoln Borglum Museum, learning about the history of this patriotic and truly American monument, before meandering through the Presidential Trail and stopping by the Sculptor's Studio.
- Crazy Horse Memorial: "My lands are where my people lie buried." Crazy Horse Memorial is a dream in progress, artistry in motion as work continues to cut, blast and carve a larger than life monument in honor of the great Native American Chief, Crazy Horse. The memorial houses a museum complex, trails and of course stunning views of the masterful work in stone, 'Crazy Horse.'

- Deadwood: One of the most notorious spots in the Wild West, Deadwood has the charm of yesteryear with top attractions and scenery for all ages. Stop by Saloon No. 10 to pay your respects to 'Wild Bill Hickok.'
- Hill City & Keystone SD
- Jewel Cave National Park: Immerse yourself in the intricate, rambling Jewel Cave – the third longest cave in the world. Delve deep underground on a cavern tour and hike above ground in the sun gorged valley of Hell Canyon.
- Wind Cave National Park: Wind Cave offers visitors the unique opportunity to stand in the midst of a confluence prairie ecosystem, while tumbling below ground to witness stunning boxwork formations. Carve out a full day at Wind Cave
- Hot Springs, South Dakota: Adventure awaits in the idyllic community of Hot Springs. Soothe your joints in one of the areas many mineral springs...take in the exquisite architecture...tour Ice Age wonder at the Mammoth Site...the possibilities are endless.
- Rapid City, South Dakota: Rapid City is a cool town and perfect vacation getaway...Kids will LOVE Dinosaur Park. Downtown Rapid City has over thirty restaurants, gardens and parks as well as museums.

Merritt & Adele will keep you informed on travel getaways in the Black Hills and beyond on the Playhouse Mystery Blog:

http://www.playhousemysteries.blogspot.com

COMING SOON

Playhouse Mystery Series:

The Ghost of the Dock Street Theatre

The stage is set as Merritt journeys to historic Charleston South Carolina for a six month stint as costume assistant at the nation's oldest theatre company, The Dock Street Theatre.

While in Charleston, Merritt stays with her friend and fellow costumer Julia Manigault. The friends delve into their first assignment: designing costumes for the theatre's upcoming production of *The Swamp Fox*, a biographical Revolutionary War drama focusing on the life and times of South Carolina war hero Francis Marion. In their spare time they soak in the city's history and culture and develop friendships with the cast and crew.

Things are going smoothly until Merritt encounters a surprise visitor in the costume shop: the ghost of former theatre costumer Lily Villepontoux Tyler. Lily, who is thought to have committed suicide by hanging herself from the theatre rafters, notifies Merritt that she was actually murdered by a member of the cast and crew. Lily's spirit, stuck between worlds until her murder is solved enlists Merritt's help to find her killer. With the help of Julia, paranormal investigator, Steve Barnwell, and Charleston police detective, Miles Barnwell, Merritt unravels a tangled web of suspects to find the real killer.

About the Author:

Adele Gibbes lives in the shadow of the Bridger and Gallatin Mountain Ranges in Bozeman Montana. Born and raised in Raleigh N.C., she graduated from Broughton High School. In high school, Adele's love of theatre blossomed. She worked for three years as a Creative Costume Consultant at Raleigh Creative Costumes. Adele graduated from Belmont University in 2009 with a degree in Music Business. She enjoys hiking, traveling, college basketball, good food, art and literature.

Join Adele online:

Playhouse Mystery Series:
http://www.playhousemysteryseries.blogspot.com

Into the Great Unknown – Travel, Music, Books and beyond:
http://www.yellowstone-explorer.blogspot.com

This Side of Paradise –Bible Study Blog
http://www.paradisevalleydevotions.blogspot.com

Facebook:
Playhouse Mystery Series
https://www.facebook.com/PlayhouseMysterySeries